DEATH IN A
HIGH LATITUDE

DEATH IN A
HIGH LATITUDE

JOHN R. L. ANDERSON

CHARLES SCRIBNER'S SONS
NEW YORK

Copyright © 1981 J. R. L. Anderson

First published in the United States by Charles Scribner's Sons 1984

Library of Congress Cataloging in Publication Data

Anderson, J. R. L. (John Richard Lane), 1911–
Death in a high latitude.

I. Title.
PR6051.N3934D38   1984   823'.914   83-20142

ISBN 0-684-18137-1

1 3 5 7 9 11 13 15 17 19   F/C   20 18 16 14 12 10 8 6 4 2

Printed in the United States of America.

For
Dick Squires

CONTENTS

I

The Cambridge Map

RUTH IS NOT what might be called a passionate supporter of women's lib; indeed, she seems to enjoy being feminine. But as Caval Professor of Mathematics at Oxford she is properly conscious of her identity and not at all disposed to feel that her role in life is to cook for me. Secretly, and perhaps not really as secretly as all that, I am immensely proud of her, though when I am introduced at academic functions as "Professor Blair's husband" I can understand the feelings of men married to Prime Ministers.

I had not in fact needed much cooking for since our marriage, partly because I am a fair cook myself, more because I was in and out of hospital. When we were married in Africa at the end of the strange affair of Eustace Quenenden*, I was just about able to walk after two operations for the wound inflicted on me by his murderer. Ruth took me home to my cottage near Salcombe in South Devon and nursed me back to something approaching fitness when my wound went bad on me and I was rushed off to hospital in Exeter. Since Ruth had to be in Oxford I was transferred from Exeter to Oxford, where I had yet another operation. I got out after a few weeks but kept on having to go back for what the surgeons called "examinations". I got through the whole of Gibbon's *Decline and Fall of the Roman Empire*. In theory I was still on the strength of Sir Edmund Pusey's Police Liaison Department at the Home Office, which acts as a kind of General Staff in the war against crime and deals with those complex cases where different authorities—police, services, customs, ministries and other bodies—overlap. I was still supposed to represent the

* See *Death in the Greenhouse*

9

Armed Services in the Department and continued to draw my pay as a colonel, but in practice I did nothing except go to the office occasionally when I was not in hospital to have lunch with Sir Edmund.

At last I seemed on the way to more than temporary release from surgeons. It was near the end of what Oxford calls Trinity and the rest of us the summer term. Ruth and I were determined to use the long vacation first to find a house in the countryside near Oxford, and then to get away from everything by going to Devon to play with my boat. We were not exactly homeless. Being an ancient institution King Alfred's College, of which Ruth is a Fellow, owns several charming houses in the middle of Oxford and we were able to live in one of these. But it was a house normally used for academic guests and although the College put no pressure on us we both felt it a little unfair to go on occupying it. Also, we wanted a place in the country, preferably on the river, where I could have some sort of boat. That evening we had finished supper and were looking through house agents' advertisements when the telephone rang. Ruth answered it. "For you," she said. "It's your boss."

I was partly pleased, partly alarmed. I was bored with myself and rather fed up, but I didn't want our plans for the vacation to be upset. "Peter Blair here," I said cautiously.

"Nice to hear you, Peter. I have good reports of you from various medical sources." (He would, I thought. So much for the Hippocratic Oath and confidentiality about patients when Sir Edmund Pusey is around.) "Don't think that I'm unsympathetic to wounds so gallantly endured," he went on. "But I was wondering if you were fit enough to undertake a small job of work."

"I'd consider it. But the long vacation's coming up, Ruth and I are house-hunting, and she needs a holiday."

"Of course. But there's still a bit to go before the end of term," (he would know exactly how much, I thought a trifle bitterly) "and what I had in mind should not occupy you for long. We could at least discuss it. Can you get to London tomorrow? We'll lunch at my flat, I think. Don't come to the office."

"All right. But I warn you that for all your medical reports

10

on me I can produce enough eminent doctors to convince even the Treasury that I'm entitled to an immediate pension, and I don't want my summer to be messed up."

"Again of course, Peter. I wholly understand. Shall we say 12:45? There's an excellent train from Oxford at 11:15 getting to Paddington at 12:20. I've already arranged for a car to meet you."

For a man with an active finger in so many pies Sir Edmund gives a curious impression of having nothing whatever to do. That is not quite true; the impression he gives is of having all the time in the world for whoever he may be talking to at any given moment. That is part of his charm, and of his un-canny success in getting what he wants. He gave me a delicious lunch, cooked by a Cordon Bleu-trained young woman, and accompanied by just the right Moselle. He talked of my affairs, of Ruth, and of house prices around Oxford, on which he seemed remarkably well-informed. It was not until lunch had been cleared away and we were sitting over coffee that he even mentioned the Department. "You know, Peter, we've missed you," he said.

"Not noticeably."

"Well, you wouldn't notice, would you? It's not so much in what we've done : we've got along all right, no one is indispens-able. It's more in the things we haven't tackled. This particular small problem that I hope you'll look into cropped up six months ago."

"Why the delay?" He didn't answer for a moment. Then he said, "Even now it's not quite clear that there's really any problem to go into. You know that I am an Oxford man. I suppose that you, too, would be considered an Oxford man now."

"When the time came for me to go to Oxford I went to Sandhurst to be trained to fight a war."

"I know that. Don't be so prickly. I was going to ask if you'd spend a few days at the other place, in Cambridge."

"As an outsider, I'm not sure that I don't prefer Cambridge. In many ways it's more beautiful than Oxford."

He gave a theatrical small wince. "You have some barbaric qualities, Peter. They come in useful sometimes, maybe. Anyway, the case, if there is a case, starts in Cambridge, if it doesn't start somewhere else."

"Don't be so damned mysterious. What's it all about?"

"That's what I want you to find out, Peter. I told you it goes back six months. What happened then was that a valuable seventeenth-century map disappeared from the Museum of Cartography in Cambridge—I should say seems to have disappeared, for it is not quite certain that it has actually been taken from the museum."

"Surely that's a matter for the Cambridge police. How on earth do we come into it?"

"We don't—yet. For all my natural Oxford instincts I have to admit that Cambridge has some things that Oxford hasn't. One of them is the Museum of Cartography. It was started with a gift from the Hudson's Bay Company in the seventeenth century and it is the finest institution of its kind in the world. The Company of Merchants Trading into Hudson's Bay was chartered in 1670, and one of the more farsighted of the founding fathers was concerned to build up a collection of accurate maps of the Arctic regions. He gave some money to a geographer friend of his at Cambridge to do the job. The museum has long ceased to be limited to the Arctic, and now houses what is probably the most important collection of world maps since Ptolemy's at Alexandria in the third century BC. The museum is associated with the university, but is not part of it; it is an independent institution with its own trustees who appoint the Curator, at present Dr Charles Wilding. His special field is early medieval cartography though he is, of course, an authority on maps in general. The missing map is outside his own particular period; it is supposed to have been made by William Baffin around 1616, during the last of his great Arctic voyages in search of the North-West Passage. It is known as Baffin's map, and although it is of somewhat specialised interest it is worth a lot of money."

"You say it is not certain that the map has been taken from the museum."

"That's one of the maddening things about the case. The map belongs to the museum, and it certainly *was* in the Arctic Room there, but it was one of a number lent to an exhibition of old maps in Hamburg last year, and it is not absolutely certain that it came back. There is no suggestion of misbehaviour by the Hamburg authorities. They undoubtedly sent it back; they insured it for the exhibition, and it is listed by the insurers in the inventory of things sent back. What is not actually proved is whether it reached Cambridge. The Curator thinks it did, and remembers checking it on a list that came to him from Hamburg, but the Keeper of Arctic Maps, the man who would have handled the map physically and been responsible for putting it back in its case, is unhappily dead. He died suddenly—he was only fifty-two—a few days after the maps came back from Hamburg."

"How was the loss discovered?"

"It wasn't until some months later. An American scholar, Dr George D. Longworth, is writing a book on the mapping of the Arctic. He was given permission to study the museum's collection of Arctic maps. When he wanted to look at Baffin's map it couldn't be found. The new Keeper hadn't any occasion to take out that particular map before. The maps are kept in drawers, in huge filing cabinets. She—the new Keeper is a woman, Dr Ingrid Mitchell—went to the drawer where the map should have been, and it was empty. The Arctic Division of the museum has a staff of four—the Keeper, her secretary, and two assistants. Between them they made a thorough search to see if the map could have been put in some other drawer, but it didn't turn up. The Keeper then reported to the Curator that the map was missing, and the Curator called in the police."

"Fairly sensational, but nothing to do with us. Odd that I don't recall reading anything about it."

"Nothing was published. The museum was rather ashamed of itself, and kept hoping that the map would turn up somewhere or other in its archives. It's a big building, and stores hundreds of thousands of maps. It was possible that on coming back from Hamburg the map was put in the wrong place, and would ultimately be found. So far it hasn't been found."

"What do the police think?"

"They don't know. They made what inquiries they could, and got nowhere."

"Was the late Keeper's death at all suspicious?"

"It was unexpected, and like everything else in the case it

might or might not be a cause for suspicion. He had been under treatment for depression, and was taking some tablets. They were safe enough in the prescribed dose, but dangerous if you took too many, and particularly dangerous if combined with alcohol. It was unusual for him to drink much, but on the night before his death he had been to a party, where apparently he did drink rather a lot of gin. On going to bed he seems to have taken two lots of tablets, and he died in his sleep. He and his wife had separate rooms. There is one child, a daughter, and apart from the man's depression they seemed a normal family. His wife found him dead when she took him a cup of tea in the morning—her usual custom. The facts were reported to the coroner, there was an autopsy and an inquest. The loss of the map did not come to light until after the man was dead, and at the time of the inquest nobody knew about it. There was no evidence of suicidal tendencies, no apparent reason for suicide, and the obvious finding was accidental death."

"If he had known about the map he might have felt that he would be held responsible for its loss. In his depressed state that might have been a reason for suicide."

"Quite. But there is no evidence that he did know about the map."

"The map may be worth a lot of money but it would seem more or less unsaleable. Any other museum or university which might be interested in buying it would know where it came from."

"Yes. The unscrupulous private collector who hoards things for the sake of hoarding them and buys without asking questions no doubt exists, but I suspect that he is a rare bird. And an old map is not quite like a picture, which may be beautiful in itself. The history of cartography is highly specialised."

"It's certainly a queer business. But I still don't see how we come into it."

"I haven't quite finished. I know that you consider me a fairly ruthless character, Peter, but I wouldn't have telephoned you last night if I hadn't felt compelled to. Even I have some concern for your welfare."

"Come off it. You're a beast, but a just beast, as somebody said about some schoolmaster."

14

"Well, thanks for at least part of the observation. Yesterday morning the chairman of Universal Oil came to see me, and he gave me this note. It is the original, exactly as he received it." Sir Edmund handed me a white envelope with a Dutch stamp, postmarked "Amsterdam". It bore a typed address to Sir Anthony Brotherton in one of those handsome streets at the back of Park Lane. "That is his private address," Sir Edmund said.

Inside the envelope was a sheet of plain white notepaper, folded once. Typed on it, in good quality typescript, probably done on an electric machine, was the message

Dr Gustav Braunschweig will be released unharmed within 24 hours of the delivery to an address of which you will be informed of the Baffin Map from the Cambridge Museum of Cartography. Failing this, Dr Braunschweig will be executed. You will be given time to make arrangements for acquiring the map before our next communication.

Sir Edmund gave me a few minutes to study the note. Then he continued, "Universal Oil is a British company with a large German holding. The headquarters of the German branch are in Hamburg. Dr Braunschweig is chairman of the German subsidiary, and deputy chairman of the main board. Four days ago he left home for his office in his own car and did not arrive. He is said to have taken precautions in varying his route and times of travel, but he always resisted suggestions that he should have a personal guard on the ground, possibly logical, that this might seem to inflate his importance and invite ideas about kidnapping him. The car has not been found. His colleagues, his family, and the German police fear that he has been kidnapped, but have made no statement about his disappearance. His staff have been told that he was feeling run down and decided to take a sailing holiday— he is a keen yachtsman—to visit various Cornish ports without any planned itinerary. This makes it reasonable that no one should be able to get in touch with him. The police have been expecting one or other of the anarchist groups in Europe to claim that he has been taken hostage, and are a little puzzled that no such claim has been made. This note is the

15

first that has been heard of him. Sir Anthony brought it to me at once. Seddon* went down to Cambridge yesterday morning and learned about the disappearance of the map. As I explained, it had not been reported beyond the Cambridge police because the museum authorities did not wish it. They were confident that if the map turned up in any saleroom they would know about it, and they still have a kind of half-hope that the map is not really lost but astray somewhere in their own collection. The museum, of course, knows nothing about the kidnapping of Dr Braunschweig."

"Would Universal Oil try to buy the map to ransom him?"

"I'm not sure. The German police hold firmly that no ransom demand should be met, but it's easier for the police to take that attitude than a man's family and close friends."

"It's utterly damnable. Has he got a family?"

"Yes, a wife, son of sixteen and daughter of twelve."

"Do they know of the ransom demand?"

"Frau Braunschweig knows that her husband has disappeared, and naturally she fears that he has been kidnapped, but she doesn't yet know anything about the note. The children, as Sir Anthony understands it, think that their father is away on business. He often is."

I thought of the appalling cases of decent men kidnapped and murdered for no reason other than some group's disapproval of society. I thought of a woman sick with anxiety, and of two children who might not know what had happened to their father but who would certainly know of their mother's distress and almost as certainly put two and two together to make a world of private misery they could share with no one. I thought of the two bullets which had torn my own inside to pieces, and of how blessed I was to be alive and to be married to Ruth. "I'd like to see Sir Anthony as soon as possible," I said.

"I knew you'd say that, Peter. We may not achieve anything, but at least we can try. As a matter of fact I've made an appointment for you with Sir Anthony at his home for six o'clock this evening."

* Assistant Commissioner Paul Seddon, the Department's representative with the Metropolitan Police at New Scotland Yard.

"I've still got my rooms in the Temple. I'll stay in London tonight and go to Cambridge first thing in the morning. I'll go to the museum before the police, I think. Can you get Rosemary* to make an appointment with the Curator for, say, ten o'clock?"

"Of course. I hope it's not going to be too much for you, Peter."

"Can but try. As you found out in your own devious ways I'm a good deal better than I was. And it wouldn't matter if I wasn't. What am I supposed to be calling on the Curator for?"

"Well, he'll expect the police to be doing something about his map, and while he won't know anything about us, and we don't particularly want him to, it's reasonable for some specialist help from London to be called in. I thought at first that you might represent the Museums Department of the Ministry, but he'll know too much about museums for that. I think you'd better belong to the Treasury—he won't know anything about the Treasury, because hardly anybody outside the top Civil Service does. You can be concerned with export licences for antiquities, anything you like. You've done all this before, Peter, and you do it rather well. I can fix things with the Treasury in case he rings up about anything."

"Rosemary had better call me Mr Blair. I don't think they run to colonels in the Treasury."

"Perhaps not, so we'll civilise you for the museum. You'll have to see the Cambridge police—I'll tell them to expect you."

I telephoned Ruth to say that I'd have to stay in London that night, and that I'd ring again after I'd sorted out what might have to be done in Cambridge. She was expecting something of the sort, because we both knew what the re-emergence of Sir Edmund Pusey in our affairs was likely to involve. We'd had a long talk about it after Sir Edmund's call. Ruth was concerned about my taking on more than I was really fit for, but she felt that it would be good for me

* Sir Edmund Pusey's secretary.

17

to have something to do : work is about the oldest therapy and it remains among the best.

Sir Anthony Brotherton's home was one of the few buildings in that part of London that are still private houses and not embassies or the discreet offices of international companies. I was admitted by a butler who took me to a charming room with bow windows on the ground floor. It was furnished a little severely, but still more like a drawing room than an office. A big desk, its expanse of polished top completely bare of papers, showed however that it was a room where business was done.

I don't know what I expected of Sir Anthony Brotherton. He was the biggest of big business, chairman of one of the top two or three of the world's largest companies, but he was not big physically. His presence was neat rather than commanding, but as soon as he spoke you were conscious of authority in his voice, and you felt his intelligent eyes taking in everything. He had a warmth of personality that was doubtless valuable, and perhaps sometimes misleading, and he was exceedingly polite. "It is good of you to have acted so quickly," he said.

"It would be shameful if we had not. Why did you go direct to Sir Edmund Pusey instead of getting in touch with New Scotland Yard?"

"Through the Foreign Office. I know the Permanent Secretary and soon as the letter came I rang him at his home. He suggested that I should take the letter to Sir Edmund at once."

"It was good advice, and has saved a little time, which may be important. I want you to tell me all you can about Dr Braunschweig."

"Gustav is an old friend, and a man of great ability. He started on the technical side of the oil industry and he is one of the ablest petroleum chemists in the business. As he progressed in the company, however, he specialised in distribution, and he is directly responsible now for supply and delivery of all our crude oil throughout the world. He controls our tanker fleet."

"From Hamburg?"

"Yes. As you know, we are a British company but German interests hold about forty per cent of our capital, and we have long worked in close partnership with the Germans. Our German subsidiary is a separate company—we have many subsidiaries—but our main board is closely integrated and Gustav is an important member of it."

"Age?"

"He is a couple of years younger than me, and I am fifty-seven. He has always kept himself fit, goes in for ocean racing and won the Fastnet race a few years back. He is not exactly austere, but he is certainly abstemious. He will have a drink with you, but not many."

"After the recent kidnapping of other leading businessmen in Germany, wasn't it foolish of him to drive himself?"

"That's hard to say. Armed guards haven't always been able to save people from being kidnapped or murdered. We've discussed it several times at board meetings. Gustav held that going around with guards was over-reacting, and might bring about the very kind of attack it was supposed to prevent. I don't know. We have unobtrusive guards around a good deal of the time, but you can be guarded to the extent of making life intolerable. I drive alone myself sometimes, and I can't blame Gustav for taking the view he did. He seems to have been wrong, but we have no idea what happened, and whatever it was might equally have happened if he'd had a couple of guards with him."

"Are you contemplating meeting the ransom demand for the Cambridge map?"

Sir Anthony thought for a bit before replying. "Left to ourselves, I think my board would probably want to buy the map and hand it over," he said. "There are a lot of old maps, and only one Gustav Braunschweig. I know nothing of this particular map, and the demand for it makes no kind of sense. I suppose it's valuable, but it's scarcely in the Old Master class—I mean, like the Mona Lisa or some priceless painting. Whether the museum would sell it I don't know—naturally I haven't asked. In the circumstances probably they would sell, but for how much I've absolutely no idea—£10,000? £50,000? Even £100,000. Whatever they asked it would be trivial in relation to Gustav's life."

19

"You say that left to yourselves you'd try to buy the map and release Dr Braunschweig. Why didn't you just do that when the note came?"

"Because we're not on our own. Almost any businessman nowadays may be the next victim. And we haven't been told yet where to deliver the map. The note itself seems a kind of declaration of intent, not a final demand. When we get a final demand we may well want to meet it to save Gustav."

"In spite of the opposition of both the British and the German Governments, and of the police?"

"Ultimately, in a company like ours, you have to take your own decisions. I'm not saying that we *would* act against the wishes of governments, but simply that we'd have to decide what to do when the time came. We might consider that we were better judges of the value of Gustav's life than anybody else, and that we had a more direct responsibility to him and his family than anybody else."

"What if the museum refused to sell the map?"

"All museums want money. Price would be irrelevant to us. I have no doubt whatever that we could acquire the map if we set out to get it. But that situation hasn't arisen yet. Whatever it does depends largely on you and, of course, the German police."

I could understand why this man was chairman of Universal Oil. I changed my line of questioning. "The key to the problem seems to be *why* anyone should go to such lengths to get hold of a map that can be studied at Cambridge anyway, and that was on exhibition in Hamburg not long ago."

"Was it? That seems to provide a link with Hamburg. Where was it on show?"

"At the School of Geography of Hamburg University. It was lent as one item in a large exhibition of world maps. The display was open to the public and was on for a couple of months."

"We probably helped to finance it—we have many links with the university. Gustav may have known about it, but not necessarily. We have a public relations division that looks after contributions to that sort of thing. I can easily find out if you like. Do you consider it important?"

"At this stage everything is important. Can you think of

anything in the operations of your company that could be related to a seventeenth-century map of part of the Arctic?"

"We have a big operation in Alaska, but that is a long way from Baffin Bay. In common with other companies we have prospected for oil in various parts of northern Canada, but we have no big development under way. That is not to say that Arctic oil will never be important—a generation ago who would have forecast the present developments in the North Sea? All I can say is that I know of nothing of any particular significance in the area of the Baffin Map, which presumably relates to some part of Baffin Bay. But I have never seen the map, and until yesterday morning I had never heard of it. In any case, the map is of some three hundred years ago. We have modern charts, and make our own surveys when we need to. The map is an antique. It can have no possible bearing on our operations."

"Yet your deputy chairman is being held to ransom for it."

"Gustav is *apparently* being held to ransom. It is possible that the group, or even individual, concerned saw the map at the Hamburg exhibition and is using it to make a grotesque opening bid. He, she or they may simply be testing our nerve before coming out with their real demands. I cannot believe that the map itself can matter much one way or another. The German police may get some sort of lead from the Hamburg exhibition."

"The police may be able to discover if an attendant noticed anyone taking a particular interest in the map. It's a slim chance, and if they do get any information it may not mean anything."

"At least it's something to go on. Are you planning to go to Hamburg? I can arrange for our people to look after you."

"That is kind of you, but for the moment I think Hamburg is best left to the German police. I shall go to Cambridge in the morning to find out everything I can about the map, without disclosing anything about Dr Braunschweig to the museum. I can rely on you and your board to maintain absolute secrecy in the matter—and please do not get in touch with anyone in Cambridge without consulting me, or Sir Edmund Pusey."

"How do I get in touch with you?"

I gave him my card. "That telephone is always manned. Ask for the duty officer and say that you want to speak to me. If I am there he will put you through, if not, he will know where I am and get a message to me telling me to ring you at whatever number you give. If it is too urgent to wait, ask for Sir Edmund. You will find that we are quite efficient."

He smiled. "I don't doubt it. I can only say good luck—you will understand the personal agony that we are living through."

"Insofar as I can I share it."

"I think you do." The warmth of the man was real. "I am at your disposal at any time. I'll tell my secretary that if you ring you are to be put through at once, whatever I may be doing. Can I offer you a drink of any sort?"

"It would be nice, but I feel that we've both got rather a lot to do. May I leave it to a happier occasion?"

"We must hope that there will be a happier occasion. Tell me frankly, do you think there is much chance of saving Gustav?"

"Of course there's a chance—how much it's impossible even to guess. On his side—on our side—there's the fact that we've been given some time, but how much time again we don't know. Against this we're completely in the dark about who may be involved. Your letter was posted in Holland, but that doesn't tell us much. Various anarchist groups in Germany seem to have associates in Holland, and it would be easy enough for an individual in Germany to get a letter posted in Holland. The letter and the envelope have gone for forensic analysis, and it is possible that the German police may be able to relate the paper or the typing to some known group, but I don't have high hopes of this, and even if it can be done these groups tend to be so elusive and their membership so vague that it may not help much. The main thing at the moment is to try to find out *why* they are interested in this particular map. You may be right in thinking that the map as such is unimportant. On the other hand it's an extraordinarily precise demand. And it's all we have to go on, anyway."

An Amber Necklace

IT WAS MISERABLY little to go on; what was worse, I couldn't even get on with it. I suppose I could have gone straight off to Cambridge, but by the time I got there it would be late at night, and since we were not disclosing the disappearance of Dr Braunschweig there seemed no adequate reason to get the Curator of the museum out of bed. The immediate problem was to get through the evening. My old rooms in the Temple were still furnished, but there was no food in the place, and it was too late to shop. I didn't feel much like eating, so I went to a pub and stood myself a large whisky and a sandwich. I enjoyed the whisky considerably more than the sandwich. Before going to the Temple I rang Sir Edmund to see if anything had come in. My hopes rose when he said yes, there was news of a sort. We didn't want to discuss the case on the phone so I said I'd call in.

"Have you eaten anything since lunch?" he asked when I arrived.

"Yes. I'm all right, thank you."

"What exactly have you eaten?"

"That's my business. You generally have some decent malt. I could use a drink if you like."

"Surely." He poured me a generous measure of one of my favourite brands of straight malt whisky, poured one for himself, and said, "How did you get on with Sir Anthony?"

"Well enough, I think. He answered everything I asked him, but I'm less sure if he told me everything he knew about Dr Braunschweig. He may have felt that there was no reason for going into things I hadn't asked about. He struck me as a very cagey sort—but perhaps that's an occupational habit of the

23

chairmen of oil companies. What's the news that you have?"

"Hamburg police have been on to say that Dr Braunschweig's yacht is also missing."

"I wouldn't put it past the oil company to have removed her to back up their story that he's gone off on a cruise."

"The police thought of that. The company says not."

"That makes it more interesting. What kind of a boat is she, and where was she kept?"

"She's quite big—a fifty-foot steel ketch. She had a mooring at a yacht club. The moorings for the bigger boats are some distance from the clubhouse, and the club runs a launch for members to get to their boats. Inquiries have had to be discreet, but as far as the police know Dr Braunschweig did not use the club launch. That doesn't mean much, because owners often take their own dinghies. Dinghies are coming and going all the time, and no one—at least, no one that Hamburg police have come across so far—remembers seeing Dr Braunschweig go out in the past few days."

"What's his boat called?"

"*Apfel.*"

"Curious name for a boat. But why not? The apple is one of the finest fruits of the earth—he may have regarded her as the fruit of his own industry. He seems to be very fond of her. How old is she?"

"Newish. She was launched just over a year ago, and Dr Braunschweig gave a big party at the club."

"Why didn't the chairman tell me about it? I suppose he thought it of no importance—maybe it isn't. But I wish he'd given me a more rounded picture of Dr Braunschweig."

"Not everyone realises the value of detail."

"You'd have thought the chairman of Universal Oil would. Perhaps he thinks so big that there's no room in his mind for detail. Anyway, the new boat and the party for her gives me a slightly more real impression of the man. And a fifty-foot steel ketch can go anywhere. If they haven't already done so, you might ask the Hamburg police to go a bit more thoroughly into the question of dinghies."

"What do you mean?"

"Well, if you have a fifty-foot boat drawing seven or eight feet moored off a yacht club you have got to get from her as well as to her. She will have a dinghy of her own carried on board, and if you use that it will be moored near the club. If no one went out to *Apfel* in the club launch, then her own dinghy was presumably used. But that implies that last time Dr Braunschweig came ashore he came in *Apfel*'s dinghy, which means that it should have been at the yacht club since *Apfel* last came in. If *Apfel*'s dinghy is still at the club, then either Dr Braunschweig or whoever sailed off in the ketch *did* go out in the launch in spite of what the police inquiries so far show, or they went in some other small boat, perhaps from somewhere else altogether. Hamburg police must have people who know about sailing. I don't know who's handling the Braunschweig affair— he may know a lot about anarchist politics and not much about boats. We want to find out everything we possibly can about *exact* movements relating to *Apfel*—how long had she been at her mooring since she last went out, what sort of dinghy does she have, when was anything last seen of it? And still more questions—what is her auxiliary engine, how much fuel can she carry, does anybody know when she last fuelled? Has other shipping been asked to look out for her?"

"I'll do what I can for your first questions, Peter—your habit of messing about in boats has come in useful before, and what seems obvious to you is not always so clear to people without your specialised interests. But the alerting of other shipping is not easy—we could only say that *Apfel* was believed stolen, and that would make nonsense of the story that Dr Braunschweig has gone off for a cruise in her. Unless the German police are forced to make a statement I think they're right to keep quiet."

"I'm with you there—I've often thought that a lot of terrorism is simply kept going by publicity. There can't be any general alert for *Apfel* at the moment. But it would help to have even a rough idea of where she is or may be heading."

Sir Edmund is inclined to be scathing about my preference either for not bothering about lunch, or being content with a sandwich, a habit which he considers uncivilised. This is not out of concern for my dietary welfare but because lunch to him is an important means of keeping up with his vast range of semi-official, semi-social, contacts. To me it is more of a

25

nuisance—I hate lunches that go on for two or three hours, however fascinating the conversation. I enjoy food at what I regard as the right times, and one of them is breakfast. With so much else in our society breakfast standards are, alas, declining, but there is one honourable exception—the breakfasts you can still get in restaurant cars on British Rail. There was a restaurant car on my early train to Cambridge, and I thoroughly enjoyed my meal. The train was not crowded and I had a table to myself. You don't actually need space for thinking in, but sometimes it helps. I had a lot to think about.

Half of me wanted to be on the way to Hamburg instead of Cambridge. That Dr Braunschweig's fifty-foot ketch should be missing as well as the man himself seemed to me highly significant—but significant of what? I wanted to know much more about the boat, about the club and the conditions in which she was kept, but it was hard to see what bearing this might have on his disappearance. And although there were lots of questions that I wanted to ask I do not speak German at all fluently, and it seemed wiser to leave the questioning to the Hamburg police while I got on with things at Cambridge. But what was I to get on *with*? Seddon's report on the missing Baffin Map was about as thorough as it could be, and while I could go over the ground again with the Cambridge police it didn't seem likely that they could tell me anything we didn't know already. The museum did not seem much more hopeful. The Cambridge CID had talked both to Dr Wilding, the Curator, and to the new Keeper of Arctic Maps, Dr Ingrid Mitchell : what could they add to me? Of course, I should be asking different questions : when the loss of the map was reported to the Cambridge police nobody had any idea of the bizarre circumstances which now surrounded it. And I should have to be careful not to give the museum people any inkling of those circumstances. Somehow I'd got to find out what conceivable interest a seventeenth-century map could have to a political terror group in Germany—that is, if they *were* a terror group. And what had happened to the map?

The Museum of Cartography is a beautiful early eighteenth-century building tucked in at the back of St John's College. There is no formal link between college and museum, but

26

many St John's men have been distinguished in exploration, and by tradition the college provides one of the trustees for the museum, the college having offered land for the building when a later benefactor added to the original grant from the Hudson's Bay Company, to enable the collection of maps to be properly housed. The entrance and courtyard remain as they were when the museum was built, but considerable extensions have been added. The museum has been fortunate in its architects, or perhaps there is something in the Cambridge air that makes for academic beauty by its river (unlike Oxford, which used the Thames for gasworks). On that early summer morning I felt that the ugly business which had brought me to Cambridge had an incongruously lovely setting.

Seddon's notes told me that Dr Wilding had been Curator for twenty-eight years, and that he would have retired this year had there not been difficulty in finding a successor, a professorship of geography and a senior post in the Map Room at the British Museum having unexpectedly become vacant at the same time. My appointment was for ten o'clock, and I reported a couple of minutes before the hour. An attendant conducted me to the Curator's secretary, who took me into a high, light room overlooking the river which had been the Curator's office since the place was built. Dr Wilding was a picture-book example of the benign elderly scholar. "It is good of you to come," he said as he rose to greet me. "I fear we cannot help you much, but if you will tell me what you want I shall do everything in my power to assist."

"You should have been told that my business concerns the Baffin Map."

"Ah, yes, of course. I fear I grow forgetful. Alas, the Baffin Map is unaccountably astray."

"I know—we have been informed of that by the police. I am concerned with the grant of export licences for works of art, and my department has been approached by a reputable dealer who wants to know if we would grant an export licence were he able to acquire the map from you. Apparently an American university has approached him in the matter."

"I am not surprised. But you have no problem because we would not sell the map."

"I am sure you would not. But you will understand that

the disappearance of the map makes inquiries about a possible export licence for it of considerable interest."

"Yes, yes. It is all most distressing. Shall we have the police here again?"

"That may not be necessary. I thought it best to call on you myself so that you can give me whatever facts you have at first hand."

"It is considerate of you." He looked at my card. "I see that your name is Blair. We had a Blair once on the staff of the museum. He was an expert on early Arab maritime maps. No relation, I suppose? No, people never are."

"I understand that the map was lent to the university of Hamburg for an exhibition there, and that as far as you know it was returned."

"Yes. The university authorities behaved most responsibly in the matter. We lent them several of our maps. They were collected by a member of their staff. Dr Steinberg travelled with the maps to Hamburg, and he travelled back here with them when they were returned."

"You checked them with him?"

"Yes. Or rather, I checked the number of packages against a list of the maps we had lent. I did not myself open them—we have an expert staff of packers and map handlers—but as Dr Steinberg accompanied the maps personally they must have returned."

"Were they insured?"

"Yes—the university of Hamburg paid the premium."

"Have you claimed on the insurance?"

"No. I have seen no reason to, because I am sure that the map is somewhere in our building."

"Yet you reported its disappearance to the police."

"In confidence. I should add that this was partly at the insistence of Ingrid—that is, Dr Mitchell, the Keeper of Arctic Maps. Dr Mitchell is a—er—quite stern young woman. She is most able, of course. Doubtless you will meet her."

"Do you ever sell maps from your collection?"

"It is a matter for the trustees, though naturally they are guided by my advice. Yes, we do sell items from time to time. Like all museums we suffer from lack of space, and sometimes

28

it is necessary to dispose of items of secondary importance to make room for additions to our collection."

"You would not regard the Baffin Map as of secondary importance?"

"Indeed, no. It is not in my own field but it is unique of its kind. I am more directly concerned with early maps of Asia. You may have come across my book, *The Asiatic Sources of Eratosthenes*."

"Surely it is still the definitive work." He almost purred with pleasure.

"You are generous to say so, but yes, I think it remains the leading authority for the period. Much good work is coming out of American universities nowadays, but on the sources of Eratosthenes I feel that we are still in the lead. Are you interested in the special problems of his location of the Caspian?"

He would have been delighted to discuss Eratosthenes all day, but it seemed unlikely that this would cast any light on the missing Baffin Map. I felt that time was slipping through my fingers. "Would it be possible for me to see Dr Mitchell?" I asked.

"Certainly. But you are so well-informed about Eratosthenes that I should like to pursue certain matters with you."

"I shall look forward to it. But we are being pressed for a decision on the Baffin Map and there are some points I should like to clear up with Dr Mitchell."

"What a nuisance!" He lifted a telephone. "Janet, could you see if Dr Mitchell is free, and if so could you take Mr Blair to her?" A minute or two later his secretary came into the room. "Dr Mitchell is free. Shall I take Mr Blair now?"

"Do you feel that you must go at once?" Dr Wilding asked hopefully.

"I fear so."

He sighed. "It has been a pleasure to meet you. It is not every day one comes across such interest in the cartography of the third century BC."

I left the Curator in something approaching despair. Obviously he knew little about the Baffin Map and cared less. His attitude to its disappearance seemed deplorable, but he lived in

29

a world of his own. Whatever his eminence as a scholar he was clearly long past his job as an administrator and for the sake of the museum I hoped that his retirement might not be long postponed. As we walked through the long corridors of the museum, making our way to the newer buildings at the back, I hoped that Dr Mitchell might live nearer to reality.

She did—embarrassingly close, I felt, when the secretary introduced me and left. "I don't understand," she said, looking at my card. "I have never heard of you. What do you wish to see me about?"

I was using one of my private visiting cards, with my address in the Temple, and which gives simply my name without any military rank. It was the best I could do at short notice. I felt instinctively that vague stories about export licences would not go down well with this sharp young woman and decided to give her an edited version of the truth. "I take it this room is secure?" I said.

"What on earth do you mean?" She was still standing at her desk as she had got up to receive me, and she seemed, understandably, a bit startled. She was quite an attractive young woman, I thought, in her early thirties, with a good figure, a slight hardness in her appearance redeemed by widely spaced, intelligent eyes. She was wearing an amber necklace, the beads of an unusually deep reddish colour that suited her dark hair with a hint of red in it, and her clear skin.

I handed her my official warrant from the Department. "You will see that I am an officer of the Police Liaison Department of the Home Office," I said. "I am not myself a policeman, but naturally I work in close association with the police. If you are at all suspicious of me ring New Scotland Yard and ask for Assistant Commissioner Seddon. He will vouch for me, and if you put through the call yourself there can be no doubt that you are speaking to the Metropolitan Police."

"I don't doubt you. I don't know what you want." She sat down. She didn't invite me to sit, but there was a chair in front of the desk and I took it. "My visit concerns the Baffin Map," I said. "You must know all about its disappearance—indeed, I understand that it was you who pressed the Curator to call in the police."

"I did."

"It has come to the knowledge of one of our embassies—I'm afraid I am not at liberty to say more—that the Baffin Map, or rather *a* map purporting to show Baffin's discoveries in the Arctic, is being discreetly offered for sale. It may be a fake, it may be a legitimate copy of your map, or it may be the original stolen from the museum. Because the diplomatic service is involved we have been called in, and it is my job to see if we can help the embassy to recover the map—if it is your map. I have, of course, a full report of the inquiries made by the Cambridge police—regrettably they do not take us very far. You will understand that the diplomatic side of the matter is delicate, and that is why I am concerned that nothing we say can be overheard."

She ignored this, and as I didn't think it at all likely that anybody was listening in I let it go at that. What she did say rather surprised me. "What are they asking for it?" she said.

"I understand it is in the region of a quarter of a million pounds."

"Then it is undoubtedly our map. Is the embassy going to buy it?"

"Hardly—ambassadors have no funds for buying stolen property. It is more a question of seeing whether the police in the country concerned can act. How can you be so sure that it is your map?"

"The price, for one thing. No one is going to pay so much without being sure of what he is buying, and inks and paper used in map-making can be dated accurately nowadays by scientific analysis. That seems to me to rule out a fake. Has your embassy seen the map?"

"No. A member of the embassy staff may be permitted to see it, and that is why it is so important to have your views on what to look for in deciding whether it is your map."

"Couldn't I see it myself? I could travel anywhere at short notice."

"Obviously that would be the best thing, but I'm afraid it's out of the question. If crime is involved it will be major international crime, and we must assume that those concerned will know all about you. For the moment it must be left to the embassy staff to handle things."

"It seems most unsatisfactory, but I suppose you have a point. What do you want to know about the map?"

"I have the description of it from the catalogue of the museum. I want to know what makes it specially important."

She considered for a moment. Then she asked, "Are you familiar with the history of Arctic exploration?"

"Not very."

"At least you're honest." She gave me a rather thin smile, but it was a smile. As if she were lecturing to first-year undergraduates she went on, "Elizabethan seamen were firmly convinced of the existence of a North-West Passage from the Atlantic to the riches of the east, and sixteenth-century capitalists, including the Queen herself, fully realised the commercial advantages of finding such a route. There were also local resources to be exploited in fish and furs. Martin Frobisher got as far as what is now called Baffin Island in 1576 and thought he had found gold, though the 'gold-bearing' rocks he brought back were found to contain only iron pyrites. In the later sixteenth century John Davis, after whom the Davis Strait between Greenland and Baffin Island is named, added considerably to knowledge of the Arctic, and in spite of the severe ice he met remained hopeful that a passage leading to the Pacific could be found. In 1610 Henry Hudson discovered Hudson's Bay, a vast expanse of water which he thought was open sea. The voyage ended disastrously in a mutiny which led to Hudson's death, but some of the mutineers got back to England with reports of his great discovery—which incidentally saved them from the gallows by exciting so much interest. William Baffin followed Hudson's exploration and after several voyages got remarkably far north in the bay that bears his name. In 1615-16 he discovered Lancaster Sound, Jones Sound and Smith Sound, all of great importance in later Arctic exploration. For the next two centuries, however, the capitalist world had other things to think about and Baffin's discoveries were largely forgotten—partly because he was thought to have brought back no map. The Hudson's Bay Company found so much profit in exploiting Arctic Canada that it saw no point in pushing northwards to the wastes of Baffin Bay. Baffin's importance as an explorer was rediscovered in the nineteenth century, when the Royal Navy after the

32

Napoleonic wars turned its attention to the Arctic and the search for a North-West Passage. Baffin's map turned out to be remarkably accurate."

"But you say he brought back no map."

"I said that he *was thought* to have brought back no map. That is the point. The map now known as Baffin's did not come to light until 1776, a hundred and fifty years after his last Arctic voyage. It was found among the papers of a great-great-nephew, whose daughter married a Fellow of the Royal Society interested in geography. She gave the map to the museum, which forgot about it until the Navy sent Parry to the Arctic in 1819. The interest aroused by Parry's voyage awakened interest in Baffin's map, and its importance was recognised."

"You believe the map to be genuine?"

"There can be little doubt. There were no other voyages from which it could have derived. It is signed 'William Baffin' in a form which corresponds to Baffin's known signature."

"Your catalogue says that a particular feature of the map is its use of coloured tints to indicate depths. Isn't that unusual for the period?"

"Yes, that is one of the things that make the map unique—and so valuable. It is a beautiful piece of work, and, as I said, surprisingly accurate."

"Have you got a copy that I could see?"

"No—I don't think there are any copies. Wait a minute, though—there was a small photograph of it in the catalogue of the Hamburg exhibition. They sent us some, and I think I've still got some in this drawer. Yes—you can keep this if you like. While I think of it, there's another photograph in Mornington's *Arctic Exploration*, but his book was published about forty years ago. It was a standard work of its time, but is now out of date. I can vaguely recall a photograph of the map, but I doubt if it's as good as the one in the catalogue."

I studied the reproduction she gave me. It was small, and in black and white, but it showed Baffin Bay clearly enough, and what I took to be the coast of Ellesmere Island. "He got very far north," I said.

"Yes. He was a remarkable navigator in ice."

33

"You reported to the Curator that the map was missing. How long did you wait before telling him?"

"One day—half a day, really. We had given research facilities to Dr Longworth, of the United States Institute of Arctic Navigation, and he wanted to consult the map. The assistant who would normally have brought it to him went to the cabinet it should have been in, and it wasn't there. She told me at once—it was lateish in the afternoon, about four-thirty. I thought that it had probably been misplaced after its return from the Hamburg exhibition, and I organised a search for it first thing next morning. When it hadn't turned up by noon I reported to Dr Wilding."

"He still seems convinced that the map is mislaid and not really missing."

"That's because he wants to think so. He's due to retire soon, and he doesn't want any sort of cloud over his retirement. He objected strongly to calling in the police."

"But you did call in the police."

"Of course we did—I went to see them myself, and then they came here, and Dr Wilding had to see them."

"What do *you* think has happened to the map?"

"Well, your story confirms what I think. It's obviously been stolen, and my own view is that it was stolen on the way back from Hamburg."

"The maps were escorted by Dr Steinberg."

"He travelled with a number of map cases—that is all he can really say about it. If you are right in thinking that some international gang of thieves is at work they could easily have somebody working for them at an airport, or in the baggage hold of an aircraft."

"I understand it was all before your time. Wouldn't your predecessor have found out at once if the map was not among those returned from Hamburg?"

She thought about this. "In the ordinary way, yes," she said, "but Charles—I knew Charles Jackson well—was ill at the time, and he may just have assumed that the map had been put back by the staff."

"Dr Jackson's death seems to have been particularly sad."

"Yes. He was the world's leading expert on Arctic geography, and he had years of important work ahead of him. But he had some domestic problems and they affected his health. I had the greatest admiration for him. He supervised my thesis for my Ph.D.—I was working on climatic change in Alaska and the Bering Straits and he was a university lecturer in geography before he became Arctic Keeper at the museum."

"Did you expect to get his job?"

"That seems to me an impertinent question. I'd been working in Charles Jackson's field and all I can say is that it seemed reasonable that the trustees should invite me to succeed him."

"I'm sorry if I have upset you—I'm simply trying to get as accurate a picture as I can of the circumstances." I glanced at my watch. "I have taken up a lot of your time, and you have been very patient. If I may, I'll report directly to you as soon as I have news of any developments."

That mollified her. "You must forgive me. Charles Jackson was my friend, and I am still shocked by his death. You must do your job as you think fit. I can only wish you luck."

"Thank you." I got up to go. "May I say that the amber necklace you are wearing is an exceptionally beautiful piece?"

She laughed, but she was pleased. "It's exceptionally interesting amber. It came from the area we've been talking about—from the shores of Baffin Bay."

The Chief Superintendent at Cambridge was clearly impressed by whatever Sir Edmund Pusey had told him about me, but I cannot say that he received me with any noticeable enthusiasm. "We're not at all sure that it is our case, or even that there is a case," he said. "We've put in a lot of police time with nothing to show for it. I can understand your anxiety for the German businessman, and of course we're at your disposal for any help we can give, but I should say that the case properly belongs to Hamburg. However, you'd better have a word with the officer who actually handled our inquiries— Detective Inspector Richards. I've asked him to stand by. I must ask you to excuse me though. I've got to attend a meeting of the Traffic Committee at three o'clock."

I was not sorry to be left with the inspector on my own. He was youngish and obviously intelligent, and he looked rather anxious. "I can't help feeling that we must have slipped up in some way," he said. "I did everything I could think of,

35

but it wasn't exactly helpful to have the Curator insisting that the map was probably not lost, anyway."

"I've read your report, and it seems to me masterly," I said. "Please don't think that I'm here to pick holes in anything you've done. What we've got to do now is to consider all the personalities involved and see if we can find any link with Hamburg, or the oil company. You knew nothing of that at the time, and you couldn't have done more than you did."

He brightened a little. "I don't have many dealings with top brass, if you'll pardon the expression, sir. But I've heard of one or two things that your Department has done, and I'm proud to be working with you."

A pleasant-looking girl came in with tea and a plate of cucumber sandwiches—she must have had everything ready in advance. "The Chief Superintendent likes cucumber sandwiches, but as you know he's had to go out. So I wondered if you might like them, they're all fresh," she said. I thanked her. The inspector poured out tea, and we each took a sandwich. The slight informality of tea and sandwiches made things easier for us. "I'd like to go back to the situation at the museum before the map was reported missing," I said. "Did the rather sudden death of the Arctic man, Dr Charles Jackson, strike you as at all suspicious?"

"Yes, sir, it did, and I went into it as thoroughly as I could. It made quite a story in the local papers when it happened because of his reputation as a scholar, though of course nobody knew anything about the map at the time. There was an inquest because he died of an overdose of drugs, but he was being treated by a doctor for depression and they were properly prescribed. The evidence at the inquest provided a reasonable explanation of how he came to take the overdose, and in the circumstances there couldn't have been any other verdict than accidental death. When I was making inquiries about the map I went into all the evidence at the inquest, and had a long talk with the sergeant who'd handled things. He thought everything was in order."

"Did Dr Jackson leave any family?"

"Yes, sir, a widow and a daughter around fourteen. The girl is being educated at a boarding school, and the sergeant thought that the widow would find it rather difficult to manage.

36

They were buying a house on a mortgage. The widow has a job as a school-teacher, but her salary won't go far with the mortgage and school fees to meet."

"Do you *know* that she was left badly off?"

"Yes, sir. I happen to know the managing clerk in the solicitor's office which dealt with Dr Jackson's will. Of course he shouldn't really have told me anything, and I didn't ask him to go into details, but he did confirm that Dr Jackson left very little, and being only fifty-two when he died there's not much in the way of pension."

"Does the widow know that the map is missing?"

"I can't say, sir. You see, with the Curator insisting that we must treat everything in confidence and not let out that there was any concern about the map I felt I couldn't very well ask her about it. I was interested in Dr Jackson's financial circumstances to see if he could have had any possible motive for trying to sell the map. There's not the slightest evidence against him, but I went into motive because if anybody had taken the map from the museum he'd have been best placed to do it, or to help somebody else to do it. He had the big mortgage and his daughter at a fee-paying school, but he earned a good salary and he added to it by lecturing. I should say he lived up to his income, but he didn't seem to be extravagant and I could find no evidence of secret gambling debts, or anything else."

"Why was he depressed? His successor, Dr Mitchell, said that he had domestic problems. What were they?"

The inspector looked worried again. "That's new to me, sir. Nothing about domestic trouble came out at the inquest. His widow said that he began to get depressed about a year ago because he felt that the quality of his lectures was falling off. She thought that he was working too hard, suggested that they should take a holiday, tried all the normal ways to jolly him along. It didn't work, and after a bit she persuaded him to see a doctor. The doctor said it was a type of depression not uncommon in academic men in middle age. He treated him with a fairly new type of tranquillising drug that he had found successful with other patients, and he thought that he was responding well. The overdose alone might not have killed him—he died from a combination of the overdose and alcohol.

37

He and his wife had been to a farewell party for a college lecturer who was going to be a professor in America, and there was evidence that Dr Jackson drank a considerable quantity of gin."

"That was unusual for him?"

"So it seemed, sir. He liked a drink, but the sergeant found nothing to indicate heavy drinking. The doctor said that a sudden turning to alcohol if it happened to be available was typical of his sort of depression."

"Funny that Dr Mitchell talked about domestic problems. But she seems to have known him well from her student days —she had actually been a student of his before he got the museum job. She may have used the phrase loosely, and not meant what is ordinarily understood by it. What do we know of her background?"

"She wasn't easy to interview, sir—she'd answer questions civilly enough, but she didn't volunteer anything about herself. My feeling was that the Curator was a bit afraid of her, and if so I'd understand it. But the main facts of her life seem straightforward. She was a student at Bristol, and by all accounts a brilliant one. She took a Ph.D. here at Cambridge, and then she got a teaching fellowship at one of the women's colleges. I'd say she was respected rather than liked. I talked to various people at the college, and they all seemed to think that she had a fair contempt for most other people, particularly for women's colleges. But there's no denying her ability. Her own special field is polar geography, and her colleagues thought it quite natural that she should be appointed to succeed Dr Jackson."

"She's quite attractive. I wonder why she's never married."

The inspector's worried look had gone again, and he laughed. "Well, I wouldn't like to be married to her, sir," he said.

"The world's a bit hard sometimes on women of outstanding ability, but I can see what you mean. Where does she live?"

"Nice little cottage out towards Cherry Hinton. Looks after herself inside, but employs an old chap as a gardener three days a week. I put a man on to watching the place for a while, but we're shortstaffed as always, and I couldn't justify keeping up a watch. She doesn't have much to do with her neighbours, though they all say she's civil enough. She enter-

38

tains a bit in the evenings and at weekends, rather fancies herself as a cook, or so it's said. Guests mostly cars with local registrations, so they're probably academic friends of one sort or another. All highly respectable. Apart from opportunity there's not a scrap of evidence to suggest that she knows anything about the map, and making the Curator call us in as she did rather points the other way."

"Know anything about her family?"

"Only from the most elementary inquiries. She seems to be an only child. Parents still alive—father's a doctor in Nottingham, and well thought of, according to the local police."

"You've been extraordinarily thorough. What about the rest of the staff?"

"Well, a sergeant and I between us have interviewed all of them, and there's nothing against any of them. Most of them, even the typists, have been there some time—jobs at the museum are reckoned good to have."

"Yet you yourself are not satisfied."

"No, sir, I'm not. I'd like to put in more time on the case, but with so little to go on, and the Curator's insistence that the map is probably not lost anyway, I can't justify it."

"He could be right."

"Of course he could, but in common sense I don't think he is, nor does Dr Mitchell. It's all very well to say that the map's only been misplaced, but where has it been misplaced? There's a staff of people called map handlers, and when a map is lent for some exhibition outside the museum the handlers are responsible for packing it in a specially made case. The cases are all labelled with the catalogue number of the map inside. When cases come back from an exhibition they go to the Chief Map Handler—he's a kind of Head Porter—and he sees that they go back to the department they came from. Once there, it is for the Keeper of that particular department to decide whether the map goes into one of his own cabinets, or is taken away for storage. There are air-conditioned storage rooms in the new buildings where maps that are not likely to be wanted very often are kept. The Chief Map Handler took the case labelled with the catalogue number of the Baffin Map to the Arctic Room himself. He knew that it normally lived in the department, but it

39

was for the Keeper—it was Dr Jackson then—to decide, so he left it there without unpacking it. That seems to be quite normal. If they don't get any special instructions they go round next day to collect the empty case. That's what happened this time. The case was left in the Arctic Room, and next day one of the handlers collected it empty from Dr Jackson's secretary. She says that she assumed that Dr Jackson had put away the map himself. He never said anything to her about it, but there was no particular reason why he should. Dr Jackson often stayed after she'd gone home—you'll recall his widow saying that he was overworking—and the secretary just thought that he'd dealt with the map after she'd gone."

"All the handlers can say is that the case was empty when they took it back. There's no proof that the map was ever in the case."

"No, sir, but that's where the university of Hamburg comes in. They say that all the maps were packed under the supervision of a representative of the insurers, and there's a signed list of all the cases, with their contents."

"So either the map was put back in its proper place by Dr Jackson and was taken some time afterwards, or Dr Jackson took it away himself."

"That's about it, sir, with such evidence as there is in favour of Dr Jackson—I mean, in favour of his innocence."

"What does the Curator think can have happened?"

"He's just vague, sir, because he doesn't want anything to have happened. He says that they've got tens of thousands of maps, and it must have been put in the wrong place somewhere."

"But surely they've looked?"

"Of course they have. All the other maps that came back from Hamburg have been checked, and they are all in the right places. It's just possible that the map may have found its way into what they call Unclassified Storage."

"What's that?"

"The old cellars, sir—they're full of boxes and bundles of maps, hundreds and hundreds of them. Mostly they are not important maps, and they're being gradually sorted out. It's a job that's been going on for years, but nobody does much to get on with it. Dr Wilding says that it's one of the things that his successor will have to do. I think he's convinced himself that one day the Baffin Map will turn up, and it's no use worrying about it."

"You think he's wrong?"

"Well, he knows the museum much better than I do, and if that's what he thinks, that's it. If the map *has* got into the Unclassified Collection it could be years before anybody comes across it. But unless Dr Jackson suddenly went mad or something I don't see any way in which it *could* have got into the cellars. Mostly they're just left locked and nobody goes there much."

"So how do things stand as far as you are concerned?"

"Just an unclosed file, sir. The new information you've brought makes it look like a serious crime, and I've been told to act on your instructions. But on the information we have there doesn't seem much more that I can do."

I liked Inspector Richards, and felt that we were lucky to have him at the Cambridge end. I wanted to call on Dr Jackson's widow before leaving Cambridge, and thought that I might as well stay in Cambridge for the moment. I phoned Ruth to tell her that I seemed likely to be stuck for a day or two. "In that case, Peter, I think I'll drive over tonight and join you," she said. "There are several small things I want to do in Cambridge, and at least we'll be together. Get a room for us, and let's meet at the University Hotel for dinner. I should be there soon after seven."

III

Death of a Geographer

AFTER FIXING UP our room at the hotel there was just about
time to find a library. I wanted to consult the Admiralty's
Arctic Pilot, but the reference section of the public library I
went to didn't have it. The librarian explained that pilot books
were a bit too specialised for them, and he recommended the
library of the Museum of Cartography. I didn't want to go
back to the museum so I asked if there was anywhere nearer,
and he suggested the School of Geography which, he said, had
a library for students, though he didn't know if they'd permit
a casual visitor to use it. I decided to have a go, talked nicely
to a young woman in the office who rang through to the
librarian. She was helpful, and found me Volume III of the
Arctic Pilot, which covers Baffin Bay. I could get the *Pilot* in
London, but I needed to have a quick look at it. The historical
notes which are such a splendid feature of the Admiralty's
pilot books confirmed what Dr Mitchell had told me of the
importance of William Baffin's discoveries. I found one point
of particular interest—the curious existence in the far north
of a considerable body of navigable open water known to the
old whaling fleets as the North Water. The reasons for the
existence of this open stretch in an area of ferocious ice
apparently remain obscure. Beyond telling me that "more than
one possible explanation has been suggested" the *Pilot* did not
enlighten me, contenting himself with saying that I could
expect to reach open water north of about the 75th parallel
and continue sailing northward until I found myself blocked
by the fast ice of Smith Sound, that desolate channel running
between Greenland and Ellesmere Island to the Arctic Ocean
and ultimately the North Pole. Interesting as this was, it

seemed scarcely relevant to the disappearance of Dr Braunschweig and the Baffin Map.

Ruth's special field is geophysical mathematics, the complex mathematical relationships of the earth movements that produce earthquakes and in their time have thrown up mountains and formed continents. According to Ruth they still do, although her timescale for the movement of continental land masses makes it unlikely that any of us will live to explore Atlantis. Earthquakes, however, are another matter, and seismic prediction is an important branch of her studies, which are also useful to geologists in the oil industry. I was so glad to see her that I was more concerned with the beauty she added to that lovely summer evening than with the geological processes of a few million years ago that formed Cambridge for us to meet in. Looking at her over dinner I wondered what made her so different from Ingrid Mitchell. Both were outstandingly able women with a mastery of abstruse subjects, yet Ruth was feminine and lovable where in some indefinable way Ingrid Mitchell was not. Or perhaps the difference was in me—I found Ruth the dearest of companions and infinitely comforting to be with, whereas on the whole I thought I shared the inspector's view of Dr Mitchell. Some men, though, might find her very attractive.

After dinner we went for a long walk along the Cam, the scent of cut lawns and flowers in the college gardens adding to the magic of Ruth's presence. I told her the whole story, and while one part of me was being a reporter another was wondering what her keen analytical mind would make of the extraordinary sequence of events. Mathematics is partly a search for patterns, partly an understanding of them—perhaps that is one reason why so many people who are good at maths (including Ruth) are particularly drawn to Bach's music. But what pattern could she find here? There must be a pattern of some sort, but so many pieces were missing that there seemed no way of putting it together.

One of Ruth's special qualities is the rare one of listening to other people. She let me talk without interrupting until I came to the inspector's remark that he knew nothing of any domestic problems in the late Dr Jackson's life.

"If Dr Mitchell is as intelligent as you make out and she said he had domestic problems then I'd believe her rather than the inspector or the evidence at the inquest," she said.

"I agree. I'm going to see Mrs Jackson tomorrow. I rang her from the police station. She's off work this week because she hurt her ankle. She teaches history, but she's also got a qualification in physical education and it seems she helps out from time to time in the gym. Anyway, she twisted her ankle or something, and she'll be at home tomorrow and can see me in the morning."

We were walking hand in hand, and Ruth gave my hand a small squeeze. "I ought to know you, Peter. Your Dr Mitchell said another funny thing—when she told you that her amber beads came from Baffin Bay."

"It was just a chance remark. She was rather pleased, I think, that I'd noticed the necklace."

"I've never heard of amber coming from the Arctic. It's fossilised resin, and it comes originally from trees. Most of the world's amber has been found round the Baltic, whose shores were thickly forested in the right geological period. It has cropped up in other places, but the Baltic is the main home of amber. Either she was trying to mislead you, or she was wrong, or the Arctic was forested in a way we don't know anything about."

"Or it was populated by a race of traders we don't know anything about. I wonder Ruth, I wonder . . ."

Typically she didn't ask me what had come into my mind and we walked on in silence for some minutes. Then I said, "I don't think she was trying to mislead me. My impression was that she was proud of her amber, pleased that I'd noticed it, and made her remark without thinking of anything except that it was interesting. But *you've* made me think. All along I've been racking my brains to try to find some point of contact between the modern oil industry and a map drawn over three centuries ago. The amber may have nothing to do with it, but you've given me a sort of amber light. Dr Braunschweig is or was an expert in oil distribution—could old William Baffin have recorded something on his map that might produce some new ideas on Arctic navigation? If so, it could be important to an oil company. There's oil in the Arctic all right, but the main fields found so far seem to be in Alaska, which is about the worst possible place for shipping oil to Europe or the eastern seaboard of America. If there were a practicable North-West Passage it would be different. If Dr Mitchell is right, old Baffin's original discoveries seem to have been largely forgotten for a couple of centuries. Could there have been some more discoveries that haven't been remembered yet? If so, is there anyone who'd so much want them to *remain* undiscovered that they'd go to the length of kidnapping Dr Braunschweig to try to get hold of the map? But again if so, why has the map disappeared? No, it doesn't make sense."

"It makes a sort of sense, Peter. There could be two or three organisations not knowing what the other's doing, or working against each other."

"I suppose there could be . . . But this is more your field, Ruth. Can anything have happened to the earth's surface in the Arctic that we don't know about?"

She laughed. "All sorts of things have happened in the Arctic, and we probably know about less than one per cent of them. The shape of the globe has changed from time to time, and the North Pole has shifted about all over the place —or at least it seems quite likely to have done so. The magnetic pole *does* shift, as you know from elementary navigation, though that is a rather different matter. If there's anything in the theory of change in the crustal shape of the globe—and there probably is—then there would have been big climatic changes with the shifting of the poles and what is now the Arctic Ocean might have been like the Mediterranean. But all this would have been millions of years ago—you're talking of three centuries. I don't think Baffin's Arctic could have been much different from ours."

"No, but he might have found things that we don't know about. Do you know anything about what's called the North Water in Baffin Bay?"

"Oh, Peter, I'm a mathematician, not a geographer. I have to know a bit about ocean floors because they're concerned in earth movements, and I know a little about major ocean

45

currents, but not much. As a matter of fact I *have* heard of your North Water because it's a curious exception to normal ice-formation in the polar region. As far as I know nobody's ever found a satisfactory explanation for such a considerable area of water so far north remaining more or less ice-free, but it's not really in my field and I've never gone into it."

"Could you find somebody who has?"

"I dare say. The geographers at your museum are on the doorstep, but I suppose you don't want to talk to them."

"No."

"Well, it would be easier in Oxford, then. I know the Reader in Oceanography, Jeremy Vaughan—he's a fellow of our college. When do we go back to Oxford?"

"I don't know. I've got to see this woman tomorrow morning, and what happens next depends on what turns up, here, in London or in Hamburg. I wish you'd come with me to see Mrs Jackson."

"If I thought it would help of course I'd come. But I feel that I'd be off-putting rather than a help. It's not going to be easy for her to talk about her husband—and you're not bad at being nice to people, Peter."

I've never been a good sleeper, and I owe most of the education I've managed to achieve to the books I've read in the small hours. That night I couldn't read with Ruth curled up beside me because the light would have bothered her, and my mind went on trying to make some sort of pattern out of the bewildering case we were landed with. What, if anything, could be called facts? Dr Braunschweig had disappeared—at least he wasn't at home and he'd not turned up at his office. His boat also seemed to have disappeared. The chairman of Universal Oil had had a letter suggesting that Dr Braunschweig had been kidnapped, and demanding a ransom in the form of a seventeenth-century map of part of the Arctic. Even if the authorities and the oil company were prepared to meet the demand the ransom could not be paid, because the map could not be found. It had been in the Cambridge Museum of Cartography for around two hundred years, and for most of that time nobody had taken much notice of it. As a map it was unique and had a considerable money value, though how that value

46

could be realised was hard to see. Probably it didn't matter, because money didn't seem to come into it—if Dr Braunschweig had been kidnapped, and if his kidnappers wanted money, it would have been easier to demand a few million pounds from the oil company.

Why should anybody want the map so much? It had been on exhibition in Hamburg, so if the kidnapping was a Hamburg affair one or other of the kidnappers could have seen the map. Or it might be the other way round—somebody in Hamburg could have seen the map and thought up the kidnapping in order to get hold of it. The Curator's belief that it had gone astray somewhere inside the museum seemed mere wishful thinking. It could have been stolen in transit, but that would not have been easy, and it seemed more likely that it had been taken after it had been returned to the museum. When? In the evening after Dr Jackson's secretary had gone home and he was working late? That would imply that it had been taken by Dr Jackson himself, for if it had been stolen by anyone else Dr Jackson would have found the map-case empty and would surely have reported it at once. But there was no reason to suppose that Dr Jackson had had anything to do with it. He might equally well have unpacked the map and put it away in its proper place. A few days later he was dead. Then came a gap of about three months before Dr Mitchell was appointed to succeed him, and then a gap of another couple of months before the visiting American scholar wanted the map and it could not be found. The map could have been taken at any time during those months. With the Curator's almost hostile attitude to police inquiries Inspector Richards had been handicapped from the start, but Dr Mitchell thought that the map had been stolen and she had not tried to put any obstacles in his way. That he had found nothing suspicious about any of the staff was not conclusive, but he was an experienced detective and it indicated that there was nothing suspicious to find. Yet he himself believed a crime to have been committed. With police resources strained and the scope for inquiries limited by the Curator's attitude, he had concentrated on Dr Mitchell herself and on what he could learn about her predecessor: that was reasonable, because whoever was in charge of the department had most opportunity

47

of removing, or conniving at the removal of, a map belonging to it. There was slight evidence that Dr Jackson had been living up to the limit of his means, but millions of respectable citizens do that. He was depressed about something, but his widow's account of things and the doctor's clinical judgement that such depression was not uncommon among academics around Dr Jackson's age tallied well enough, and certainly there was nothing so far to invalidate the coroner's finding that his death was an accident. Well, I should soon be seeing his widow, and it was pointless to speculate on what she might be able to tell me. With that I managed to doze off, and slept until nearly seven.

Ruth had been invited to deliver the Granage Lectures at Cambridge in the autumn, and she wanted to discuss one or two details with the university people. She went off soon after nine-thirty. My appointment with Mrs Jackson was not until eleven. I rang Sir Edmund. Nothing that seemed important had come in, but he had answers to some of my questions about Dr Braunschweig's yacht. "He disappeared on June 1 and the ransom note was delivered to Sir Anthony Brotherton in London on June 5," Sir Edmund said. "Hamburg police discovered that the yacht was missing on June 2, but it wasn't necessarily significant until the ransom note turned up. His staff had been told that he'd gone off on a cruise, and for all the police knew at the time it was just possible that he had. They were chiefly concerned in trying to trace his car, and didn't begin serious inquiries about the yacht until they learned of the ransom note on the morning of the fifth. They were—they still are—hampered by the need for secrecy. People's memories about when they last saw a yacht at a mooring are vague at the best of times. However, the police think they have established that she was definitely there on the first, and not there on the morning of the second. Before that they can't be certain, but they think that she'd been lying at her mooring for about a fortnight, since she came back from a weekend cruise. She has two dinghies—a ten-foot clinker-built tender and an inflatable rubber dinghy. Neither is at the yacht club, and there's no reliable information on when they were last seen there. As for going ashore from the last cruise, Frau

48

Braunschweig thinks they didn't take their own dinghy, but used the yacht club tender. She says she can't swear to it because they've been out in the boat so often, but she thinks she's right about the club boat because she remembers they had to wait a bit after signalling for it. Your questions about fuel are more difficult. The boat has a high-grade diesel auxiliary, but except for going in and out of port he doesn't use the engine much, and takes a pride in maneuvering under sail—doubtless you will understand that, Peter. Frau Braunschweig can't say for certain when the boat was last fuelled, but thinks that it may have been before the weekend cruise in May. She says the engine was used hardly at all on that cruise, so if the tanks were full then they'd be nearly full now. Assuming an average of around six knots she carries enough fuel for about two hundred miles—not a great range, but she's a sailing boat. She was designed specially for Dr Braunschweig, and he didn't want to give up space to fuel tanks."

"A proper attitude, and nice to see it in an oil man," I said.

"Well, I don't know that it gets you anywhere, but you wanted the information."

"Nothing gets anywhere at the moment. The whole of this case is navigating in dense fog—and without a compass or a lead-line."

I told Sir Edmund that I'd ring him again after I'd seen Mrs Jackson, and probably come back to London in the afternoon. Unless something new turned up I thought I'd probably go on to Hamburg.

I had half an hour or so to wait before I needed to get a taxi to go to Mrs Jackson, so I walked into Clare gardens and found an entrancing little sunken lawn to sit on. I wanted to concentrate on what I was going to say to Mrs Jackson, but I kept thinking about Dr Braunschweig and his yacht. There was nothing to indicate that he was with her, but somebody had taken her from her mooring. Could she have been taken off singlehanded? Probably, but to take a fifty-foot ketch from a crowded mooring singlehanded implied someone with a good deal of experience, and it seemed more likely that at least two people were involved. How had they got out to her? Her own dinghies were not at the yacht club, which fitted Frau

Braunschweig's recollection that *Apfel*'s party had gone ashore from her last cruise in the club launch. If so, then the dinghies were probably still on board. I had no idea of *Apfel*'s deck arrangement, but there would be room for a ten-foot tender and a rubber dinghy on a fifty-foot boat. I doubted whether there would be comfortable room for a third dinghy. What had happened to the dinghy that *must* have gone out to *Apfel* to put on board whoever sailed her away? She might be towing it, but a towed dinghy is a nuisance, particularly if the towing yacht has only a minimal crew. A simpler explanation was that somebody had stayed in the dinghy and taken it back ashore. Assuming that two people had been put on board to handle *Apfel*, that meant three people in the dinghy, and someone may have noticed a dinghy with three up in the vicinity of the moorings on June 1 or 2. If there hadn't been anyone left to take away the dinghy it might have been cast off and abandoned as soon as *Apfel* was safely out of sight from the club—if so, an abandoned dinghy ought to have been washed up somewhere.

The Jackson house was Victorian and detached, and it must have had at least six bedrooms. There were signs of neglect—the woodwork needed painting, and the big garden was overgrown and untidy, with weeds in the drive and a lawn beginning to look like a hayfield. Mrs Jackson's first words on opening the door were to apologise for the lawn. "I was going to cut it last weekend, but I couldn't," she said. Her left ankle was in plaster and she was using crutches. When I thanked her for agreeing to see me in spite of her injury she laughed. "It's not nearly so bad as it looks. They think I may have broken a small bone, but it doesn't hurt now, and I can get around all right. The main trouble is that I can't drive. If I can find somebody to take me in I shall be back at school next week. I get frightfully bored being on my own. But you don't want to talk about me. I've no idea what you've come about, and I probably shan't be able to help in any way, but do come in. Would you like a cup of coffee?"

I accepted the coffee, followed her into the kitchen and filled the kettle for her. "You seem to be house-trained," she said.

"Not really—you don't need much training to fill a kettle for somebody who's walking on crutches, particularly when you're going to share the coffee."

"Do you mind if we have it in the kitchen?"

"Not a bit. You've made it a most attractive room." Originally it had been a kitchen and scullery; now the scullery part had sink, cooker and refrigerator, and the rest of the old kitchen was furnished as a dining-cum-sitting room. We sat at a nice pine table. "My daughter's away at school, and when I'm on my own this is my living room," she explained. "I let as much as I can of the rest of the house, mostly to students. It would be better not to have students because there wouldn't be the bother of vacations, but Charles and I both wanted to help students if we could—that's one of the reasons we got such a big house. The rent from letting rooms helped to pay the mortgage, and when Charles was alive it was nice to have the place to ourselves in the vacations. It's different now, but I still haven't sorted myself out properly. And I still don't know why you've come, or even who you really are, apart from the fact that you have something to do with museums."

"I don't have much to do with museums as such. As I explained when I telephoned yesterday I belong to a small government department that's concerned with antiquities, and we're interested in an old map that was in your late husband's keeping."

"But surely they can tell you all about it at the museum?"

She was alert and intelligent. She must have been considerably younger than her husband, no more than in her early forties, and she was, or could have been if she bothered a bit more about her appearance, distinctly attractive. I had to make a quick decision. "The trouble is," I said, "that the map, which is a valuable one, is missing."

She looked suddenly rather haggard. "Isn't that a matter for the police?" she said.

"Yes. I was at Cambridge police station when I telephoned you."

"Then you're just a policeman, and all that talk about a department of antiquities was a lie to get me to see you without suspecting anything. It's damned unfair. I've never liked it when students call policemen pigs, but now I think they're right."

"It's not as simple as that. I *am* from the Home Office and I am *not* a policeman, although as you may know the Home Office is the ministry responsible for the police. I have told you no untruth. I should like your help in trying to discover what *is* the truth about this missing map, but if you are in any doubt of my credentials please ring Cambridge police and ask for the Chief Superintendent. I should prefer you to be satisfied about me before I say anything more."

She looked even more haggard. My impression was that although she was worried about something she was not worried about the map. She was sitting across the table from me, her coffee untouched. Suddenly she put her head in her hands and broke down sobbing. After a minute or two she dabbed her eyes with a handkerchief. "Sorry," she said. "I'm not going to telephone about you. Either I trust you or I don't, and I think I'm going to trust you."

"It might even make you feel better."

"You're not unperceptive, are you? I've been living with all this for months, and there's been absolutely nobody I could talk to."

"Your daughter's too young?"

"Susan's only just fourteen. She adored her father, and I don't want anything to hurt her memory of him. Besides, I don't *know*—I've never *known*."

"You suspect that his death was not an accident?"

"I don't know what I suspect. I only know that Charles changed suddenly. It was about a year ago. I can't explain it properly—you have to live with somebody to notice changes in behaviour. It was a lot of little things. Charles always worked hard, but he loved what he was doing, and he was an optimistic, cheerful person. He always enjoyed breakfast—suddenly he didn't want any breakfast. He took to coming home late, and often he didn't want any dinner when he did come home. We started having rows—we'd never had any sort of rows before. We've always had to worry about money, wanting to send Susan away to school, paying to keep Charles's old mother in a home, but we never used to have rows about it. Then I spent a few pounds on material to make some new curtains and Charles was furious—scarcely spoke to me for two days. It was then that I got seriously worried about him, and

52

persuaded him to see a doctor. I wish I hadn't."

"You didn't tell any of this to the police?"

"How could I? Charles was dead—it could have been suicide, which would have been awful for Susan to live with. There wasn't any doubt that Charles was suffering from a clinically diagnosed depression—the doctor helped there. I answered all the police questions, but I couldn't tell them of the things that worried me, because I wasn't even sure of what they were."

"Did you suspect that another woman might have been involved?"

She didn't answer for some time. Then she said, "Yes, I think I did, sometimes. But it would have been totally unlike Charles—I mean, he might have fallen in love with somebody else, but if so he would have told me. At least, the old Charles would, but then everything was out of character in that horrible last year."

"Did you go to the party the night before he died?"

"Yes. I'm afraid I rather encouraged him to go. I felt it was good for him to go out as much as possible."

"Do you remember who was there?"

"It was the usual sort of Cambridge party, given by a geography lecturer called Jack Eastman who was going to a professorship in the States. We knew him well. Several of the museum staff were there, including Ingrid Mitchell who got Charles's job—of course she wasn't at the museum then, she had a tutorial fellowship, and geography was her subject. It was quite a crowded party. Deliberately I didn't stay with Charles—I wanted him to get out of himself and talk to other people. There was some food, and a lot to drink—it wasn't a dinner party, you just helped yourself to food and ate it where you could. About eleven o'clock I looked for Charles to go home and I was horrified to find him nearly drunk. Ingrid Mitchell was looking after him, and she helped me to get him out to the car so that people wouldn't notice too much. Then she came home in the car with me, and helped me to get Charles into the house, and put him to bed. I was so thankful to get Charles to bed that I didn't think about his pills—if I had thought I'd probably have felt that he was too far gone to bother about them. They were on a table by his bed, and he normally took two. The doctor thinks he must have taken his usual two, and then forgotten he'd taken them and had some more, probably several more. I ought to have taken them away, but I didn't."

"Have you always had separate rooms?"

"No. It was all part of his illness, or what I call his illness. He took to not being able to sleep, and he'd want to read, or get up and work half the night. So I moved out into what had been our spare room. It was quite friendly—he agreed that it was better for him to be on his own."

"If it's not too painful for you, could I see the room?"

"Why not?"

She got up and led me out of the kitchen back into the hall by which we'd entered. "Susan's bedroom is on the first floor, but Charles and I lived on the ground floor," she explained. "I told you we let some of the other rooms. This was Charles's room. Originally I think it was a music room. It opens on to the garden, and as you can see it's a nice room."

It was. There were french windows leading to the garden, and other windows to each side of them, so that the whole room was full of light. For all that it had a sort of musty feel about it. "You don't use it now?" I asked.

"I haven't since Charles died. I suppose I could let it, or move back into it myself, but I just haven't wanted to."

"So it's much the same now as it was then?"

"Pretty much. I've taken away clothes and things, but I haven't moved any furniture."

A double bed stood against the wall facing the french windows. The room was big enough not to seem cluttered. A table with a reading lamp was beside the bed, and in one corner stood a big desk, also with its own light. The wall by the desk was lined with bookshelves, and there was a bookcase against one of the other walls. There were a couple of armchairs and two or three attractive prints. There was no washbasin—apart from the bed it was a study rather than a bedroom.

"Did he take his pills with water?" I asked.

"Yes. I always put out a glass of water for him. The police took away the glass, and there were only his own fingerprints on it."

I walked over to the french windows and looked out at the

54

untidy garden. Even with the long-haired lawn and the weed-filled flower beds it was a pleasant outlook. At the bottom of the french windows an edge of carpet had become untacked. "Do you keep the french windows locked?" I asked.

"They are now. They weren't then. Sometimes when he was having a particularly bad night Charles would wander round the garden."

Something caught my eye in a fold of the loose bit of carpet. I picked it up—it was an amber bead.

"Is this yours?"

She took it from me and studied it. "No, I've never seen it before. It may have been there for ages—I'm afraid I haven't cleaned out the place very thoroughly." She did not seem much interested.

"May I keep it for the moment?"

"You can have it if you like."

"Thank you. Can I finish my coffee?"

"It will be cold. I'll make some more."

"Please don't bother. I rather like cold coffee. The coffee doesn't matter, anyway. I just want to talk to you for a few minutes more."

"And you'd be happier in the kitchen?" She spoke almost brightly.

"A bit, yes. I don't want to hurt you more than I have to."

"You're not hurting me now—you're making me rather interested. I still don't know who you are, but I said I'd trust you, and I'm not going back on that."

I found it easier to talk in the kitchen than in that room with its dreadful memories. But the room raised several questions.

"When you and Dr Mitchell brought your husband home, did you get him into the house by the door, or by the french window?"

"The window. After we'd got him out of the car Ingrid Mitchell kept him standing up while I ran in and opened the window, so we could get him directly into his room."

"Dr Mitchell came home with you in your car. How did she herself get back?"

"Her own car was parked near the party. After we'd got Charles safely to bed I drove her back to where her car was

55

parked. I thought it was all right to leave Charles, and I wasn't away long."

"But there was a time when your husband was alone in the house. About how long, do you think?"

She passed her hand across her forehead. "It's horrible to think back to it all, and it's hard to remember things exactly. I had to drive back into Cambridge, but I came home as soon as I'd dropped Ingrid Mitchell by her car. I may have been away about twenty-five minutes."

"Did you leave the french window locked after you had put your husband to bed?"

"I can't say for certain, but I think probably not. I can't remember locking it."

I changed the subject. "Did you know much about your husband's work?" I asked.

"Yes—at least I did before his illness. One of the changes in him was that he stopped telling me about his work. Before that we more or less worked together. We were quite a good partnership, you see, he was a geographer and I'm a historian. I mean, I've got a history degree and I teach history, though I'm not really a historian in Charles's class as a geographer. But I could understand what he was doing, and sometimes I could help him a bit."

"What was he doing?"

"He was interested in climatic change in the Arctic. It's a highly specialised subject, and I think I could say he was one of the world's top authorities on it. Now his book will never be published. Dr Mitchell has taken over his work and I expect she will edit the papers that Charles left. I'd like to do it myself, but I'm not good enough. It's all immensely complicated, but in the old days when Charles talked to me about it I found it fascinating."

"When you say climatic change, do you mean over historical time?"

"Partly. There's one theory that the climate in southern Greenland a thousand years ago was slightly milder than it is now, and that this encouraged Norse settlement from Iceland. The settlements disappeared around the fourteenth century, and some people think that this was because the climate got severe again. But all this is rather marginal. Charles was concerned with the fundamental geography of the Arctic, possible movements of the Pole with changes in the earth's crust, and the consequences in terms of climate. These are changes over millions of years. I'm not up to the maths and physics involved."

"Where are your husband's papers now?"

"At the museum. We both made wills soon after we were married, leaving everything to each other. Charles never changed his will, so the papers are mine, and I control the copyright. But I know he'd have wanted his work to go on, and I can't carry it on. Dr Mitchell and the museum people can. When it comes to publication I suppose I shall be consulted, but that's probably a long time ahead. Sometimes I think that perhaps Susan will follow her father—she's got his sort of mind, I think. But she's only fourteen."

"I hope she does. And if she's proud of her father I think she can be equally proud of you."

"What do you mean?"

I got up to go. "Precisely what I said—that your daughter can be very proud of both her parents. There's a great deal that I don't know, but I can assure you of one thing—there is not even a possibility that your husband committed suicide."

"If only I could believe that!"

"You can. I can't explain any more now because I don't know, but I think you may find that what you call his illness was wholly creditable to him."

"You're an extraordinary person. I'm glad I talked to you. Shall I see you again?"

"I hope so. I can't say when I shall have more to tell you, and it may take time, but I promise to come back as soon as I can."

She smiled. "Well, you've given me something to look forward to. Since Charles's illness I haven't looked forward to anything except with dread."

I walked back to the hotel. I had much to think about. There was remarkable new evidence in what Mrs Jackson had told me, which meant that Charles Jackson could not possibly have taken his own life. And what was to be made of the amber bead now in my pocket?

IV

A Trip to Hamburg

CAMBRIDGE POLICE LAID on a car to take me to London Airport and I flew to Hamburg that same afternoon. I did not take up Sir Anthony Brotherton's offer of hospitality by Universal Oil, feeling that it would be better to be on my own.

I was met at the airport by a plainclothes officer and taken straight to police headquarters. There an impressive reception committee awaited me—a senior official from the German Ministry of Justice, the chief of Hamburg police, and the head of their equivalent of our Special Branch. To my shame their English was infinitely better than my German and we had no need of an interpreter. It was just on six o'clock when I got to the police building. My hosts provided wine and a substantial spread of Scandinavian-type open sandwiches, which meant that we could get to business straightaway without spending time on a more formal meal.

The man from the Ministry of Justice, Herr Hans Teck, opened our conference. "We are very glad to see you, Colonel, for we are all of us becoming more and more puzzled by this case," he said. "It is unlike any of the other kidnappings we have experienced. First, the ransom demand is extraordinary, and secondly, no one has so far claimed responsibility. If it had not been for the ransom note, I should be inclined to feel that Dr Braunschweig had suffered some sort of breakdown and gone off suddenly on his yacht without telling anyone, but the ransom note, strange as it is, cannot be dismissed. We are hoping that you can indicate some line of approach for us."

I gave a quick summary of my doings in Cambridge, as I had reported to Pusey. "Clearly the Baffin Map has been the object of criminal attention for some time," I said. "The evidence points to its having been stolen, either on the way back to the museum from Hamburg, or, I think more probably, from the museum itself after its return. The death of Dr Charles Jackson, who was Keeper of Arctic Maps at the time, is highly suspicious. He died from an overdose of sleeping pills, supposedly self-administered, combined with the effects of alcohol. There was a glass of water by.his bed, and only his own fingerprints were found on it. But I learned this morning that the glass had been put there by his wife in accordance with her normal practice. If there had been no interference with the glass her prints should have been on it as well as her husband's. They were not, and this seems to me conclusive evidence that someone wiped the glass clean of fingerprints and imposed Dr Jackson's. In view of what has happened since, it seems almost certain that Dr Jackson's death was in some way connected with the map : either he took it himself, and some associate decided that he could not be left alive with the knowledge of what had happened, or he was murdered so that the map could be taken by somebody else without its disappearance coming to light at once."

"All this is new to us and very interesting," the Special Branch man, Rolf Keller, said. "But you have not shown any connection with Dr Braunschweig."

"Apart from the ransom note linking his kidnapping with the map, I know of none so far. There *must* be a connection, but I think it can be found only in Hamburg. What do you know of him as an individual?"

Franz Schumann, the Chief of Police, answered. "Not very much, other than that he is one of our leading industrialists, respected and liked by his colleagues. He takes little part in public life, though his company—and I suppose this to some extent reflects his own interests—is generous in civic matters, particularly ,in anything relating to the university. We knew that the Baffin Map had been exhibited in Hamburg before we were told by London. As soon as we learned of the ransom note one of my officers recalled that there had been a recent exhibition of maps here and we obtained a catalogue. The costs of the exhibition were largely met by a grant from Unol —Universal Oil—but it is hard to see that this connects Dr Braunschweig with the map itself in any way."

"You did well to get on to the exhibition so quickly." Herr Schumann was pleased, and I went on "I have discussed Dr Braunschweig with the chairman of Universal Oil who, one would think, must know him well, but either he is not really intimate with his deputy, or he is unable to convey his qualities, for I have only a sort of passport picture of him, and no impression at all of his personality. What are his private interests? Is anything known of his domestic life?"

"I have talked with Frau Braunschweig, a charming and intelligent woman, and I should say that she and her husband are most happily married," Keller said. "Their home has a— I am not sure of the right English word—a sense? an air? an atmosphere?—of stability and contentment. A policeman must beware of subjective feelings, but often they are all you have to go on."

"Your English is excellent, and I should trust your feelings here. But what of the man himself? Has he no interests outside the oil industry?"

"He is devoted to his home and family, and he is greatly interested in his yacht and sailing. Frau Braunschweig shares these interests. They spend all the time they can together on their boat."

"Do you suspect any known group of organising his kidnapping?"

Keller ran his hand through his hair in a worried way. "There are, alas, many fanatical groups, some of which we know, some we do not. They are loose groupings, mostly of young people who share a hatred of society, and whose aim, if they can be said to have an aim, is to destroy in order that from the ruins of our social system some better order may emerge. They need money for their activities and they obtain it by bank robberies and other crimes. Some members of these groups act from a contorted sense of idealism, but they attract others whose motive is just greed—violence is a sadly easy way of getting money. Our difficulty always is that the organisation is so loose. It is like tackling—how shall I say it?— a jellyfish. You can cut away this piece or that piece, but poison remains in the rest. In addition to the more or less political groups there are also many nationalist groups promoting the aims of various movements outside Germany—

some of these may attempt kidnapping to put pressure on some Government. Since we have not found Dr Braunschweig's car, and have no witnesses to say what happened, there is nothing to indicate how he was taken. And the ransom demand is so unusual that I think we have to deal with some group hitherto totally unknown."

"Until this morning—or rather until yesterday—I thought that too," I said. "Now I am less sure. We have no known linkages, but we have a train of circumstance which, if we could understand it, offers the possibility of a clear link of events. Dr Braunschweig is concerned with the distribution of oil, and that is primarily a matter of sea routes. He is himself a sailor, in possession of an ocean-going boat. That boat has disappeared with him. Whoever has taken him is demanding a map of a little-known part of the world for his ransom. The map has also disappeared, in circumstances that suggest that its value to someone is so great that he or she is prepared to stick at nothing to get it. To go farther we must make certain assumptions. I think we can reasonably assume that at least two different sets of people are concerned, those who stole the map, and those who have taken Dr Braunschweig. If his kidnappers already have the map, or even know that it has been stolen, the demand for it as a ransom would seem absurd."

The three Germans were listening intently. Keller, who was the most experienced policeman, shook his head. "That is not necessarily so, Herr Colonel," he said. "They might know that the map is stolen and seek the resources of the oil company to recover it."

"That is a good point, but such facts as we have suggest that if those responsible for the ransom note know that the map is missing they must think that the oil company has possession of it. That is not impossible, but from what we know of Dr Braunschweig it seems unlikely that he would be concerned in a criminal conspiracy to get hold of the map. Besides, the ransom demand refers specifically to 'the Baffin Map *from the Cambridge Museum of Cartography*'.

"There is another possibility—that what was originally one group determined to steal the map has split into two factions, one of which has the map while the other has Dr Braunschweig. That would imply that someone has reason to think that threatening Dr Braunschweig's life may influence whoever has the map. It would imply further that Dr Braunschweig has some direct interest in the map and that link in the chain of evidence is so far missing."

"If your reasoning is anywhere near the truth it is the vital link," said the Ministry of Justice man. "You have constructed an ingenious theory—but why should any modern terrorist group have any interest in a seventeenth-century map?"

"Again, I am not sure. I have no more facts, but I can see a possible connection between Baffin's map and the present-day oil industry. Instability in the Middle East is a constant threat to oil supplies to Western Europe and the eastern part of North America. There are rich oilfields in the Arctic, but all that have been developed so far offer relatively easy routes only to the Pacific coast of North America. The search for a North-West Passage from the Atlantic to the Pacific dominated the thinking of navigators for centuries. It sent Baffin to the Arctic. For various reasons the apparent value of such a passage subsequently declined and its final achievement by Amundsen in 1905 was a sort of historic footnote. It was followed by no commercial development—indeed, his route is one so difficult that it offers no prospect of practical use. *Suppose there is another, unknown, route?* Suppose that something in Baffin's map provides a clue to it? That would be of immediate importance in two ways : it would be of immense direct value to the oil industry, and anyone intent on destroying Western civilisation would wish to deny Europe easy access to Arctic oil."

No one spoke for several minutes. Then the Special Branch man said, "It is a breathtaking suggestion, Herr Colonel, but it seems to me capable of proof or disproof almost at once. Have you consulted copies of the map? For scientific purposes they would be as good as the original."

"That is the trouble—as far as I can discover there are no known copies. Although the map has been used to illustrate one or two textbooks the illustrations are only smallscale photographs. The most recent was used in the catalogue of the Hamburg exhibition. I wonder if they still have the negative?"

"I shall talk to the Director this evening—I know him

slightly, and I can ask him about the photograph without explaining precisely why we want it," said Schumann, the police chief.

"Excellent. It will be interesting to have an enlargement but it may not help us much. The photograph is in black and white, and one of the important features of the map is its use of coloured tints to indicate soundings. Since Baffin had no echo-sounding devices, his soundings imply the existence of open water, which may be of significance. It may also be significant that the map disappeared before an American scholar who is making a study of the region was able to see it."

"The School of Geography here is considered one of the best in the world," Schumann said. "To what extent can I disclose your theories about the map? Their experts may be able to give practical help."

"It is your territory, and primarily your case," I said. "I should not presume to suggest how you handle an interview. My own feeling is that as we have not so far disclosed Dr Braunschweig's disappearance, and no one in Hamburg, apart from yourselves, knows that the map is missing, we should still keep quiet about it. To disclose our line of thought might be to warn one of the very people we want to find, and perhaps still further endanger Dr Braunschweig."

"I agree—I was only seeking your opinion," replied Schumann. "I shall tell the Director that we have learned of the possibility of forgeries of old maps being put on the market, and ask if he can put us in touch with experts who can tell us what to look for. I have a catalogue of the exhibition, and I can talk about the photograph quite naturally."

"That will be splendid. Now I want your advice on a number of matters concerning Dr Braunschweig's yacht."

"You may ask, Herr Colonel, and we shall do everything we can, but we are none of us ourselves sailors," Schumann said. "I have heard something of your own record and you will know much more of sailing boats than we do. Of course, we have some good sailors in our police force, and we can call on expert help. What is your particular concern here?"

"It is not a matter of sailing experience but of straightforward police work," I said. "The disappearance of Dr Braunschweig's yacht *Apfel* at the same time as the man himself is too much to be dismissed as coincidence. I think we must assume that the two events are related. Moreover, to take a kidnapped man to sea in an ocean-going sailing boat that has no need to put in anywhere for fuel is an effective means of keeping him hidden. Then the fact that there is no news of his car suggests that it has simply been left in some garage in or near Hamburg. I agree that a search of private property would be difficult to mount without disclosing our concern for Dr Braunschweig, but it might be done by announcing a hunt for *another* car. His car was a grey Mercedes : you could say that the police were anxious to find a blue Citroen believed to have been used in a jewel robbery. That would provide a reasonable excuse for house-to-house inquiries. The whereabouts of the car may be important, but of equal importance is the question of dinghies. Your inquiries so far indicate that Dr Braunschweig did not use the club launch to get out to his boat. He has two dinghies of his own, a wooden boat and an inflatable one. Neither has been found, which implies that they are on his boat. But to get there they must have started from somewhere, and since neither seems to have been at the club for some time the probability is that they were on board the yacht. This suggests that a third dinghy must have been used. There is no dinghy left on *Apfel*'s mooring, so either the dinghy which took Dr Braunschweig to the yacht was rowed ashore afterwards, or it was towed away by *Apfel* herself. If so, a further consideration follows, because a third dinghy would be a nuisance, and I should expect it to be abandoned on the way out to sea. You will have people with expert knowledge of the mouth of the Elbe—can you find out where a dinghy cast adrift soon after leaving the yacht mooring would be likely to come ashore, and whether any such dinghy *has* come ashore? We can't neglect the possibility that it was rowed ashore. If so a boat containing three or four men would have gone out to the yacht and returned with only one man. Someone may have seen this—it is surprising how much is observed on any waterfront. If we can get a line on the dinghy we have at least a starting point for the hunt for the people involved."

"That is all realistic deduction, and we ought to have thought of it ourselves," Keller said.

"There was no reason why you should. I happen to have had long personal experience of getting to and from small boats. You were properly more concerned with trying to discover the political motive behind the kidnapping. I have suggested a possible motive, but I have been able to do so only because I have been dealing with the missing map. If my theory is worth pursuing we can assume, I think, that the kidnapping is unlikely to be the work of any known terrorist group, and must concentrate on the logistics of the thing itself. Inquiries about the dinghy and a local search for the car seem to me of the most immediate importance. They can be done only by you, and it is for you to say whether they are worth doing."

The police chief got up. "Keller and I will go to work forthwith," he said. "Your theories may be wrong, Herr Colonel, but you have given us something to go on and I feel that we can now act. I feel also ashamed that we made no such deductions ourselves."

"You couldn't, because you didn't have the facts until I brought them."

"That may be so, but we had some facts and we deduced nothing from them. Come, Rolf, you and I know precisely what to do. Let us meet here again at nine o'clock tomorrow morning."

The next step forward was due to Keller, with a fine piece of analytical detection. He greeted me with it when we met at the chief's office in the morning.

"I don't know what, if anything, to make of it, but I've come across something rather interesting," he said. "In my job I have a fairly wide range of contacts, and one of them happens to be a leading chart agent—as a matter of fact we were at school together. Acting on your principle of trying to work out events from the logistics required to bring them about, I wondered if we could make a guess at the present whereabouts of the yacht from the charts she might have on board. So I went to my friend. I did not tell him anything about Dr Braunschweig—I said we had reason to believe that a group of international terrorists was planning some sensational piracy of rich men's yachts this summer. We had no

65

idea which yachts, but in cooperation with other national police forces we'd worked out a list of possible victims and were proposing to ask the NATO naval forces to keep an eye on them at sea. The problem was that we did not know where the yachts were likely to go. We could ask the owners, but that would invite panic and perhaps create publicity. Most cruises are planned in advance and the planning must include purchase of the necessary charts. Could he possibly analyse sales of charts to leading yachtsmen over the past six months? I explained that I was concerned only with German yachtsmen and that similar inquiries were being made in other countries. Of course they could not be conclusive—yachts might already have charts of voyages their owners intended to make. But a yachtsman rich and important enough for the attention of international terrorists might be expected to use only up-to-date charts, and recent purchases would provide at least some idea of forthcoming cruises.

"He could do nothing about cash purchases, but assuming that most rich yachtsmen have credit accounts the information was obtainable from his ledgers. I've been up with him most of the night and I've filled a notebook with useless lists—*but among his customers is Dr Braunschweig.* During last winter he made considerable purchases of charts for Greenland, the Canadian Arctic, and the Arctic Ocean. He wrote a letter with his order for charts saying that he particularly wanted the most recent information on the coasts of Ellesmere Island, Smith Sound and Kane Basin. It was such an unusual letter that the clerk handling the order brought it to my friend, who was puzzled because it is a part of the world mostly un-navigable and extremely dangerous for any yacht. However, Dr Braunschweig is an important customer, so my friend did his best, but with the charts he wrote a note stressing the difficulties and dangers from ice. He thought that Dr Braunschweig may have wanted the charts for some study, and not for any possible cruise in *Apfel*."

"Your information may be of the highest importance. The trouble is that it's a huge and inhospitable area, next to impossible to search, unless one had some indication of where to look. In any case, even if *Apfel* is bound for the north of Baffin Bay she couldn't be there yet."

"How soon do you think she could get there?"

"Hard to say—I'd have to work out a detailed route plan. If you have an atlas we could make a rough estimate of time and distance."

Assuming that *Apfel* had left Hamburg bound for Greenland I reckoned that her best route would be down the Channel, south of Ireland, and then north-west. But if whoever was navigating her didn't want to be seen he'd probably keep away from the busy shipping lanes of the Channel and take an alternative passage across the North Sea, sailing on between Scotland and the Faeroes. By any route it was a fairly long way, roughly 2,300 miles to south Greenland, and then another 1,500 miles or so northwards to Smith Sound. And no sailing boat can sail direct to anywhere.

After some work with atlas and ruler I said, "I don't know *Apfel*, or what she's capable of doing. She's fairly new, and I expect fast—at least we know she has gone in for ocean racing. If she takes the northerly route instead of going west about the British Isles she could escape the prevailing westerlies in the North Atlantic—the old sailing ships on passage from Liverpool to the United States used sometimes to go a long way north in the hope of fair winds. But there's no certainty about the wind. Given some strong easterlies she'd race along, but she couldn't expect fair winds the whole time, she might run into fog, and I've no idea of ice conditions at the moment. We can find out these things from the Met people. At a guess, and it's a very rough guess, she might do it in a month, but she might take twice as long. A lot would depend on what sort of crew she has, and how many they can use for watch-keeping."

"So if she is making for the Arctic and has Dr Braunschweig on board nothing much can happen for another three weeks," Keller said.

"If . . . But it makes some sort of sense. Assuming that Dr Braunschweig had come across something in the Baffin Map, or in some research of his own that we don't know about, to indicate the possibility of an Arctic route for oil transport, he might well have planned to go there secretly in his own boat to investigate. That would explain his purchase of the charts, and the fact that he did so privately instead of simply asking for charts from the shipping division of Universal Oil. He was in a position to get any charts he wanted, and at first I wondered why he should bother with a chart agent. Now I see that there could be several reasons. If we're right in any of this, we've got to make another assumption—*that someone else knows about the route and is determined that Dr Braunschweig and Universal Oil should not use it.* There could be a political motive to deny cheaper oil to Western Europe, or it might be commercial rivalry. But something has gone wrong. The map has disappeared, and Dr Braunschweig already knows enough to plan a voyage to the Arctic to see for himself. So he is kidnapped, and the kidnappers decide to use him and his boat to find out just how much he knows and to try to keep him quiet by threatening his life."

"But why the ransom note demanding the map?" Keller objected.

"Yes, what I've just been thinking can't be right—or it may be on the right lines, but I've drawn the wrong conclusions. I don't know. It might make sense if Universal Oil had the map—but that would imply that Dr Braunschweig or someone acting for him had gone in for criminal conspiracy at Cambridge. And if the company knows anything about possible Arctic oil routes why didn't the chairman tell us about it when he got the ransom demand for his colleague? None of that makes sense. I feel that we've put together one or two pieces of a jigsaw puzzle, but all the other bits are still a hopeless jumble."

"Not hopeless," said the police chief. "You and Keller have already made something out of nothing. We must find"—he paused—"some more nothings."

"That will not be difficult," I said.

We all laughed.

The first thing to be found was far from being a nothing—it was the car, which was found around mid-day in the garage of a house temporarily unoccupied. It was across the river from the yacht club and barely a quarter of a mile from a piece of hard-standing where a number of dinghies were parked, with a small jetty much used by sailing people. The car showed no signs of a struggle and gave no indication of anything other than completely normal use. Even this, though, was information of a sort, for it suggested that Dr Braunschweig had stopped probably of his own accord, perhaps to give someone a lift. Keller and I discussed this after lunch. "I don't like the idea of stopping to give someone a lift," he said. "Dr Braunschweig liked to drive himself and refused to go around with guards, but he was an intelligent man and knew well enough that he was sufficiently important to be a candidate for kidnapping. He wouldn't have stopped for some hitch-hiker, nor for a man or woman standing by an apparently broken-down car. Those are the obvious ways of stopping a driver to attack him."

"Unless he knew whoever stopped him," I said. "Don't you think there are slight indications that he knew, or thought he knew, what he was doing, stopped, and later went out to his boat quite willingly?"

"Perhaps. I think I would agree with you about the stopping. It was in the morning, there must have been plenty of people about, and there is no evidence that anyone heard a shout for help. As for going out to the boat—we don't know. That may have been at night, and he may have been drugged."

"Open mind on that, then. But there's a more positive question. How did they know that the house where they put the car was empty?"

"Earlier reconnaissance—they wanted an empty garage, and looked for one."

"Do we know who the house belongs to?"

"Yes, Schumann's man went into that while the car was being brought in. The house belongs to a man called Baumgarten, who is a director of an engineering firm. He is youngish—in his middle thirties—married, with no children. He is a professional engineer himself and often travels abroad to supervise work done by his company. Sometimes his wife goes with him. He is at present in Brazil, and he travelled accompanied by his wife. They have been away about a fortnight, and are not expected back for another month."

"Where is the Baumgartens' own car?"

"In a garage near the airport. If he goes away alone his wife drives him and brings back the car."

"So the people making your preliminary reconnaissance

69

would have had to find out not only about Herr Baumgarten, but about his wife's movements, too. It wouldn't have done for her to come back to find the garage occupied. High-grade intelligence on their part and, if I may say so, high-grade work by Hamburg police in learning so much about the Baumgartens so quickly."

"That wasn't difficult—we had only to get in touch with his firm. Franz is a good policeman, though. He won a scholarship that took him to a college in the United States— as a matter of fact, so did I. It was a useful experience. I'd already graduated at Heidelberg but it was a help to get a US doctorate. The most valuable thing, though, was to be able to talk in English as we are talking now."

"You put me to shame. The English aren't much good at languages. Too lazy, perhaps."

He laughed. "You are not bad at logical deduction."

"We may get all the answers wrong. Still, I'd like to know a bit more about Herr Baumgarten. You've been to see Frau Braunschweig—could you find out if they know the Baumgartens? And I may think of one or two other things when I get back to England."

"When are you going back?"

"I shall stay in Hamburg tonight in case anything else turns up, but I'd like to get the first flight to London in the morning. Could you get me booked on that?"

"Yes, and I'll arrange a car to take you to the airport. I'll try to see Frau Braunschweig later this afternoon. Can you have dinner with me tonight?"

"That's nice of you. If you go off to Frau Braunschweig I think I'll call on Herr Schumann."

Schumann‚ was delighted that our theories about the car had worked out so well and he had more news for me—the dinghy, or at any rate *a* dinghy, had also been found. "It was adrift off the mouth of the Elbe not far from Cuxhaven," he said. "The marine police spotted it and brought it in. It has no name or number so there's no means of identifying the owner yet, but the forensic people may come up with something."

"Can I have a look at it?"

"Of course. It's been put in one of the Customs boathouses,

some distance from here. I'll take you out."

The dinghy was a fourteen-foot boat, clinker-built of good planking, not plywood. There was a mast-step in the forward thwart, but no mast. She had clearly been built for sailing for she had a centre-plate, but the plate was up, and without a mast she could not have been sailed when she went adrift. She had rowlocks but no oars on board—indeed, she was remarkably bare for she did not even have a painter. Marks on the wood of the transom indicated the use of an outboard bracket, but there was no outboard engine in her. She seemed generally in good condition, and a boat that an owner would have tried to recover if he knew she had gone adrift. "Dinghies do break loose from moorings, and I suppose in Hamburg as in England boats are sometimes stolen. Has anyone reported the loss of a boat like this?" I asked.

"We have a number of reports of missing dinghies. I've been through the list but there's nothing whose description matches this," Schumann said.

"The absence of a painter is curious. If she'd broken loose from a mooring I'd have expected the painter to come away from the mooring rather than the boat," I said. "If she'd been left carelessly hauled up on some beach where the tide could reach her she'd normally have had her painter with her. An owner leaving a boat moored or hauled up might reasonably take away mast and gear but he wouldn't take away the painter—if she was on a mooring, he couldn't."

"What do you think happened?"

"Well, all sorts of things *might* have happened, but the condition of the boat fits the possibility that she was abandoned from a yacht. At fourteen feet she's biggish for a tender, and I'd say she was used as a sailing dinghy in her own right. If there's anything in our theories of the boarding of *Apfel*, and this was the dinghy used, she could scarcely have been rowed back because there are no oars. She'd be too big to be carried with the other dinghies on *Apfel*'s deck, so she would have been cast off when they'd towed her far enough to feel it safe to abandon her. The absence of anything on board rather suggests that she was abandoned—the people on the yacht would have kept warps, line, oars, outboard, anything which might come in useful, before casting her off. *If* she was the

71

dinghy used for *Apfel* she'll have been at sea for a week. I don't know anything about tides and currents at the mouth of the Elbe. You might ask your marine police if they can work out from where she was found where she might have been set adrift a week ago."

"I can certainly do that. And the scientists may find something to tell us about her occupants."

"We can hope, and while you are about it, you might get samples of dust from the treads of the car's tyres analysed and see if there are any similar traces in the dinghy. It's a long shot, and it may not mean anything if there are, but it seems worth trying."

Keller lived in Bonn but his organisation had a discreet flat for its officers to use in Hamburg, and he had dinner sent in for us from a first-rate restaurant. There were just the two of us—Schumann had to attend a meeting he couldn't get out of, and the Ministry of Justice man had gone back to Bonn. The food was set out on a hotplate, so there was no waiter or anybody else to overhear our conversation. "I'm not clear why you suspected it but the Braunschweigs *do* know the Baumgartens," he said. "Baumgarten's engineering firm does some specialised work on valves for pipelines, so there's a business connection. There's another link, too. Baumgarten is also a sailor and they are members of the same yacht club."

"I didn't suspect—it was one of the things I just wanted to know. I'm puzzled by the efficiency of what you called reconnaissance. Of course the absence of the Baumgartens could have been discovered by anyone who really wanted to find out, but they had not only to be absent, but away together, and for some time. Now you've established that it could have been discovered *through* Braunschweig, or perhaps through someone else in Universal Oil. It doesn't follow that Baumgarten was involved in any way—it's hard to see how he could be, because he was already in Brazil. But a personal relationship between Braunschweig and Baumgarten seems to strengthen the probability that we are dealing with a somewhat closed group."

"Have you talked to any of the Unol people about this?"

"No. I didn't even tell them that I was coming to Hamburg.

There may be all sorts of politics involved—inter-office politics, and oil politics in the wider sense. There are lots of things that I want to ask his colleagues, but I want to know much more before approaching them."

Keller was silent for some time. Then he said, "You almost make me feel that you regard the kidnapping as a put-up job."

"I think I do—but put-up by whom, and for what purpose, I can't so far even begin to work out. You must remember that I've been more directly concerned with the mystery of the map—when, or if, we can relate that to Dr Braunschweig I shall feel that we are really getting somewhere."

"Franz and his Hamburg police are in touch with the oil company, and I have met the two senior directors. It is important to our Government that they should feel that we are doing everything we can. You may be right to keep out of sight, but we can't. What do you think we ought to do?"

"I shall be in the same position in London—Sir Anthony Brotherton will expect some report on our activities. I feel that until we know a lot more we should keep everything we *do* know, or even think, to ourselves. We need some playacting, or to use a politer term, diplomacy. As far as possible we should tell the truth, but not the whole truth. I should be inclined to tell them, in strict confidence, of the finding of the car, but I should not disclose where it was found. Meanwhile I'd like you to go as thoroughly as you can, without giving anything away, into the private lives of Dr Braunschweig's staff and immediate colleagues. How many of them knew the Baumgartens? Did his secretary have any dealings with them? How many are members of the yacht club, or go in for sailing? These are some of the things that I should like to know, but I can't instruct you to make the inquiries."

"You don't need to. My instructions are to cooperate in every way possible with you, and I know I speak for Franz as well when I say that the results of our collaboration so far have been impressive. We shall do everything you ask, and when it comes to diplomacy—well, perhaps we are not bad at it."

A big envelope was waiting for me at the hotel, and in it was an enlargement which Schumann had had made of the photograph of the Baffin Map from the catalogue of the Hamburg exhibition. The enlargement gave me a much sharper *sense* of the map. It was, of course, in black and white, but the coloured tints of the original showed reasonably well as shadings. I wanted to compare the map with charts and globe—and I wanted to know the outcome of Ruth's researches. I couldn't discuss things on the phone but although the drive from Oxford meant an early start she insisted on meeting me at the airport.

V

A Theory of the Arctic

RUTH SEEMED MORE concerned about me than about the
Arctic. I had to tell her three times that neither of my old
wounds was hurting, that I'd been fed more than adequately
and that I was not overtired. It wasn't until she was reassured
on these matters that she asked, "Where do we go now?"

"Anywhere I can talk to you. Have you had any breakfast
yet?"

"Well, I had a cup of coffee before I started. What about
you?"

"They gave me the standard continental breakfast on the
aeroplane. Why you can't get a proper breakfast anywhere
across the Channel I don't know. Let's find somewhere and
have breakfast."

When we'd both eaten and were enjoying our coffee I asked
Ruth if she'd managed to get hold of her oceanographer. "Yes,
Dr Vaughan gave me dinner last night—very respectably, his
wife was there too," she said. "It was a bit difficult because
I didn't really know what to ask him."

"About changes in the Arctic climate."

"Oh that, of course. But I thought I'd start off with Dr
Jackson—I can't help thinking about that woman you went
to see. Dr Vaughan knew Charles Jackson—he said his death
was a dreadful loss to polar studies. He asked me if I knew
what had happened to his papers."

"I didn't have time to tell you that; according to his widow
they are at the museum."

"I was diplomatic and said that as it was only on the fringe
of my field I didn't know, but that I could probably find
out. I explained that an American scholar had been in touch
with me about the geophysical mathematics of polar shifting.

75

I'd heard of Dr Jackson as a leading geographer on the Arctic but when I tried to get in touch with him was shocked to learn that he was dead—that was why I'd turned to Jeremy Vaughan."

"You couldn't have done better—the only thing is I must make sure you never get into Pusey's clutches as a diplomatic —er—diverter of the truth. What did Dr Vaughan say about polar movements?"

"Well, he told me what I knew already, that there have been changes in the earth's crustal shape with consequent shifting in the position of the poles and profound effects on the climate of both the Arctic and the Antarctic. What I didn't know is that there is a new theory that parts of the Arctic seabed remain affected by the older tilt of the earth and are warmer than present surface glaciation would suggest."

"Does this have any practical effect?"

"Yes and no. It upsets some of our present theories about the Gulf Stream. If there is anything in what has been called the Arctic Calorific Syndrome it may mean that certain currents of water relatively warmer than the surrounding sea which occur between Greenland and North America are not, as thought at present, offshoots of the Gulf Stream but are brought about by warm springs welling from the seabed. Such springs may explain your North Water, for instance. But the work has so far been almost wholly theoretical—seabed research in the polar regions would be prohibitively expensive, and extremely difficult, anyway. Some people think that the successful underwater navigation of the North Pole by the US nuclear-powered submarine *Nautilus* in 1958 indicates that there may be something in the theory, but clear water far below the ice may simply mean that there is a natural balance between frozen and unfrozen sea, a temperature gradient if you like, maintained by salinity and the insulating value of surface water and sea ice itself. The unexpected discovery made by that voyage was the immense depth of water underneath the Pole. It goes down to more than thirteen thousand feet, much deeper than had previously been thought likely. That *could* be a vestige of an older shape of the earth's crust, but it could equally have been brought about by many other geological factors."

76

"Could William Baffin in the seventeenth century have found open water where there is none now?"

"I didn't ask Dr Vaughan that—I thought it might be a mistake to start talking about your Baffin Map. Baffin certainly *could* have found conditions that no one else has come across since—the Arctic is a huge area, and the tracks of all the ships that have ever navigated, or tried to navigate it cover only a small fraction of the whole region. But you must be careful here, Peter—you mustn't confuse two quite different things. Surface conditions of the Arctic ice change from year to year, often from day to day—what may be open water today may be completely blocked tomorrow. I've been talking about the fundamental structure of the globe. It does change, yes, it's changing all the time, but changes that separate continents or alter the character of oceans take place over millions or hundreds of millions of years."

"But the structure of the globe must determine conditions on the surface."

"Of course. There is snow on mountains because those mountains have been thrown up by some structural upheaval. But the mountains have been there through human history."

"What is human history? Wasn't there a land or land-and-ice bridge across the Bering Strait from Asia to Alaska when there were men and women alive to walk over it to populate America?"

"Probably. But that's still a matter of surface conditions. And even there the Bering Strait has been much as it is now for twenty or thirty thousand years."

"People discover things. Australia was *there,* but it didn't mean much until it was discovered by European seamen. I don't see why a seventeenth-century navigator shouldn't have come across something that nobody has noticed since. I think there's some evidence of it in his map. I haven't shown you this yet—I've got an enlargement of a photograph of the map taken for the catalogue of the Hamburg exhibition."

"And you think this may be relevant to modern oil transport? Is that your amber light? It's a good piece of Peter imagination, but as a mathematician I fear the odds are against you."

"There *must* be some connection between the map and the

77

oil industry. Oh, Ruth, why isn't Dr Jackson alive?"

"Because you may be right, my darling—or if you are not right somebody else may have made the same mistake. Now the chances of *that* are mathematically much higher!"

That remark of Ruth's made me feel better. It didn't really matter whether I was right or wrong, as long as somebody else had had the same sort of ideas about the Baffin Map. But who? And precisely what ideas? My own were still of the vaguest—I merely thought that William Baffin must have come much nearer to discovering a practicable North-West Passage than anyone had given him credit for, and that this could be deduced in some way from his map. But I hadn't got his map. I hadn't even got a facsimile of it, for the colouring seemed all-important and I had only a black-and-white photograph. Still, it was a good photograph. "Let's go and talk to Pusey," I said, "and then I think I'll have to go back to Cambridge."

I rang Sir Edmund and he suggested an early lunch in his flat. After our excellent breakfast neither Ruth nor I was much interested in lunch, but the flat was a convenient place to talk, and I knew that he had a globe because I'd often admired it. But he wouldn't have charts of the Arctic. I asked him to get Admiralty charts of the whole Arctic region and to have these ready for us when we came. "There's scarcely time to send out to a chart agent, and in any case I don't know the sheet numbers, but you can borrow charts from the naval branch of the Ministry of Defence," I said. Sir Edmund is good at these things.

"You seem to have done all right, Peter," he greeted me. "I've just had a private phone call from the German Ambassador who says that his Government is much indebted to you for leading to the recovery of Dr Braunschweig's car."

"Hamburg police did that. Have you got the charts?"

"He thinks you told the police where to look. Yes, I have got the charts."

"I want your globe, too. It will be a help if we can have it with the charts."

He brought the globe and the three of us studied the North Pole. "If you forget flat maps you can see what a marvellous route there is from Alaska across the Arctic Ocean to the north of Ellesmere Island, then through Kane Basin and Smith Sound into Baffin Bay. And from there it's straight sailing to the whole of the eastern seaboard of North America, and to Western Europe," I said.

"The disadvantage is that the Arctic Ocean is mostly ice," Sir Edmund said mildly.

I'd forgotten that he hadn't been doing my thinking about the Baffin Map. I gave him a hurried summary, and produced my photograph. "It's maddening that it's not in colour because Baffin used tints to indicate soundings," I said. "But you can tell from the shading of the photograph where the tints change, and you can tell roughly from the shaded key in the corner what depths the changes show. The important thing is that they show *soundings*. Baffin had to sound with lead and line— he couldn't sound through ice. And the map shows that he got soundings of some sort in a rather wiggly pattern right through Kane Basin. It's astonishingly far north for the seventeenth century."

"What do you think it means?"

"That everyone else who looked for the North-West Passage tried too far *south,* being led astray by inlets like Lancaster Sound. And this applies equally to the known routes by which the passage *has* so far been accomplished, routes that are just possible, but of great difficulty. The secret is to go *north,* almost to the Pole."

"There's nothing in this photograph of Baffin's Map to suggest any practicable route from the north of Ellesmere Island across the Arctic Ocean. Why do you think there's any chance of such a route?"

"Because of Ruth's discovery of the Arctic Calorific Syndrome and the immense depth of some sort of trench across the Arctic Ocean. Sorry, Ruth didn't really discover any of this, but she discovered it for me from one of her experts at Oxford."

"It was the US submarine *Nautilus* that learned about the depths in 1958," Ruth said. "I'm bound to add, Peter, that there's not the slightest indication that surface ice north of

Ellesmere Island is any less severe than has always been supposed."

"I'm relying on old Baffin. He knew what he was doing in charting his route so far north. For all we know there's another map of his dealing with the Arctic Ocean that has never come to light."

"That is pure speculation," Ruth said.

"It's all speculation. But you pointed out that it doesn't matter if I'm wrong as long as someone else has made the same mistake about the map."

"You're going far beyond me," Sir Edmund said. "All I know about the map is that it has been demanded as a ransom for Dr Braunschweig and is apparently missing from the Cambridge museum to which it belongs."

"Again I'm sorry. I've been so living with the thing that I keep forgetting that you haven't. There *must* be something to relate the map to Dr Braunschweig. He is head of the distribution network of one of the biggest oil companies in the world, and if the map suggests a feasible route to transport oil from Alaska to the West it would be of the highest importance to him—and to anyone who wanted to stop either Universal Oil or the oil industry in general from making use of it."

"And you think he has been kidnapped in an effort to get hold of the map?"

"I don't know what to think—it seems to me that it's much more complicated than that. I think that Dr Jackson, the expert at the Cambridge museum, was murdered, either because of the map itself, or of some work he was doing in connection with the Arctic, probably this theory of the Arctic Calorific Syndrome. I think that Dr Braunschweig has gone off, or been taken off, in his ocean-going yacht *Apfel* to look for something in the Arctic. There is evidence that he was planning a voyage to the Arctic in the charts that he bought recently. That links Dr Braunschweig with the map : what I haven't found is *anything* to link the map with some third party who could feel strongly enough about it to murder Dr Jackson. There's a vital link still missing."

"And you hope to find it in Cambridge?"

"I don't know where else to look. The carrying out of what-

80

ever plot there was took place in Hamburg, and the very able German police are doing everything that can be done there. But I don't think the *reasons* are in Hamburg. They may not be in Cambridge either, but Cambridge must come into the chain of events at an earlier stage than Hamburg, and it's only by working backwards from Cambridge that we can hope to break into the chain."

Sir Edmund has some tiresome characteristics but they are more than made up for by unshakeable loyalty to those who work for him. He may have been wholly sceptical of my wild assumptions about the Baffin Map but he didn't waste time in cross-examining me. My reasoning might get us nowhere, but it had produced at least *prima facie* evidence that Dr Jackson's death was a graver matter than had been supposed. He agreed to see Sir Anthony Brotherton himself, to keep him diplomatically in the picture without disclosing any details of the picture as we saw it. I wanted to get back to Cambridge, but first I wanted a word with Seddon at New Scotland Yard. Ruth had to return to Oxford and I arranged to ring her in the evening.

Paul Seddon is an Assistant Commissioner of the Metropolitan Police, with vast experience as a detective and an accumulated wisdom that makes his police skills doubly valuable. He acts as the Department's special representative at the Yard, and also as consultant in cases concerning fraud or financial crime, which was his own field of detection before he was recruited by Sir Edmund. We were old friends. Ruth dropped me at the Yard on her way out of London.

"I thought the boss would call you in on the Cambridge case and I'm delighted to see you back at work," he said. "We certainly get some sticky ones. I spent a day at Cambridge as you know, and I've seldom met a case that had less to go on. I felt sorry for that young Inspector Richards. He's a good man. He rang me about your discovery of the finger-prints, kicking himself for not having got on to it but glad to have evidence to reopen inquiries."

"He has no cause to blame himself—with his limited time and facilities he was extraordinarily thorough," I said. "The trouble was that the picture someone wanted the police to see

—depression, properly prescribed drugs, death from a sad combination of drugs and alcohol—was too well painted. Glass of water beside bed with man's own fingerprints on it, everybody wanting a verdict of accidental death—what more was to be looked for? It was chance that Mrs Jackson told me she was in the habit of putting out her husband's drinking water for him."

"Well, you found out, but we can leave it at that. What do you want me to do?"

"I want you to go drinking with some of your old City pals. Universal Oil's share price seems well up, but with the oil market as it is that may not mean much. I'd like to know if at any time in the past couple of years there's been a hint of boardroom rows, or any talk of a possible takeover. The company is too big to make a takeover bid seem likely, though I suppose there could be a merger of interests with one of the other giants. But I'm equally interested in any takeovers, actual or considered possible, *by* Universal Oil."

"I'll have a go, but Unol's the bluest of blue chips in the stock market, and oil companies tend to live in a world of their own, respecting one another's secrets. Takeovers *by* Unol should be a bit easier. The company certainly acquired Arabian Sands, one of the smaller Middle Eastern outfits, not long ago, and there may be other deals in the pipeline. It would be a help if you'd give me an idea of what you suspect."

"That's the trouble, Paul—I don't know. I told you that the picture of Dr Jackson's death seemed too pat. I have rather the same feeling about the kidnapping. Dr Jackson certainly died and Dr Braunschweig may well have been kidnapped, but the extraordinary ransom note, and such bits and pieces as we have been able to put together about the probable sequence of events in his disappearance make me feel that we're meant to put two and two together and make four—whereas the real sum may be two plus or minus some completely different figure. I've no evidence to indicate that we should look inside the oil company for the unravelling of events, but somebody is determined that we should look *outside* it, and it is this that bothers me. Sending the ransom demand to the oil company at once makes it look like a political kidnapping. It may be, but like Dr Jackson's death

82

the picture somehow seems too neat. And if the kidnapping is an attempt to get hold of the map it doesn't make sense. A great oil company can obviously afford to buy the most valuable of maps in return for the life of its deputy chairman, but in this case the map can't be bought because it can't be found. *Suppose that whoever sent the ransom note knows that the map is unobtainable and that the demand can't be met.* It's cleverer than asking for money, which can be bargained about. Either the map is produced, or Dr Braunschweig is killed. And since the map can't be produced that's equivalent to a death sentence."

"You've got to assume that somebody has a compelling motive for getting rid of Dr Braunschweig."

"That's why I want you to go drinking in the City—in the hope that you can pick up something that may give us a line on motive."

"Some hope! I do know one or two people in the oil market but it's a cagey business, and I've got to be careful—it doesn't need much to start some rumour that sends share prices tumbling with a lot of innocent people getting hurt. How much time do you think we've got?"

"That's anybody's guess, but if I'm right about the general feel of things without necessarily being right in any of the details—I reckon we've still got a few weeks. I think that Dr Braunschweig alive is still valuable to somebody, and will remain so until his boat has got to wherever she may be going. The critical time will come when she's run her distance, which, if I'm right, will be around the end of the month."

"But you don't know where she is."

"No. The NATO air and sea forces are looking out for her, but a fifty-foot boat is a tiny speck in the North Atlantic and I doubt if there's much chance of spotting her. But we can make a reasonable guess at the area she's bound for. It's a vast region, but I'm hoping that research into the map and more inquiries in Cambridge may narrow it down a bit, and we may be able to intercept her. By that time you may have filled in some of the real picture, not the one that we're supposed to see."

I'd talked to Paul Seddon with more confidence than I felt.

His record in ferreting out financial scandal was remarkable, and if there was any funny business going on inside the oil company I'd every confidence in his ability to sniff it. Where I had less confidence was in myself. The car and the dinghy made it seem reasonably likely that Dr Braunschweig *was* on board *Apfel* bound for the Arctic, but why, and who was with him, remained x and y in a still insoluble equation. My maths is not Ruth's, and I thought back to my schooldays about equations with x and y in them. As far as I remembered the best way of solving such puzzles was to find two sets of equation—simultaneous equations—which could provide values for x and y because they told you different things about them : you could solve two equations together when you couldn't solve either of them alone. Could I find two equations here? Well, at any rate there seemed two problems—the murder, for I was convinced it was murder, of Dr Jackson, and the disappearance of Dr Braunschweig. And there was a common factor in both—the Baffin Map. If we could make any progress in the Jackson case we might begin to see light in the Braunschweig affair.

There was no nice breakfast on this journey to Cambridge because it was the wrong time of day, but I had more than enough to think about as the gentle landscape of East Anglia slipped past. Too neat a picture . . . was that another common factor in the Jackson and the Braunschweig cases? I had told nobody so far of the amber bead I had found in Mrs Jackson's house. Was this another stage property, added to the scene-setting to provide an insurance policy in case the police had *not* taken everything about Dr Jackson's death for granted? Ingrid Mitchell was his successor at the museum, she wore an amber necklace, and she could be considered to have a motive for getting rid of Dr Jackson in order to obtain his job. Sufficient for murder? Doubtfully, but ambition can be a terrible driving force and even in these days an able woman can see herself passed over for a job she is well qualified to do. Dr Mitchell had reasonable hopes of succeeding Dr Jackson, and she may have felt that if the vacancy could occur before that pompous old fool of a Curator retired she would have a better chance of getting it. She was with Dr Jackson at the party and knew the state he was in. Why not slip into his room through the french window and help him to an overdose of tranquilliser? Necklaces can break, and a bead from an amber necklace might be damning evidence against her. Again I thought, "Too neat." And then my whole reasoning was upset—the amber bead couldn't provide the police with a readymade suspect at the time of Dr Jackson's death because it had not been found. It came to light by chance when I visited the house some months later and could have no possible bearing on the case. I was wasting time over it. But the thing nagged at my mind and I decided that I was not *necessarily* wrong in thinking that it might have some connection with the case. The fact that it was not found at the time of Dr Jackson's death was not proof that it was not there to find. It was more or less hidden under the edge of carpet, and had I not been studying the surround of the french window with particular attention it might be there still. Amber was already connected with a woman who had played some part in Dr Jackson's life, and who was with him on the night he died. I couldn't have things both ways—if I was trying to deduce things from what seemed an unreal neatness in the pattern of events I couldn't dismiss the amber bead because it now seemed too neat. The fact that it had not been found did not rule out its value in offering the police a readymade suspect. As it happened it was not needed, because the police were not suspicious. If they *had* been suspicious they would have searched the room more thoroughly and the bead would have been found.

I badly wanted another talk with Ingrid Mitchell but by the time I got to Cambridge it was too late to call at the museum. I had not found her easy to talk to, and an unexpected visit to her home, assuming that she had not gone out for the evening, was about the worst possible way of opening an interview. But I also needed to see Inspector Richards. I rang his home number and he invited me to his house. "If you don't mind a scratch meal I'd be delighted if you could stay for supper," he said.

Inspector Richards offered to drive to the station to collect me but I wouldn't let him and got a taxi instead. He had a

85

pleasant small house on the outskirts of Cambridge. He introduced me to his wife and two young children, a boy coming up to four and a girl of about two. Either tactfully, or because it really was their bedtime, Mrs Richards went off with the children, leaving the sitting room to her husband and me. I brought him up to date with the German side of things and he was impressed by the finding of the car and dinghy. "You seem to have a knack of finding things, if I may say so, sir," he said.

"You can cut out the 'sir' and forget about knacks—it was straightforward police work, and the German police seem highly efficient."

"Better than we are, I'm afraid."

"Come off it. With hindsight I think Dr Jackson's death merited a rather fuller investigation than it got, but the coroner was satisfied and the university people must have been thankful to have the whole business cleared up so quickly. I had much more reason to be suspicious."

"Well, you certainly stirred things up. I can't say that the Super was all that pleased, but he's a good policeman and he took me off everything else to concentrate on the Jackson case."

"How does it stand now?"

"To be honest, just as it was before. I've been to see Mrs Jackson—she's an intelligent woman and seems to like you, though she doesn't know what to make of you. I had to check your report on the glass, and it's just as you said—she is prepared to swear that she filled the glass and put it on the bedside table. We examined the glass for fingerprints at the time, of course, and found only Dr Jackson's on it. That seemed natural enough in the circumstances as we knew them then. I've tried to find out who was at the party where he had too much to drink—I thought the other guests could be interviewed to see if anyone recalls seeing him being deliberately encouraged to drink. But it's not easy. The people who gave the party are in the States, and that sort of Cambridge party has a lot of coming and going. Mrs Jackson remembers some of the people there, but she wasn't with her husband all the time. I haven't talked to anybody else yet because we can't have those sort of interviews in Cambridge without people talking, and it's only a matter of time before all sorts of rumours start flying around."

"You're right to be careful. We may have to announce a murder inquiry and invite help from the public, but that's the last thing we want at the moment. Apart from Mrs Jackson, nobody outside the museum even knows that the map is missing, and apart from a few high-ups in the oil company nobody knows yet about Dr Braunschweig. *Somebody* must be very anxious to know just what we're doing. . . . The less we give away the more chance there is of that somebody trying to be too clever and making a mistake." I outlined my theory of how a plausible picture of Dr Jackson's death had been put together and then I told him about the amber bead.

I still had the bead in my pocket and I handed it across to him. "She didn't mention this to me," he said.

"No reason why she should—she didn't seem to think anything of it. And perhaps she regarded it as a reflection on her house-keeping, though it's understandable that she shouldn't have wanted to go into the room more than she had to."

He turned over the bead in his fingers, studying it with a slightly puzzled look. "I've a feeling that I've seen a bead like this somewhere fairly recently," he said.

"Yes. Dr Mitchell wears an amber necklace—at any rate she was wearing one when I met her."

"That's it." He was suddenly excited. "You know, she could have a motive of sorts—after all, she got Dr Jackson's job." Then his face fell. "But you must have thought of all this already," he said.

"I've thought *about* it, but as with everything else in this case I don't know what to think. If we are now treating Dr Jackson's death as murder then that bead needs explaining, and Dr Mitchell may have a lot of explaining to do. But like the rest of the picture it bothers me—somehow it seems just too pat."

"In my own experience the obvious often turns out to be what did happen."

"It didn't in the first explanation of Dr Jackson's death. . . . We thought what somebody meant us to think, and it's wrong. I can't help wondering if the bead is *meant* to direct us to Dr Mitchell."

The inspector looked rather unhappy. "Are you telling me about the bead officially, sir?" he asked. The return of the "sir" was a measure of his unhappiness as the CID man in charge of the case.

"Yes. Probably I ought to have told you sooner, but there was so little time before I left for Hamburg."

"You may be right in feeling that it could be a plant, but I don't see how I can ignore it. Dr Mitchell is already mixed up in the case to some extent, and she's got to be questioned about it."

"I agree. But if you don't think I'm interfering too much I wonder if you'd let me do the questioning? I'm going to try to see her first thing tomorrow. You can come with me if you like, though if you feel you can trust me my instinct is that we may do better without too formal a police invasion."

"I'm sorry. For someone in your position you've been wonderfully good to me, and now it looks as if I'm picking holes in what you say. I'm not, but I've got to report to my own Superintendent and already he's feeling a bit let down because none of our force went into the matter of the glass as well as we should. The bead is evidence of a sort involving Dr Mitchell and while I take your point that somebody may be trying to hoodwink us again I'd be failing in my duty if I did nothing about it. If you're going to see Dr Mitchell, sir, there's no problem. You'll be far better with her than I could be, and of course I won't come with you. I've never met a boss before who asked if I could trust him."

I was much moved by this. Richards had been remarkably good. I had been impressed by his thoroughness, and I was now even more impressed by his courage in telling me that I might be being too clever by half. I was quite ready to believe him right. I slipped back into slight formality myself. "I do not think for a moment that I can handle Dr Mitchell any better than you could," I continued, "but I've been making the most detailed study I can of what is known of the map and of modern charts of the area, and I hope—I can only say I hope—there may be a better chance of listening between the lines, as it were, if I talk to her alone. I can promise you that when the time comes for our own report on the case I

88

shall take particular pleasure in recording the ability with which you have dealt with things."

Dr Mitchell was dictating letters to her secretary, whom she had taken over from Dr Jackson. She did not seem enthusiastic about my visit but appeared to accept it as one of the inevitable chores of life. "That will do for the moment, Joan," she said to the secretary. "I'll ring through as soon as I'm free."

When the young woman had gone she asked frostily, "Have you recovered our map?"

I took a long shot. "Actually, no. But then I scarcely could without breaking into your house," I said.

VI

Ingrid Mitchell's Story

HER COLOURING WAS not the sort to go white. Her rather dark honey-tinted skin turned an unhappy grey, and she put a hand to her throat. She was not wearing her amber necklace. Then, instead of protesting, she said, "If you know so much perhaps you can solve my problem."

"If I knew what your problem was, perhaps. I am rather looking to you to help in solving mine."

"Aren't you going to arrest me?"

"I don't think so—not immediately, at any rate. You have committed a number of offences, including wasting police time. Did you know that that is an offence? You could be held on various counts if necessary, but whether you are or not depends mainly on you. I should warn you that you are not compelled to say anything. If you prefer it so, I can take you to the police station, where you will be detained. But I have a curious feeling that we are really on the same side, and my private view is that it will be much better for you in the end if you cooperate. I can't make you any promises, I can merely give my own opinion. Whether you accept it or not is a matter for you. I must add that I think the map will be safer in my possession than in yours, and I shall want you to hand it over. I'll give you a receipt for it."

"You guessed quite rightly—the map is in my house. I don't think I can stay here anymore today. Would you be willing to come home with me?"

"Certainly."

"Then I'll just tell my secretary. Will you agree to come in my car?"

"Why not?"

She rang through to the secretary and picked up her handbag. We went out through a door opening straight to the passage, not through the secretary's adjoining office by which as a visitor I had been taken to her. As we got into the car she asked. "Aren't you afraid of letting me drive? I could easily kill both of us."

"You could, but I don't think you will. I think you want to solve your problem."

"You're a strange person. But I've not met many policemen."

"I'm not a proper policeman. As you know, I'm attached to a special department of the Home Office."

Her colour had come back as we talked. She was on edge, but she did not seem particularly worried. She drove well, and in spite of Cambridge traffic we were at her house in under half an hour. It was an attractive place, two eighteenth-century cottages knocked into one, standing back from the road with a short semi-circular drive and a white painted gate at each end.

I got out to open the gate for her and she drove up to the front door. As I walked up to the car she leaned out of the window and said, "If you are going to arrest me it would be tidier to put the car away. If you open the garage door for me I'll go in—the door just swings up."

"I should leave the car where it is for the moment."

"Come into the house, then."

As with many converted cottages there was no hall. The front door was sheltered by a substantial porch, doubtless built on during the conversion, and it opened straight into a lounge. All the paintwork was white, which set off the black beams exposed across the ceiling, and a staircase of dark wood in one corner of the room. There was a door in the opposite wall of the room.

"Entertaining the police is outside my experience," she said. "If you were anybody else I'd offer you a cup of coffee, but I don't know if you'd consider that suitable."

"I'd love a cup of coffee."

"Then I shall have to go into the kitchen—it's through that door. You can watch me to see that I don't run out at the back, and don't put poison in the coffee."

"A woman of your intelligence could poison a cup of coffee

without being noticed. You may have made the necessary preparations, but I shall go on trusting you."

She smiled. "I'm a geographer, not a toxicologist, though there are times when toxicology might come in handy. This isn't one of them. I'm going to grind the beans—I always grind them fresh, so don't be startled by the noise."

She left the kitchen door open, but I didn't particularly watch her. I looked at her bookshelves and pictures. "Is this the only sitting room?" I asked.

"No. It was the kitchen of one of the old cottages. I have a study upstairs which I use as a kind of drawing room when I have people. But mostly I use this downstairs room— it's handy for the kitchen and the garden."

"Why haven't you got married?"

"That's part of the problem."

When she had brought the coffee she said, "It would help if you would tell me just how much you know."

"I know that you were rather in love with Charles Jackson once, but that was some time ago, when you were a student. He was a bit in love with you, but you were both exemplary and I suppose old-fashioned in your views on marriage, and as Charles Jackson was married you decided that yours could be only an academic friendship. I suspect that Charles Jackson gave you your amber necklace, but I don't know." She nodded, and I went on, "Fortunately your iron self-discipline worked and you fell out of love, though you retained a high regard for Jackson's work, and I think for the man himself." Again she nodded. "Then you met someone else with whom you fell quite desperately in love, and with whom you had a passionate affair. I don't know who he was, and I think he passed out of your life."

"He was murdered."

"Can you tell me about it?"

"I know he was murdered, but it was supposed to be suicide. His death was a bit like Charles Jackson's, but there was no history of depression and he died from an overdose of barbiturates. That's one of the reasons why I know it was murder, because he was not on any kind of sleeping pill, and why he should have had the drugs at all was never satisfactorily explained. He left a letter to his parents saying that he had decided to take his own life and he was sure that they would understand and forgive. They were just shattered, and didn't understand."

"There was no doubt about his handwriting?"

"There was doubt about everything. Adrian was in the habit of typing letters, and this was typed. The signature seemed all right, but I was never convinced by it."

"Where did this happen?"

"Adrian was working in Hamburg, and it all happened there. I tried to get our Embassy in Germany to have the case reopened, but I think they didn't want to get involved. From their point of view a British subject had committed suicide, the German police were satisfied, and the less said about it the better. And I had no real standing in the matter."

"Why weren't you and Adrian married?"

She took a sip of coffee, put down the cup and clenched and unclenched her hand. "Because I was silly, I suppose. It is not easy to be a woman sometimes. Adrian was a mathematician, and a really brilliant one. He had a job with a big oil company, Universal Oil, which is partly German—at any rate it has big offices in Hamburg. Adrian was concerned with economic forecasting and he was so good at his job that he had his own department and could run things as he liked. I wanted to stay in Cambridge, to get on with my own job. I didn't want to be tied down in marriage. I still don't know if I was right or wrong. Adrian might have been murdered anyway, but as his widow I'd have been better placed to get justice done to his memory."

"What was his surname, and when did he die?"

"Does it matter? It's got nothing to do with the map."

"It may matter very much indeed—and you may be nearer justice than you think."

"He was Adrian Stowe, a Fellow of Magdalen College, Oxford, and he died in February last year, not quite eighteen months ago."

"Now tell me about the map." I hated to go on driving questions at her, but in a curious way she seemed almost to welcome them. She didn't reply at once and fiddled with the coffee pot. Then she shook her head, as if trying to shake off some unhappy memory, and went on in the same detached, unemotional way. "It's harder to talk about than Adrian because it's not my story and I can only guess at some of it," she said. "You know that Charles was brilliant—that was one of his problems. Sheila, his wife, is an awfully nice person, but intellectually she's not in the same league as Charles. I don't suppose you've ever heard of a geographical theory known as the Arctic Calorific Syndrome."

"As a matter of fact I have. It concerns the possible retention in the Arctic substructure of warmth from an earlier period when the earth's crustal shape was different, and the North Pole was not where it is now."

"That makes it a bit easier." She did not ask how I came to be informed on such a specialised subject. "Well, Charles really invented the theory. I worked with him on it for a time, but when we decided that there was no future in our own relationship, I got more involved with college work, and he carried on by himself. We kept in touch, though, and after I met Adrian things became rather easier between us, if you can understand that."

"Yes."

"You've got to understand, too, that Charles was a very *good* person—exceptionally gentle, and kind to anyone he thought he could help. He should never have taken the museum job, though—he was rotten at admin and not very practical in his own life. He was a tower of strength to me when Adrian died, the more so because there was never any question of going back to our old relationship. I suppose I'd grown out of it, and so in a way had he. His daughter was growing up intelligent, and she meant everything to him."

She seemed to be talking to herself as much as to me. I didn't interrupt her, and let her go on in her own way. After a longish pause she sighed, and continued, "About a year ago Charles invited me to lunch. He seemed worried about something and I could see that he wanted to talk to me. He said that a friend of his was being blackmailed, that he had been helping with money, but the sums were getting bigger and he couldn't afford to go on. I told him to go to the police. He said he couldn't, because it wasn't his business.

"That first conversation was rather inconclusive. I went on

94

seeing him from time to time, and he looked iller and iller. Then he told me that he'd been offered a way of settling the blackmail problem once for all—by stealing the Baffin Map from the museum. To anyone like Charles this was unthinkable, but whoever suggested it to him had worked out quite a clever plan. The map was going to the Hamburg exhibition, and it was to disappear when it came back. The insurance company would pay in the end so the museum wouldn't really lose anything."

"Except the map."

"Except the map. That was what worried Charles. He didn't know just what was being planned so he stayed late on the day the map came back and when the rest of the staff had gone home he took the map himself and gave it to me. I was nothing to do with the museum then, and Charles thought that if anyone was thinking of stealing it they wouldn't be able to find it. His idea was that I should keep the map safely out of the way until it could be returned. Two days later he was dead."

"Why didn't you return the map when you were appointed to Dr Jackson's job?"

"Because I didn't know enough about it. Charles had been really worried, and for all I knew the map might still be in danger. Nobody noticed that it was missing until that American asked for it, and then I had to do something. I knew that the Curator wouldn't want a fuss just before his retirement, and as long as the map couldn't be found it couldn't be stolen."

"Where is the map now?"

"In my bedroom. I'll get it for you."

She went upstairs and was back in a moment with a flat cardboard map-case. She opened it to show me that the Baffin Map really was inside. I longed to be able to study it, but there were a lot more questions to be asked first.

"Did Dr Jackson tell you who was this friend of his who was being blackmailed?"

"No."

"And you didn't ask him?"

"Of course I asked him, but he didn't want to tell me. He felt that loyalty was concerned, and if you had known Charles you would understand that to him that was final."

"Did you suspect anything about his death?"

"Yes, and I still do, just as I do about Adrian. But I had nothing to go on, no evidence that I could give to the police."

"You had the story of the blackmailer and the map."

"Can you see the police believing me? And I had the map."

"It's easy to be wise with hindsight, but you gravely underrated the police. You are telling me everything now."

"It's not quite the same. And at the time I was frightfully mixed up. I wanted to be loyal to Charles, and I wanted to keep my job at the museum. I knew the map was safe as long as I had it, and I didn't know that it was all going to come up again."

"Do you know why it has come up again?"

"No. You came to me with a preposterous story, but having reported the map as missing I had to pretend to believe you."

"It was partly because someone as intelligent as you believed such a preposterous story that I thought you probably knew a lot more than you admitted. When did you break your amber necklace?"

"What on earth has that got to do with it?"

"You must just accept that it has, and that it may be important."

She shrugged her shoulders. "You really do have an extraordinary amount of information. Yes, the necklace did break, one day when I was visiting Charles at the museum. As he'd given it to me originally he was a bit upset, and helped me pick up the beads."

"Was that before the map came back from Hamburg?"

"Yes, some weeks before."

"And you were one bead short."

"How can you know that?"

"Because I have the bead." I showed it to her, but did not let her take it.

"Where did you find it?"

"In Dr Jackson's bedroom."

I let this sink in, and went on, "You appear to have been remarkably frank with me, and I should like to be equally frank with you, but there are many things that you have not explained, and that need explaining. I must tell you that the police now have reason to believe that Dr Jackson's death was not an accident. I'm afraid I can't disclose the evidence for that, but since you also suspect that his death was no accident you can accept what I say. You will appreciate that the finding of your bead in the bedroom could be regarded as evidence against you. So far, I am disposed to believe what you have told me, but there must be much that you have not told me, for your story as such is even more preposterous than my account of the missing map's being offered to a British embassy."

She put her head in her hands. Then she shook herself again, and with a touch of her old insouciance remarked, "To be accused of Charles's murder would have elements of real comedy, or more accurately of farce."

"Nobody has accused you of Dr Jackson's murder. I said that what you have just told me, coupled with the finding of one of your beads in his room, could provide a *prima facie* case against you. A prosecuting lawyer could certainly make a good deal out of it. What really happened on the night of Dr Jackson's death?"

"You know about the party. There was a woman there I didn't know—about my age, and I suppose most men would call her attractive, but I'm sufficiently anti the exploitation of women as sex symbols not to care much for those very low-cut dresses by which women exploit themselves. She attached herself to Charles. I moved around a lot talking to people and fairly late in the evening was horrified to find that Charles was more or less drunk. I'd never seen him like that before. The woman left him when he began to get drunk. I stayed with him until Sheila came, and between us we got him home."

"Did you go into his room?"

"Yes. I helped Sheila get him to bed."

"Did you go in by the door or the french window?"

"The garden door—what you call the french window. Sheila ran in and opened it, and then I helped her get Charles into the room. It was easier from the garden, for we more or less had to carry him. I didn't stay long—it was embarrassing for Sheila, and for me."

"Now I must go back a bit. I think you have told me nowhere near the whole truth. I find it impossible to believe

97

that you were willing to be an accomplice in extracting a valuable map from the museum simply because Dr Jackson said that a friend of his, whom you don't know, was being blackmailed."

"It wasn't only that. I thought I'd explained that it was mainly to protect the map."

"Why did you think the map needed protecting?"

She was silent again for what felt a long time. Then she seemed to come to a decision. "You're quite right, there was much more than the map," she said. "It is easy to be wise afterwards and I think now that I ought to have gone to the police long ago, but I couldn't talk to the policemen I've met as I'm talking to you."

"You should have more trust in the police. They would probably have put you in touch with my Department."

"Maybe. But I didn't know that. And it was the German police more than the English police. You see, Adrian was doing the most vital secret work that might have transformed the oil industry. Only Charles Jackson and I really knew what he was doing—oh, there was Dr Braunschweig who was head of his company in Germany, and who trusted him enough to give him a free hand in his work. But Dr Braunschweig only knew part of it, some of Adrian's conclusions, but not all the scientific data on which he made them. After Adrian's death Dr Braunschweig came to England to see Charles, but Charles was a bit suspicious of him and didn't tell him much. Charles was a scholar, not an industrialist. He trusted Adrian because Adrian was a scholar, too, but Charles didn't want his work to be exploited commercially before he was satisfied that he'd got things absolutely right. And he wasn't, yet."

"What was this work?"

"I thought you knew—it was the Arctic Calorific Syndrome which, if we could understand it properly, would, or rather might, open sea routes around the North Pole. Adrian believed that it would be practicable, and his calculations about oil transport were of immense economic and strategical import-ance. But he died—I think was killed—before he knew enough to translate theoretical calculations into practical action. No-body knows quite enough yet, though Charles and I have

98

learned a good deal more since Adrian's death. Now that Charles is dead I'm the only one left, and I want Charles and Adrian to have the recognition that is due to them."

"Where are Charles's papers?"

"Sheila still has them. They don't matter very much to me because I know what he was doing and I've carried some of his work still farther, but I want Sheila to let me edit them for publication one day. I think she will, but I haven't wanted to distress her by seeming to want to grab at the papers."

"Do you know that Dr Braunschweig has been kidnapped and that his life is threatened unless the Baffin Map is handed over to his kidnappers? Here is a copy of the ransom demand. It is a strange document."

She took the sheet of typescript from me and studied it intently. "What a fool I've been," she said. "It looks as if Dr Braunschweig may have been on our side."

"I think probably he was. But who is on the other side?"

"I don't know. That's where I've been a fool. I thought I could protect Charles's and Adrian's work by keeping it to myself, but all I seem to have done is to endanger other people. If I'd gone to the police long ago this might never have happened."

"It has happened, and we've got to find Dr Braunschweig before he is murdered, too. That's why your help is vital. What makes the map so important that somebody is prepared to murder for it?"

She frowned. "But I don't think the map is particularly important. It's valuable as a rare example of early seventeenth-century cartography, and it has a bearing on the Arctic Calorific Syndrome in that William Baffin seems actually to have met some of the streams of slightly warmer water that the theory supposes to exist. My own view is that it was meeting a calorific stream that enabled him to get as far north as he did. But of course he knew nothing about the theory, and the theory wasn't developed from his map. Only a handful of scholars really know anything about the theory—I'm astonished that you seem to have heard of it. One or two papers have been published, but they're highly speculative, and the only detailed work has been done by Charles, Adrian and me. On what has been published so far I think it's fair to say that most geographers reject the theory."

"Yet somebody has wanted the map for some time. On your own story Charles Jackson was asked to steal it in settlement of his friend's debt to a blackmailer."

"Well, it's worth quite a lot of money."

"But you know that it couldn't be sold openly. You can't have thought that it was simply a matter of money."

"No . . . but yes, in a way . . . I did think that the blackmailer wanted money, but I also thought that he wanted Charles to steal the map so that he would have a hold on Charles. You must remember that it wasn't Charles who was being blackmailed—it was a friend of his."

"And you expect me to believe that? And that you don't even know who the friend is?"

"What you believe is up to you. I can only tell you what I know. I've tried to explain that it was entirely in keeping with Charles's sense of loyalty that he should not disclose his friend's name, and it was entirely in keeping with my relationship with Charles that I should accept what he told me and not try to cross-examine him."

"Did Charles Jackson have any personal knowledge of the Arctic?"

"Of course he did. He was quite a distinguished explorer before he settled down to academic work and he led two expeditions to Northwest Greenland and the north coast of Ellesmere Island, which is known as Grant Land. My amber beads came from there—he picked up a fine piece of amber from a beach which he found unexpectedly ice-free near the Robeson Channel entrance to the Lincoln Sea."

"Some evidence that the coast was once forested."

"Perhaps, but the amber could have been carried there by currents in the sea. There's better evidence in some seams of coal, a sort of lignite, that Charles also came across. I think there isn't any doubt that the area was once warm enough for trees, but that was millions of years ago. What is still questionable is whether geothermal systems from this once-warm Arctic exist to influence the pattern of ice formation today. Charles and Adrian believed that they do. I want to try to complete their work, but there's a great deal still to be done."

I wanted to get back to London. I also wanted to return to Hamburg. Another visit to Mrs Jackson seemed almost equally urgent, but I thought that might be left to Inspector Richards. I felt desperately sorry for Ingrid Mitchell—she'd done some silly things, but she must have been wretchedly lonely and unhappy and she did not know enough about either the English or the German police to know where she could have turned for help. For all the strange aspects of her story I believed her; and I respected her for trying to be matter-of-fact about events that were agony for her.

"I'd better take the map," I said. "I shan't give it back to the museum yet. It seems to have done enough harm—it will be safer with us for the moment."

"Aren't you going to arrest me?"

"Certainly not. I'd much prefer to regard you as an ally."

She rang for a taxi, and the Baffin Map in its cardboard case travelled with me by train to London. It was an awkward shape for the luggage rack, so it stood on the floor beside my seat. One man nearly tripped over it, but nobody else took the slightest notice.

I wasn't much of an ally for Ingrid Mitchell. Ten minutes after I got to Sir Edmund Pusey's office the phone rang. "For you Peter," Sir Edmund said.

It was Inspector Richards to tell me that Dr Mitchell was dead.

VII

The Second Note

THERE WAS NO doubt that Ingrid Mitchell's death was
murder because she had been shot. If there was a pattern in
the killings connected with the Baffin Map it was continued
here, for a .28 pistol was in her right hand with her forefinger
bent round the trigger, to give an appearance of suicide. It
was a poor performance; the wound was in the left temple,
not easy to inflict with a pistol held right-handed. Furthermore,
there were no burn-marks round the wound, indicating that
the shot had been fired from a distance of at least several
feet.

It was chance that her death was discovered so quickly. A
man had called to read the electricity meter, and rang the
bell at the front door. No one came, and this puzzled him
because of the car standing in the drive. He rang again, and
when there was still no answer he became slightly uneasy and
tried the door. It was unlocked, and as it opened straight into
the lounge he saw the body as soon as he had opened the
door a few inches. He was an elderly ex-serviceman who had
seen death, and it took him only a minute or so to decide
that he could do nothing. Using the telephone in the cottage
he rang the police, and waited until they came. Inspector
Richards was at the house with a doctor and a constable in
ten minutes. He telephoned me from the house. He knew that
I had planned to see Dr Mitchell at the museum that morning,
but he did not know that I had been to her house. "What
time did you leave?" he asked.

"Soon after midday, say about 12:15," I said. "Dr Mitchell
telephoned for a cab for me, and I got to the station at 12:35
—I know the precise time, because I was hoping to get the
12:34 for London but the cab was held up in traffic and I

missed the train by just one minute. I had to wait for a later train—that's why I have only just got in."

"We were called at two-twenty p.m. and were there by two-thirty. The doctor can't give a precise time of death, but he estimates that she could not have been dead for much more than an hour. That would mean she was shot around one-thirty."

"I wonder why the front door wasn't locked."

"It's an old-fashioned mortice lock, with a biggish key. It doesn't lock automatically. The key wasn't in the lock, but we found it in Dr Mitchell's handbag, in her bedroom upstairs. If she stayed at home after you left, presumably the door was unlocked when she opened it for her murderer—or the murderer took a chance and found the door unlocked. I suppose he didn't lock it afterwards because he didn't have the key."

"I can't get back to Cambridge for the moment but I *must* talk to you. Can you come to London tonight?"

"I could drive up. I could get to London by about seven-thirty."

"Splendid. Come to the Department in Whitehall, and we'll look after your car. Then we can have some supper and I can put you up for the night. Can you see if you can find any working notebooks or files, papers of any sort dealing with what is called the Arctic Calorific Syndrome?"

He repeated the phrase and promised to do his best. "By the way, I've recovered the map," I said.

While Sir Edmund was arranging for Seddon to meet Inspector Richards with us I got on the phone to Keller in Hamburg. He had news that took us one stage farther. The edge of one of the dinghy's thwarts was slightly splintered, and in a crack in the wood was a tiny thread of fabric. On analysis it was identified as coming from a material widely used for men's summer suits. He had been to see Frau Braunschweig and she thought that her husband had been wearing such a suit on the day he disappeared. Keller thought this established a strong probability that the dinghy had been used to take Dr Braunschweig out to *Apfel*.

This was useful as far as it went, but I had an urgent job for Keller. I told him of the apparent suicide of Adrian Stowe and asked if he could look up the records and perhaps go into the case again. "On the face of things it is rather similar to the death of Dr Jackson in Cambridge. That was assumed to be an accident, with a possibility of suicide, though we now know that it was murder. Adrian Stowe was working for Universal Oil in Hamburg, but he was also engaged with Dr Jackson on geographical research relating to the Arctic. There's been another murder in Cambridge—no doubt at all this time, a woman killed by a bullet in her head. We have a conference about all this tonight. We've recovered the map, though we're not saying anything about it at the moment. It's a long story—I'll tell you later."

Keller understood the pressure we were under without having to be told. He didn't try to question me. All he said was "Right, I'll get on to the Stowe case straight away. Good luck."

We began with a drink of Sir Edmund's whisky, which we all needed. Richards at first was inclined to be overawed by so much of what he would have called Top Brass, but Sir Edmund is at his best on such occasions. After I had outlined my own interview with Dr Mitchell the inspector told us about his day. "To deal with your question, sir," he said to me. "I looked everywhere I could in the cottage, but I couldn't find any notes or papers on that Arctic Syndrome you mentioned. Dr Mitchell's desk wasn't locked, and it looked as if someone had been through the drawers. Dr Mitchell herself seems to have been a neat person, and her clothes were all beautifully tidy. The drawers in the desk were a mess—papers all mixed up, and things that had obviously been in alphabetical order shoved in any old fashion."

"You're probably right. She must have had some papers on the Arctic, and it seems likely that whoever killed her took them. Maybe he or she was also looking for the map. There's one thing I'm thankful about. When I first talked to Dr Mitchell about the map I said I'd give her a receipt for it when I took it away, but in the end I didn't. She trusted me by then, I think, and didn't ask for one. So there was nothing to show that we have it."

"That was a stroke of luck. It had better remain missing for the moment," Sir Edmund said.

"Yes, we still don't know *why* there's all this apparent interest in the map—the Arctic papers seem far more important. I can't help feeling that it has been brought in to confuse the picture. Where are Dr Jackson's research notes? Mrs Jackson said they are at the museum, but Dr Mitchell told me that Mrs Jackson still has them. When you get back to Cambridge, Inspector, I'd like you to check Mrs Jackson's story. I'm fairly sure that she herself believes the papers are at the museum, but my own view is that they were taken on the night her husband was killed—I think probably that is why he was killed. You might have a look at his desk or filing cabinet to see if there are any signs of its having been rifled. After all this time there may not be much to find, but you may spot something."

"I can try, anyway," Richards said. "How did you know that Dr Mitchell had the map?"

"I couldn't *know*, but for a woman of her intelligence to swallow my story about the map's being offered to a British embassy was too much to believe. If she'd thought that this really was a chance of getting back her precious map, she'd have moved heaven and earth to know where the embassy was, and although she did suggest rather tepidly that she should go there herself, she didn't press the point. And there were other things that didn't make sense. When she insisted on calling in the police about the map she calmly accepted the doddering old Curator's reluctance to have any publicity. You'd have thought she'd have wanted every museum and art dealer in the world alerted. She didn't even have a proper description of the map available when I went to see her—she was ridiculously casual about it."

"How much of her story do you believe?"

"Pretty well all of it, but I can't understand her reasoning. When she got Charles Jackson's job she could have put back the map without any trouble at all. Why didn't she? I'm absolutely certain that she wasn't hanging on to it because she wanted to steal it—I feel more and more strongly that she was an honourable woman in a situation that became too much for her. She was trying to play a lone hand as a detective. She regarded herself as the trustee of the work of Charles Jackson and Adrian Stowe, and she guessed that somebody was threatening that work. But she didn't know who. Someone had tried to involve Charles Jackson in stealing the map, presumably to get a permanent hold over him, and I think she may have hoped that whoever it was would try the same thing with her, which would give her a chance of discovering his identity. Outside the museum, remember, nobody knew that the map was missing.

"Let's turn to the papers on the Arctic Calorific Syndrome. Dr Jackson's seem to have disappeared, and now Dr Mitchell's have gone, too. *I think there is a third set of papers, dealing with the work of Adrian Stowe.* Where are they? Dr Mitchell seems to have suspected Dr Braunschweig, but the note demanding the map in return for his life shook her profoundly. I wish now I'd told her about it before—we can never know just what she thought. Whatever her previous thinking about Braunschweig, certainly the ransom demand changed her mind. But she was genuinely puzzled about the map—in her view it wasn't really of much importance."

"What do you think?"

"I don't know. It must be important in some way, but I think it's probably not important in the way we're meant to think it is. We must leave that until we know more about it. Dr Mitchell's death is a major new fact. What do you make of it, Inspector?"

"How it fits in, sir, I can't pretend to guess, but as murder in furtherance of robbery—of those Arctic papers, maybe—it seems straightforward. From the position of the body Dr Mitchell was shot near the foot of the stairs. It looks as if she had just come down, perhaps because she heard someone at the door, and whoever it was walked in and shot her. There were no signs of a struggle."

"Whoever killed her must have put the pistol in her hand. Is there anything in the way of fingerprints?"

"Not on the pistol—except the dead woman's own. It must have been wiped over before being placed as it was. There are some prints on the desk that don't belong to Dr Mitchell, but they may be there quite innocently, of course, and if they were made by some friend of hers we may never be able to identify them. But it's early days yet. I left a photographer and fingerprint expert at work when I came to see you. There's a good team on the job, making inquiries to see if anyone heard a shot or noticed a car drive up."

"It would be around lunch time—that may help people to remember. Perhaps there's another fact; it seems probable that she knew her killer."

"Why?"

"If your reconstruction is right she was shot by someone standing at the door as she came down from her bedroom or her study upstairs. If someone she didn't know wanted to steal her papers there was no need to kill her. She lived alone, she was out a good deal, and the cottage would not be difficult to get into. Normally she would not have been at home at the time she was killed—she would have been either at the museum, or having lunch out somewhere. It was pure chance that she was at home today, because she took me there. Assume the murderer wanted to go through her papers. Lunch time would be quite a good time when she was likely to be out. Before breaking into the place the murderer tried the door, and was delighted to find it unlocked—it hasn't got a snap lock, and she might easily have forgotten to lock it. To be on the safe side he rang—then he heard her coming down. Why kill her? All he had to do was to say that he was selling something, or looking for a house called 'The Cedars' and did she know where it was. A minute's polite conversation and he could have gone off, kept an eye on the house, and returned when he saw her car go out. If she knew her caller the situation was different. It might have been much harder to offer a reason for calling—the murderer may have wanted the fact that he'd visited the house at all to remain unknown. So she was killed out of hand."

"He'd come prepared to kill or he wouldn't have had a pistol," Sir Edmund said.

"True, and that seems to strengthen the case that she knew him. If she was out, well and good, but if she was at home she had to be killed."

"I agree with Peter," Seddon said. "But it's the inspector's case—what does he think?"

"I would say that Colonel Blair has a strong argument, but only if the intention was to steal papers or perhaps to look for the map," Richards said. "I don't know enough about the background—someone may have wanted her killed for some quite other reason. I must carry on with all the routine things. She must have had friends, but it's not easy to know where to start—her colleagues at the museum, I suppose."

"Please don't think I'm trying to interfere with your case, but I'd be very discreet about the museum," I said. "It may not come into it at all, but I can't help feeling that the museum side of things has been nowhere near explained. Find out everything you can about the other museum people and where they were at the time of the murder—the Curator, the heads of the other departments, Dr Mitchell's secretary, everyone. But don't say anything about the Arctic, or the map. She was an attractive woman—if they like to think that you are looking for a jealous husband, let them."

It was Seddon's turn. "Peter's guess that there has been trouble of some sort on the Unol board seems to have something in it," he said. "I had a bit of luck in getting hold of the right man in the merchant bank which advised the Arabian Sands Oil Company during the Unol takeover. The City thought that Unol needed Arabian Sands to strengthen its position in the Middle East after the various troubles that have upset production in other fields there. The board of Arabian Sands, which is one of the smaller concerns, reputable but a bit short of capital, was quite willing to be taken over, and the Unol deal seemed to them to make sense. But in the negotiations that went on over the price to be paid for Arabian Sands there was a snag—Unol just couldn't be brought to offer what the Arabian Sands people considered reasonable. At first they thought this was just normal commercial bargaining, but according to my man it gradually became apparent that there was a strong influence in Unol which didn't want to have anything to do with the deal. Oil companies like to play their cards close to their chest and you must understand that what comes next is largely guesswork. But a good merchant bank's guesses tend to be well-informed. My man thinks that there was a fairly powerful minority on the Unol board, led by the deputy chairman, Dr Braunschweig, which held that the company was already over-dependent on Middle East oil, and that instead of buying more production there they should be putting everything they could into other parts of the world

—the North Sea, Alaska, West Africa, anywhere outside the Middle East. You can make a case for this, but if a company wants oil *now*, and Unol does, then it's not easy to get away from the Middle East. Anyway, the Braunschweig policy, if that is what it was, didn't work, and the full board accepted the Arabian Sands offer at a price which certainly pleased Arabian Sands shareholders. But my man says that this took a lot of hard work and discreet lobbying in the right places. The trouble was that Arabian Sands wasn't sitting all that pretty. They had to find a large sum for advance royalties on a concession they hadn't yet worked, and they just didn't have the cash. No money, no new concession, and they'd have been in big trouble. There were other possible bidders, but they wanted to pay in shares. Arabian Sands needed cash, and Unol was about the only outfit with the cash to spend. So it was important to a lot of people that the Unol merger should go through."

"None of this came out at the time?"

"No. There were ups and downs in Arabian Sands share prices as speculators thought that the deal was on or off, but that's normal. Naturally Arabian Sands didn't want to say anything, and it would have been against all Unol tradition for any hint of differences in the board room to be made public. But I think things probably happened much as my man said. What bearing, if any, it may have on the Braunschweig kidnapping is another matter. It's all over and done with, anyway."

"Still, it's interesting."

Sir Edmund suggested that we needed another drink, and there was no dissension on our board. The inspector's earlier tension was now relaxed, and I could ask him without seeming patronising if he wanted any help that we could give in Cambridge. "Well, I want all the help anyone can give in getting to the bottom of the Mitchell murder and what looks like the Jackson murder, but you're doing everything you can already," he said. "As far as the routine work goes, we can manage. And the Super's so fed up by what we missed in the Jackson case that he'll give me every man I can use for the Mitchell business."

"I'd like you to see Mrs Jackson about her husband's papers yourself, if you can fit it in."

"Of course. I'll give that priority as soon as I get back to Cambridge."

Seddon wanted to get home, and as there seemed nothing more that we could usefully pursue at the moment Sir Edmund took the inspector and me out to dinner. Afterwards I took Richards back to my rooms in the Temple for the night. We were having an early breakfast when the phone rang. It was Sir Edmund. "There's been another Braunschweig letter," he said. "Sir Anthony Brotherton is bringing it to me straight away—he should be here in about ten minutes. Can you come?"

Obviously I had to go. There didn't seem much point in bringing the inspector, and he was needed back in Cambridge. So I left him to finish breakfast and was lucky enough to pick up a cab almost as soon as I got to Fleet Street.

Sir Anthony Brotherton may have been disturbed, but he did not show it. He was impeccably dressed for his day in the City, his greying hair beautifully groomed, his air of distinction unshaken. I felt that he would present the same unruffled front whether he had made or lost a few thousand million pounds. His warmth of personality that had impressed me when I first met him was again impressive now. He seemed to convey a feeling that Sir Edmund and I were doing him a favour by letting him come to see us. He took an envelope from his pocket. "Here is the letter, just as it was delivered this morning, except that I have opened the envelope," he said.

Sir Edmund glanced at the envelope and the note inside it, then handed both to me. Envelope and notepaper seemed precisely similar to those of the first ransom demand. As before, the envelope was postmarked Amsterdam. The note it contained was now more threatening. It read:

You have had time to acquire the Baffin map from Cambridge. It must be delivered by hand to 16, Ilmgasse, Vienna, at noon precisely on June 30. The map is to be packed in a flat case, not rolled up. There must be no attempt at conversation with the person who accepts the map. When these instructions have been carried out Dr Braunschweig will be released. If you fail to carry them out Dr Braunschweig will be executed as an example to other capitalist maggots gorging themselves at the expense of the workers in society. The map must be delivered by a single person acting alone. If any attempt is made to invoke the police the execution will be carried out.

As before, the note was typed, and it was unsigned.

"What do you make of it?" Sir Anthony asked.

"I served briefly in Vienna in my Foreign Office days, but I can't recall an Ilmgasse," Sir Edmund said. "That doesn't mean much. 'Gasse' in Vienna is normally used for a small side-street, or alley, and there is no reason why I should have come across this particular one. Do you know Vienna, Sir Anthony?"

"I have been there, of course. We have offices there, which I visit from time to time. But I have had no business which has taken me into side-streets, and I have never heard of the Ilmgasse. My main reason for wanting so urgently to see you is that I feel the time has come to approach the Cambridge museum in order to buy the map. It may be an interesting old map, and it may be worth a lot of money, but neither is important in relation to Gustav Braunschweig's life."

I remembered that Sir Anthony Brotherton knew nothing of the disappearance of the map from Cambridge, and I hoped that Sir Edmund realised this too.

"Today is June 12 and the note demands the map on June 30, so we have still nearly three weeks," I said. "It is too soon to contemplate giving in to the kidnappers' blackmail. I am sure that the German authorities would also take that view."

"I would put it even more strongly," Sir Edmund said. "The German Ambassador has conveyed his Government's opinion that it is imperative to resist demands for ransom, and I may say that that is equally the view of Her Majesty's Government. To give in to this sort of blackmail can only encourage other blackmailers, and might have lamentable international effects."

"I understand the international implications, but as a human being I cannot feel that they really outweigh the value of Gustav's life," Sir Anthony said unhappily.

Sir Edmund tried to comfort him. "So far as we know Dr

Braunschweig has not yet been harmed and with time in hand we have no reason to abandon hope of finding him."

"Yes, but where? It is agony for his wife, as it is for us, his friends. I appreciate that you cannot go into details of the secret work that is doubtless going on but I shall be grateful for anything I can tell my board to relieve our anxiety. We have a treble responsibility. It is in our power to ransom Gustav, and naturally we want to exercise that power. At the same time we must accept some measure of responsibility to the world of international business—you do not need to stress the threat to all businessmen in senior positions. Thirdly, we feel a human responsibility for Gustav's wife and family."

"I am sorry if our advice seems hard, but we, too, have a heavy burden of responsibility," Sir Edmund said gently. "As for giving in and trying to buy the map from Cambridge—you have no guarantee that delivery of the map will help Dr Braunschweig. Indeed, past experience of such kidnappings suggests that readiness to meet a ransom leads to the escalation of the demands. In this case the demand for the map is so extraordinary that it seems almost certain that it is merely a preliminary to something else. You can tell your board that they are not being heartless in standing firm—they are doing the best possible thing for your colleague."

"You are right, but it is hard."

"There is another reason for not approaching the Cambridge museum at the moment," I said. "I take it you did not hear the seven o'clock news on the radio this morning."

"No. My day starts early and I get up soon after six. My post is specially collected, and is brought to me about six forty-five. As soon as I saw the letter I could think of nothing else. Why do you ask?"

"Because the Keeper of Arctic Maps at the museum, the department responsible for the Baffin Map, has been found murdered at her home."

For all the power of his personality he seemed suddenly drained. "What devilry is going on?" he asked.

"We do not yet know. The demand for a map for which she was responsible may have an important bearing on her murder. It is imperative that nothing about the map should get out—

the murderer must not be allowed to know what action is being taken about it."

"You refer to the Keeper as 'she'—is it not unusual for such a post to be held by a woman?"

"I don't know enough about museums to know how usual it is, but I should say it is not uncommon nowadays. Dr Ingrid Mitchell is a distinguished geographer."

"Can you be sure she was murdered?"

"Yes. She was shot."

"People have been known to shoot themselves. . . . I'm sorry, of course you would know the details in the case, and it is not my business. You must forgive me for being so shaken."

"You have nothing to apologise for, it is wholly understandable," Sir Edmund said. "Can we return to your letter? Can you suggest any reason why the scene of action should apparently shift to Vienna?"

"No. Administratively our Vienna offices come under Dr Braunschweig, but it is our policy to allow our various national companies a high degree of independence, and the Austrian company would not have much to do with Hamburg in day-to-day affairs. We have offices all over the world. I can only suppose that the gang which kidnapped Gustav has some links with Austria. Will this knowledge help in any way, do you think?"

"It may. Colonel Blair is already in close touch with the German police and he will discuss the Viennese location with them. Is there anything else you would like to say to us now?"

"I don't think so—you have been most patient. Thank you again for your consideration." He got up to go. Sir Edmund put an arm on his shoulder and went with him to his car.

As soon as they had left the room I rang Hamburg, and was fortunate to get hold of Keller at once. I told him briefly of the letter and said that I should probably be coming to Hamburg later in the day. "It's odd to be given a precise address so far in advance," Keller said. "I know the head of security in Vienna, and I'll ask him to have a discreet look at 16 Ilmgasse. Maybe I shall have some news for you when you come."

Sir Edmund returned while I was speaking to Keller. When

113

I put down the phone, he asked, "Was I all right?"

"You were marvellous," I said, and meant it. "We've been thinking so much about the disappearance of the map that I was terrified you might say something about it. I should have known you better."

"You're generous this morning, Peter! What a mess it all is—do you think you're really going to get anywhere?"

"Well, already I've got a man on the way to 16 Ilmgasse. I don't believe a word of it."

"No . . . And I'm surprised that a man as intelligent as Sir Anthony seems to take it all at its face value. But I've met this before—men who are supremely able in one field can be simpletons in another. And to be fair, he's going through a bad time."

"Not so bad as Frau Braunschweig, or Mrs Jackson. I wonder to what extent his board does what he tells it to."

"If Seddon's right, not always . . . or rather, not always without a struggle. In this case, though, I should think they'll do whatever he suggests, which is what we are asking, anyway."

"Yes . . . Keller's getting on to the chief of security in Vienna to have a look at 16 Ilmgasse. My guess is that it will turn out to be a harmless café. I think we're intended to put in a lot of time watching the place and making inquiries in Vienna while something else goes on somewhere entirely different. I've even half an idea where it may be."

"You mean the Arctic?"

"Yes. And when I've had a couple of hours with the Pilot Book I may be able to narrow down the area. If only Ingrid Mitchell hadn't been killed. . . . Perhaps that's why she *was* killed. I think I shall have to go there, but I want to talk to Keller first. If you approve I'll go to Hamburg this afternoon, and probably to Greenland from there—either your influence or Keller's should provide an aeroplane. And I must talk to Ruth."

"As always, Peter, I'll back you whatever you do. The thing that bothers me now is whether you're fit for gallivanting in the Arctic."

"You must be getting old! You haven't worried much about my fitness in the past."

"Not for the first time, Peter, you pretend to an ignorance you don't have. I may appear to take people for granted, particularly, perhaps, those who mean most to me. If I have sometimes seemed to drive you hard it is because we serve a cause greater than ourselves."

"I don't doubt you. If you asked what I really want to do I should tell you that I want to enjoy the summer with Ruth. But there's some particularly dirty work going on here and a lot of innocent people are going to suffer if we can't clean it up. So that's that. My fitness will have to take care of itself."

I was reckoning without Ruth. When I told her on the phone that I was off to Hamburg again and might not be back for some time she knew perfectly well what I was thinking of, and she flatly refused to have it. "I shall get your surgeon to telephone Sir Edmund and tell him that you are not up to all this. If necessary, I'll get him to order you back to hospital," she said.

"My darling, you just mustn't. I'm not as bad as all that. I agree that no one is indispensable, and that if I dropped dead other people would have to carry on. But I haven't dropped dead, and while I'm on my feet it isn't conceited to say that probably I can do one or two things that other people mightn't think of. And it isn't conceit that makes me feel it's my job to carry on. Ingrid Mitchell's been murdered and other lives are at risk. I wouldn't be any use to you as a husband if I gave up now. We may not win, but we can try. You're a trier, too, and it's no use pretending you're not."

"All right, but wherever you go from Hamburg I'm going with you."

"Fine—you're the best partner in the world, and between us we're a pretty good partnership. Can you get to London Airport for two-thirty?"

"Yes. What shall I bring with me?"

"The thickest pullovers you've got."

VIII

An Expedition

KELLER MET US at Hamburg, with two pieces of news. As I'd expected, 16 Ilmgasse in Vienna was the address of a small café. "The security people are keeping an eye on it," he said, "but as far as they know it's a perfectly respectable place, with a clientele mainly · of musicians from the Opera House. If nothing happens before June 30 we can send a man there with a flat parcel the size of the map, but for myself I doubt if it has anything to do with the case except to divert our attention." His second piece of news was unexpected—Frau Baumgarten was English, born Hilda Stevenson. She had worked for a time at the Unol offices in London where, presumably, she had met her husband when he was over on some business connected with his pipeline engineering firm. This seemed mildly interesting, but there was no reason why Heinrich Baumgarten should not have married an English girl, and it was hard to see what bearing, if any, it might have on the case.

We learned these two facts in brief conversation while Keller drove us to the hotel where he had booked a room for us. On dropping us at the hotel he invited us to supper, and arranged to pick us up. It didn't take long to unpack, and we had an hour or so to ourselves before Keller was due back. I was grateful for the chance to talk to Ruth, told her about my meeting with Ingrid Mitchell, and outlined the circumstances of her death.

"Poor woman, she didn't have much luck," Ruth said. "I can understand just how she felt about the man Adrian Stowe

—wanting to marry him, and not wanting to marry him. If I'd met you differently I think I should have felt much the same about you. You've been very good, Peter, in not trying to stop me being a professor, but what's so difficult about being a woman is that only half of me really wants to be a professor —or rather I *do* want to be a professor, but another me wants to cook and make curtains and even knit socks for you."

"My poor child, I've been ill most of the time since we got married. You've looked after me marvellously—and you ought to know how proud I am of Professor Ruth."

"I don't think I'm looking after you very well now."

"Well, I think you are. Just as I don't want to stop you being a professor so you don't want to stop me from trying to get to the bottom of this appalling case."

"Half of me, perhaps more than half, does want to stop you. But there's a bit that understands. Oh Peter, how difficult life is for practically everybody."

"We make things difficult for ourselves. It's not man's bad luck or hard struggle that really deserve pity—it's his sheer damned stupidity. Greed is a form of stupidity. Fortunately the greedy are also stupid in other ways. I think there's been a certain amount of stupidity in this case, but I can't see yet where it fits in. You're a mathematician, Ruth, and so was the man Adrian Stowe Ingrid Mitchell was in love with. Tell me how a mathematician fits in with the geographers in studying the Arctic."

"Could be all sorts of ways, maths comes into everything somewhere. I've been doing some work for you. I've been reading up the little that has been published on this Arctic Calorific Syndrome and there's an immense field for mathematical research. Given the shift in the North Pole and a change in climate coupled with heat retention sufficient to affect sea temperatures somewhere still, you'd have to identify and calculate the other variables before you could find out much about it. There was some maths in a paper by Dr Jackson published in the *Proceedings of the Geophysical Society* about a year ago. He touches on the maths only briefly, simply to show how complicated it is. Among his variables are rock formation and topsoil—that is sand, mud, remains of countless millions of sea-creatures—on the seabed, varying depths and insulating characteristics of this topsoil over the floor of Arctic seas, shelving of the land mass where it meets the sea, which has a bearing on currents and the movement of ice near the shoreline, rate of formation of surface ice, wind, temperature gradients in the atmosphere . . . and a lot more. He doesn't go into the details but says that promising work was being done by Adrian Stowe, whom he names, up to the time of what he calls his tragic death. He describes Stowe's work as brilliant and says that it will be the basis of all future work on the subject."

"I wonder where it is. I don't think Ingrid Mitchell had it."

"From the Jackson monograph it's obvious that Jackson himself had been following it closely, and one would expect at least copies of Stowe's theoretical reasoning and calculations to be among Jackson's own papers. You said that they were at the museum, awaiting editing."

"That's what Mrs Jackson told me, but Ingrid Mitchell said that all the papers were still in Mrs Jackson's possession, and that she hadn't wanted to worry her about them. Inspector Richards is going into the question of the papers with Mrs Jackson, but it looks to me as if they're missing. One would think that they may have been stolen on the night of Dr Jackson's death, and perhaps that was the real reason for his murder."

"We don't know enough about it yet. Stowe must have left papers—what happened to them? Is anybody going into that?"

"I heard of Adrian Stowe for the first time yesterday and I got on to Keller about him as soon as I could. He promised an investigation of all the circumstances of Stowe's death. Maybe we shall hear something about it this evening."

In spite of Hamburg traffic Keller was punctual to the minute. Ruth had ignored my suggestion about pullovers, deciding that she could buy what she needed in Hamburg, and had brought only one small suitcase. From this, however, she extracted a dress that looked stunning and I felt immensely proud of her. Keller was considerate and polite as always, but he worried me by seeming slightly ill at ease. Over a drink before supper he came to the point, saying frankly, "Tell me,

Herr Colonel, to what extent we can discuss highly secret matters before your wife."

"I have no secrets from Ruth," I said. "We have worked together before and although she is not a member of my Department—she is Professor of Mathematics at Oxford—she is accepted as a valuable colleague. I respect your scruples, the more for stating them so openly, but I can, assure you that you have nothing to fear from Ruth—indeed, we may all gain from her own intelligence."

His manner changed and he poured us all another drink. "That makes things easier. I should have known that you would not have brought your wife for merely social reasons. But I have known important men who have had to make concessions to their wives."

Ruth laughed. "I sometimes think that men are really happiest in monasteries or ships at sea where there aren't any women. And yet we have been known to come in useful."

Keller bowed. "*Gnädige Frau*, you must forgive me. I am a victim of my training in security."

"Judging by results it seems to have been an admirable training," I said. "Before you came this evening Ruth and I were talking about Adrian Stowe, the man whose death I asked you to look into. Have you been able to make any progress there?"

"I have looked up the files. It was a curious case. He had a good position in the research division of Universal Oil, and he seems to have been much respected. Frau Braunschweig knew him quite well—he worked closely with her husband, and came to their home quite often. She liked him very much. His suicide astonished as well as grieved them. It puzzled the police at first, but the note he left seemed to be genuine. It was his habit to drink a cup of chocolate before going to sleep, and since he was slightly worried about becoming overweight he sweetened it with saccharine instead of sugar. On the night of his death he added a powerful barbiturate drug to his chocolate—a deliberate overdose, which would inevitably prove fatal. There was a small empty bottle that had contained the barbiturate tablets on a table in his bedroom. They were apparently obtained in England, for the bottle bore the label of a London pharmacist. It was thought at first that his death might have been an accident, that he might have put the barbiturate in his chocolate in mistake for his normal saccharine tablets. But there was saccharine in the chocolate, too, so he must have added two lots of tablets. The note he left ruled out accident. It was addressed to his parents and began by expressing his love for them and his sorrow at the distress his death would cause. He wrote that life had become insupportable for reasons he did not wish to explain, though he could promise they were not dishonourable. He concluded by saying he was sure his parents would understand.

"The note was puzzling in not being more explicit—suicide notes more commonly attempt to justify the action, and tend to be self-pitying, or to blame someone. Inquiries among Mr Stowe's colleagues, however, showed him to be a man of deep reserve, accustomed to keep his feelings to himself. He did not have a full-time secretary—his work was in mathematical research—but he would sometimes dictate letters and reports. When he needed secretarial help the same girl was accustomed to work for him, and had done so for nearly two years. She got to know him slightly, and said she thought there was a woman in England whom he wanted to marry but for some reason could not. His father came to Hamburg—his mother was too upset to accompany him—and to some extent he confirmed this story. He said he had known that his son wished to get married, but understood that there were difficulties in the way. He described his son as not exactly secretive but reluctant to discuss personal matters, even with his parents. The officer who interviewed Mr Stowe senior found him also exceedingly reserved. He did say he did *not* understand why his son should have taken his own life, but in the circumstances there seemed no alternative to a finding of suicide."

"The letter was typed, not handwritten?"

"Yes, but that was in keeping—apparently Mr Stowe always typed in preference to writing by hand. The letter was typed on a machine that was in his bedroom. The signature was accepted by his father, by the bank he used in Hamburg, and by the girl I mentioned who typed office correspondence for him."

"The barbiturate tablets were supplied in London—did you discover the doctor who prescribed them?"

"No. You must understand the circumstances at the time. All that was in England. As far as our police were concerned it seemed a clear case of an unhappy man's suicide. I think our man made as thorough an investigation as seemed justified. Everything was reported to the British diplomatic mission, and they were satisfied. Knowing what we do now I agree that far more exhaustive inquiries should have been made in England as well as here, but that did not seem necessary at the time."

"We must make those inquiries. It is the Cambridge case all over again, a reasonable cause of death and no obvious reason for suspicion. Do you know how Adrian Stowe spent the evening before he died?"

"Yes, that was gone into. He attended a small dinner party —curiously enough given by the Baumgartens, whom he knew because they are friends of the Braunschweigs. I haven't been able to talk to the Baumgartens because, as you know, they are abroad, but they were interviewed at the time. They said that Mr Stowe seemed perfectly normal, left shortly before midnight and drove back to his flat in his own car. The doctor's estimate was that he took the barbiturate tablets at about one a.m., so the times seemed to fit all right."

"Everything fits, yet I'm quite sure that it fits an entirely different picture and that Stowe was murdered like Charles Jackson in Cambridge."

I have no doubt that Keller gave us an admirable supper, but I have no recollection of what we ate. We talked far into the morning, trying to make sense of things. The cases of Dr Jackson, Ingrid Mitchell and Adrian Stowe seemed to be linked with the work that all were doing on the theory of the Arctic Calorific Syndrome and the discovery of a usable North-West Passage, a route that would have as much importance to the world today as Elizabethan seamen realised in their search for an Arctic passage to the riches of the East. We asked Ruth if she could assess the mathematical probabilities of such a route's existing. She said that given Adrian Stowe's theories and calculations she might be able to, but without them she didn't know where to begin. That raised another point—who else may have thought that there was something of the utmost value in the Jackson-Stowe-Mitchell theories? As their records seemed to have vanished, it seemed a reasonable assumption that they had all been murdered by some individual or group of individuals who wanted to get hold of their work. There was a sort of pattern in the killings, with the deaths of Charles Jackson and Adrian Stowe disguised as accident and suicide, and an incompetent attempt to make Ingrid Mitchell's murder look like suicide. All this seemed reasonable reconstruction, but how did any of it relate to the disappearance of Gustav Braunschweig?

"The Vienna in the second ransom note seems an absurdity but there is one thing in the note that I think we must take seriously—the date," I said.

"You mean that *something* is going to happen on June 30?" Keller asked.

"Yes. As I see it the kidnappers don't really expect the map to be delivered, and do intend to murder Gustav Braunschweig on the excuse that their demand has not been met."

"The map is now in your possession. The demand could be met."

"I don't think it would make any difference. I think a decision to kill Braunschweig has already been taken, and that the whole kidnap-ransom story is intended to put the blame on some anarchist group that will be named when the 'execution' is announced. It may be an entirely imaginary group."

"Why demand the map instead of the release of political prisoners, or something more in keeping with the activities of anarchist groups?"

"Because somebody wants to draw attention to the map. I don't know why, but I can suggest a variety of possible reasons. When the killing is announced the map will attract enormous publicity. Ingrid Mitchell told me that the map itself is only marginally relevant to the North-West Passage theory. Suppose someone wants to demolish the whole theory —promote interest in the map, and then use it as a basis for showing that wherever old Baffin got to he was no nearer to finding a North-West Passage than anyone else. The three experts on the theory are all dead. There's opposition to their views, anyway, and a little skilled academic manipulation could do the rest."

"Possible, perhaps, and an interesting bit of speculation, but

I don't see any anarchist group going in for kidnapping and murder simply to demolish an academic theory," Keller said. "They wouldn't. They could say that they chose the map as a typical example of a useless museum piece maintained in the interests of capitalist culture instead of being sold for the relief of poverty, to provide money for working-class education, for anything else you like. They could go on to say that they've deliberately started with a highly specialised old map to prepare for similar demands for the *Mona Lisa,* Leonardo's *Last Supper,* Rembrandt's masterpieces, the treasures of museums and art galleries throughout the world. There'd be terrific publicity, and quite a few people might have a sneaking sympathy for the idea."

"You'd be dangerous as an anarchist public relations officer. . . . I suppose it could be something like that. But you destroy your own case, because the rest of your theory implies that there aren't any anarchists involved."

"I said only that they *might* be imaginary. I'm trying to make sense of what seems a meaningless jumble of murders and an absurd kidnapping."

"You've recovered the map, and I think we all accept your view that he is on board the yacht, bound probably for the Arctic."

"And due to get to wherever he's going around the end of the month. That's why I'm bothered about the date June 30 in the latest ransom note."

My mind went back to the schoolboy algebra I'd played with on the train to Cambridge. We had, I thought, two separate but related cases, the murders and the Braunschweig-map affair. Two cases, two equations? What common factors did they have. I turned to Ruth. "Look, you're a real mathematician whereas my maths stops at elementary algebra," I said. "Can you formulate two equations from the muddled data that we have? Let's call the murderer or murder-group x and Dr Braunschweig's group—they may be kidnappers, or they may be voluntary companions—y. What can we say about x and y?"

"You can say that both are concerned with the Arctic. You could express it algebraically as x plus y equals some Arctic enterprise."

"All right, that's one equation. Now we need another to enable us to try to derive some values for x and y. How would you express x minus y?"

"If what you call the Braunschweig group didn't exist the murder-group would presumably have got what they wanted —say all the known facts about the Arctic Calorific Syndrome. If the first equation is to be valid we must assume that *because of* the existence of the Braunschweig group—our y—the murder-group—x—*hasn't* got what it wanted, and can't get it without taking Dr Braunschweig to the Arctic, or going with him to the Arctic; from the point of view of the maths it doesn't matter whether he is on a voluntary or involuntary trip. What does matter is that he is in some way imperative to something connected with the Arctic that x wants to secure. So you could say that x minus y equals success in something or other."

Keller was listening keenly. "I think that's really illuminating," he said. "True, it's merely algebra, but it's a good way of thinking clearly and it does suggest that the murder-group regards the Braunschweig lot, or Braunschweig alone, as in some way inimical to its interests. Inimical—but at the same time important. That would explain the various gaps in time which have puzzled me all along. The murder-group *needs* Dr Braunschweig for something, but hopes, or expects, that by June 30 it will have got what it wanted from him."

Ruth shivered. "After which he will be disposed of," she said.

"It looks rather like it. We need some more assumptions. What can Braunschweig have that the murder group wants?" Keller asked.

"Adrian Stowe's calculations," I suggested. "Stowe worked for Braunschweig and they may have had a close relationship. I think Stowe was murdered for his calculations, but perhaps the murderers couldn't find all they wanted. Perhaps they thought that Braunschweig had them, or knew about them. That may be the reason, or part of the reason, for the murder of Ingrid Mitchell. We can assume that she knew a good deal about Stowe's work, and perhaps the murder-group felt safer with her out of the way."

"The assumptions seem reasonable," Keller said. "The immediate point is, What do we do about them?"

"Go after Dr Braunschweig and find him before he is murdered."

There was a long silence. We were all tired, but all too much worked up to think of breaking off. Finally Keller said, "Agreed —a splendid course of action. But where, and how? What is the next step in mathematical detection?"

"Simple," Ruth said. "All we have to do is to go to the place p."

Keller laughed. "I like mathematical detection. But I'd like still more to get murder-group x locked up. How do we set about finding the place p?"

"We have some clues," I said. "First, there's the map, which for all Ingrid Mitchell's dismissal of it as of no great importance does indicate some kind of navigable route through Smith Sound and the Robeson Channel to the Lincoln Sea and the Arctic Ocean. Of course it doesn't follow that what may have been possible in the ice conditions of the seventeenth century will be practicable now, but at least it's a starting point —we can assume that is the general area of our place p. Regrettably, it's a big area, and even an air search may not spot a small boat. But we have two other clues—Ingrid Mitchell's amber beads, and her statement to me that Charles Jackson came across a seam of coal during his own travels in the region. I've not had time for much research and I've never heard of amber in the Arctic, but the coal undoubtedly exists. A seam was discovered by the Nares Expedition in 1875-76, and it's mentioned in the Admiralty's *Arctic Pilot* as being exposed in a ravine about a mile inshore from the western coast of Hall Basin—that's a stretch of water lying between Smith Sound and Robeson Channel. The coal is not far from Cape Murchison in Latitude 81 degrees forty-five minutes North, Longitude 64 degrees seventeen minutes West, and it ought still to be identifiable. More important it suggests that wherever we're looking for is on the west, or Ellesmere Island coast of the sound, and not on the Greenland side. If we could get any idea where the amber came from we might narrow the area of search to quite a small district."

"The coal implies the existence of forests at some period in geological time, and amber is a fossilised gum from trees," Ruth said. "I'm not a geologist, but it would be reasonable to suppose that the climatic conditions which provided the vegetation for coal continued long enough to enable trees to produce the gum for amber."

"We can say a bit more than that," I went on. "Charles Jackson was interested in the sea, and he was studying the coast. The coal is near the coast, and he must have picked up the amber somewhere on the coast. Therefore it seems probable that if we follow the coast northwards from Cape Murchison we shouldn't go too far wrong. It's an appalling coast, with sheer cliffs rising to a thousand feet or more, and often no sort of beach. That may help in a way, for if there's hardly anywhere a boat can get to, we shall have to look only for the few places where there is some kind of open water near the shore. My guess is that we shall find *Apfel* somewhere near the Lincoln Sea end of Robeson Channel. The cliffs there fall away, and there's a short stretch where the heavy Arctic ice runs aground up to a couple of hundred yards offshore, leaving a narrow channel between ice and shore. One of the ships in the 1875-76 expedition lay there for eleven months, and horrible as the place sounds she was quite safe. This strange channel may, indeed, have given rise to the idea of a navigable passage so far north. That's where I think we have to go."

"How do you propose to get there?" Keller asked.

"The only practicable way is by air. There's not enough time to attempt the route by sea, and we have none of the specialised knowledge that Dr Braunschweig may have obtained from Stowe. According to the *Arctic Pilot,* which is all I've had a chance to study, a bit south of where we want to go there's a place called Gould Bay which was visited by an Oxford University expedition in 1935. They found a big patch of gravel, about two miles square, at the head of the bay. The gravel bank had a hard, smooth surface, with occasional patches of snow. They thought that it would make a useful landing place for aircraft. I'd suggest that we make for Gould Bay by air, taking a helicopter with us. The helicopter could be assembled at Gould Bay and from there the rest of the area we want to search would be within the range of quite a small helicopter. This would need cooperation from the Services, but in the circumstances I'm sure we'd get it."

"I could get help from our German authorities without any difficulty. They'd welcome the exercise as an unusual form of training," Keller said.

"Well, let's go ahead and do it. If the German Air Force will help and we can fly direct to Gould Bay in an aircraft big enough to take a helicopter we don't need to let more than a handful of people know what we're doing. And since we've no idea how widespread the conspiracy we're up against may be, the fewer people who know about our plans, the better."

"Right. I don't think I need to get anyone out of bed, but I'll start first thing in the morning. I shall come with you, if I may."

"Of course. You will be invaluable."

"And I shall come too," Ruth said.

We both tried to dissuade her. "*Gnädige Frau*, I am no believer in the superiority of men—I am conscious always of the work that women have done in war, and in my own trade as a policeman," Keller said. "But there is a fitness in things, and this job is not fit for you. You have heard what your husband said—it is a terrible place, and we may have to meet some terrible people."

"My name is Ruth. If we are going on an Arctic expedition together you will have to call me Ruth," she said.

"It's all very well, my darling, and I know how tough you are, but you have no experience of conditions in the Arctic," I tried to argue.

"You haven't either. All right, you've put in a lot of time in small boats and you're good at sea, but the Arctic isn't just sea. We're not going there by sea in any case. And you are not fit. If you make any more difficulties about my coming with you I shall do what I said I would, and get your surgeon to tell Sir Edmund Pusey that you must go back to hospital."

That was that. "There may be some trouble with the Air Force. You and I have official positions, but what can we say about the lady?" Keller said.

"You can say that I am one of your investigating team— after all, I *am* your mathematical detective. Peter will have to fix it with Sir Edmund to get me put temporarily on the strength of his Department."

I was afraid Sir Edmund would agree. When I rang him later that morning he accepted Ruth with a readiness I found alarming.

Having decided on a course of action Keller pursued it with the efficiency and thoroughness I'd come to expect from the German police. By that afternoon the Air Force had agreed to put a plane at our disposal, and got down to the job of working out details. They wanted two days for an aerial survey of Gould Bay, and said that if the landing area proved suitable the rest of the plan could be carried out. They would provide a transport aircraft capable of carrying a helicopter and fuel for it, and a pilot and co-pilot for the helicopter.

Keller and I had to decide on the strength of our party. "Our assumptions may be wildly wrong, but as they're all we've got to go by we must stick to them," I said. "We're assuming that Gustav Braunschweig has taken *Apfel* to the Arctic for some purpose that we don't yet understand, though in a sense that doesn't matter because what *does* matter is to find him before June 30. My further assumption is that he had made up his mind to sail to the Arctic voluntarily, but was put on board *Apfel* somehow or other by other people, and made, or persuaded, to sail with them. He must have at least two others on board with him, possibly as many as four— I don't think there can be more than four, because the dinghy would have been a bit crowded and more noticeable. Whether he knows it or not—we still don't know whose side he's on— his companions include at least one person who is determined to murder him. I think it's more likely that the whole crew are related to our murder-group *x* and in the plot to do away with Braunschweig, but we don't know that. What we must take into account is that up to four people may be hostile, ready to use any violence to resist our attempt to rescue Braunschweig."

"We must assume that they will be armed," Keller said.

"Yes. On the other hand we should have the advantage of complete surprise, and our helicopter will be much more maneuverable than their boat. A party of six should be enough to deal with them."

"Including the pilot and co-pilot?"

"That's a point. We might want to send back for reinforcements, and we couldn't risk both pilots being injured. But we could use one of them."

The matter was settled for us by the size of the helicopter which the Air Force wanted to use. It had to be transported to Gould Bay, and the machine judged most suitable was a smallish one with a carrying capacity of six people, including the pilot. The experts considered that Ruth could safely be added, so with Keller and me and the two pilots we could take two other men. There was some discussion about whether they should be airmen or police, and it was decided that as this was a police operation they had better be policemen. Keller selected two men from Hamburg. The big transport plane would have an Air Force crew augmented by half a dozen extra men, so that if necessary the helicopter could be sent back for help. The expedition was to carry a doctor and, partly, perhaps, out of politeness to Ruth, a nurse. They would stay at Gould Bay while we went forward with the helicopter.

While these arrangements were being made an aircraft was dispatched to Gould Bay to inspect the landing site. We used the time collecting kit, and studying everything we could get hold of about the region. Kit was not much of a problem, for the Air Force equipped us with the most up-to-date survival clothing, specially designed for air crews who might be forced down in conditions of extreme cold. It was light, comfortable, completely weatherproof and beautifully warm.

Weapons had also to be selected. All of us, including Ruth, were to carry small automatic pistols, and we decided to take rifles as well. We might have no need of such armament, but if we didn't need rifles they could be left in the helicopter, and if by any chance we did need them it would be as well to have them with us. Keller's Hamburg men were police marksmen, and he and I could both handle a rifle. The helicopter carried its normal complement of machine guns, so we should be a heavily armed party if it came to a fight.

IX

Accident

IF THIS WAS death, I thought, then it was a lot more painful than being dead is commonly supposed to be. I opened my eyes, but could see nothing but a swirling whiteness. There was an intolerable weight across my chest. I ached all over, but found by experiment that I could move my fingers. My left hand was in a glove and still quite warm, but my right hand was gloveless and rapidly getting frozen. Using arms and shoulders I tried twice to shift the weight from my chest, and couldn't. But unless I were dead and this was some peculiar form of hell I couldn't stay where I was. Making a tremendous effort I pushed and heaved and wriggled until the weight was across my stomach, then my thighs, and at last I was free. I could kneel, and stayed on my knees for a time, panting. Then I got to my feet, at first swaying groggily, but steadying after a minute or two. As my eyes became accustomed to the murk of fog that engulfed me I could see a few yards. The weight across my chest was in the snow beside me—it was a bit of one of the blades from the helicopter's rotor. Wreckage was everywhere. I thought despairingly that I was the only one to have survived the crash, and knew that I could not survive long.

Then I heard a faint call, more a sort of moan than a call. Groping my way in the fog I stumbled over a body, practically buried in snow. I scraped the snow away with my hands and found that it was Keller, still alive and, after I had dragged him from the snow, able to talk. "Who is it?" he asked.

"Peter. We've had a crash, and God knows if there's anybody else alive. I'm bruised all over, but I don't think anything's broken. What about you?"

He moved first his head, then his arms, then his legs. "I think I'm probably undamaged," he said. "I suppose the snow saved

130

me. But I can't get a grip on anything. If you can give me a hand I'll try to stand."

He was badly shaken, but determination, and such help as I could give, got him to his feet. He even managed a faint grin, which distorted as it was by the mist, was cheering. "Well, there are two of us, anyway," he said. "The first thing we've got to do is to see if there's anyone else."

I was sickened about Ruth—it was my fault that she was here. Search seemed hopeless. As far as we could make out the helicopter had crashed into a mountain, and the slope on which we were trying to stand was excessively steep. The two of us were in a narrow gully filled with snow. Keller seemed able to think more clearly than I could. "It's no use looking uphill—if there's anybody alive they'll have rolled down," he said.

The mist seemed thinning a little. It was daylight, about four o'clock in the afternoon, and what had wrecked us was the sudden swirl of fog. In theory we had been flying at a height sufficient to clear all known peaks, but the whole region was so remote and desolate that it was not easy at any given moment to make out precisely where we were. Perhaps something had gone wrong with the helicopter's instruments; perhaps we had struck a mountain whose very existence was unknown. None of that mattered now—our concern was to see if we could find any other survivors.

The first place to look was in the wreckage itself, and in the twisted body of the helicopter we found three of our companions, the two pilots and one of the Hamburg policemen. All were dead, and appeared to have been killed instantly. In the pocket of the flying suit worn by one of the pilots I found a pair of gloves. It was vital to me to have a glove for my right hand, so I took them.

As far as we could make out the helicopter had struck a rock face on the mountainside. Keller and I were alive because we had been flung out into soft snow. Neither Ruth nor the other Hamburg man was in the wreckage, so presumably they also had been flung out. But where?

We began a systematic search downhill. I call it "systematic" because we tried to follow a system of keeping on the same line of slope about ten yards apart, but it didn't work because the ground was so broken. We worked down the gully that had saved us but could see nothing but snow. There was another gully running roughly parallel to ours and about thirty yards to the right of it. Here I found Ruth, bleeding from a cut on her forehead, unconscious, but still alive. Between us we got her out of the snow and carried her to a small platform of more or less level ground a little below the wreckage. Whatever had struck her on the forehead had knocked her out, but the cut did not seem too bad and I bandaged it with a handkerchief. Soon after I had got the bandage on she came to. "Lord, it's cold," she said. It was scarcely an inspiring speech, but I doubt if any words ever spoken have sounded lovelier. I put my arms round her to warm her as well as I could, taking care not to press on anything that might be broken. She snuggled up to me, and like Keller, she managed a smile. "I can wriggle my toes, and my fingers," she said. "I think I'm all right."

While I was looking after Ruth, Keller found the second Hamburg man. With us he had been thrown out of the helicopter but he had not been lucky. Instead of being thrown into snow he had been hurled against a rock and his neck broken.

With all the crew accounted for we took stock of the position. "I don't know how long we were lying in the snow before we recovered ourselves, but I don't think it can have been long," Keller said. "Say ten minutes to a quarter of an hour—if it had been much longer I should think we'd have suffered from frostbite, your hand, anyway. My watch is still going, and I looked at it when we started our search. That was just on forty minutes ago. So it will be roughly an hour since the crash. The people at Gould Bay will be worried to be out of radio communication with the helicopter, but radio doesn't always work well in these high latitudes, and they won't necessarily expect disaster. If the crash happened about an hour ago we'd been up for about three quarters of an hour. We gave no estimated time of return because we were going to search, but they'll expect us back within four hours or so. That's about two hours from now. When we don't come back they'll begin to get very worried indeed, but they will think we've probably made an emergency landing somewhere, with our radio out of action. The big transport plane is not an ideal search aircraft, but I should think it almost certain that they'll go up to have a look for us. And they'll radio for another helicopter. It will be at least a day before it can be flown out, but the big plane should have spotted us by then. It can't land anywhere near us, of course, but they can send down some help by parachute. It seems to me our best course is to stay by the wreckage and hope to be rescued."

"I agree, but I don't know how long we should stay here. At this time of year there is virtually no darkness, so as soon as the fog clears we've a chance of being spotted. But the fog that wrecked us may wreck our chances. I think we should stay here for twenty-four hours and if we've seen no aircraft by then we shall have to reconsider things. The first job is to see what we can find in the wreckage in the way of food and shelter."

The helicopter had been well supplied with a day's food for seven people, and in addition carried emergency ration packs that would last the three of us for several weeks. The problem was whether we could find any of it. To my relief Ruth was fit enough to join the search, and it was she who discovered a big carton of ration packs half-buried in the snow of the gully where she had fallen. That solved the immediate problem of food. There were rations for twelve men for forty-eight hours, including two dozen cans of self-heating soup.

The helicopter had not caught fire in the crash, so her stores were more or less intact, though scattered over a wide area of snow-covered broken ground. The pilot's cabin had taken the full force of the crash and the instruments were shattered—compass, navigating instruments, radio, all useless. However, my wrist compass seemed to be undamaged, and Keller had a pocket compass. The two more or less agreed with one another, so we assumed that they were probably all right.

We were wearing our small automatic pistols, and several of the rifles that had been on board seemed usable. There was also a box of ammunition, and although the box was broken the cartridges packed inside were unharmed. So we were well off for firearms, though what we needed more was a spade. We had nothing in the way of a tent, and shelter of some sort was imperative. Both Keller and I had served in the army and been on survival courses, although mine, many years ago, had been no farther north than Scotland. Keller, however, had been on a course in northern Norway and he thought that he could build a snow house if we had a spade. We didn't, but I remembered the broken rotor blade which had fallen across me and I thought

133

that this might serve. It was not ideal because it was too long but it could be used after a fashion, and while Keller got to work trying to make rough blocks of snow Ruth and I searched the wreckage for smaller pieces of metal. We found several, all of which made better digging tools than my original rotor blade. Keller showed us what to do and a circular snow-house began to take shape. The walls rose quite satisfactorily, but the snow was too soft for good building blocks and after two or three attempts at a roof it was obvious that we were not going to win. Bits and pieces of wreckage solved the problem. We used them to make a framework for the roof of our house, and then covered and packed the frame with snow—important for insulation to conserve the heat of our bodies inside the house.

The work kept us warm and when our house was finished we were rather proud of it. We had not thought about food while getting on with our building work, but with the house usable we felt ravenously hungry. We were also thirsty, but although we had food we had no water, and for the moment no means of melting snow. The helicopter had carried a small tank of water, but that had gone in the crash. We had matches and I thought that we might get a fire going from burnable wreckage; the fuel tanks had burst and the fuel spilled out, though there were dregs left to ignite what could be burned. But we didn't want to use what was burnable in case we needed a fire to attract the attention of rescuers. For our first meal we had to try to quench thirst with soup, and afterwards by taking mouthfuls of snow. We could survive on snow, but it is a poor substitute for drinking water. We filled the empty soup cans with snow and put them between our legs in the hope that the heat from our bodies would melt the stuff. We got a miserable amount of greyish water from our soup cans in the end, and it was a slow job, one of the problems being that our admirable cold-weather clothing was so well insulated that little body heat got through it. This was invaluable for keeping warm, but an obstacle to snow melting.

There were some lifejackets in the emergency equipment carried by the helicopter. We laid these over the trodden snow that formed the floor of our hut and they made it quite comfortable to sit or lie on.

It wasn't until we'd eaten that the horror of things really struck us. We'd been kept going by having work to do, and

134

collecting what seemed useful from the wreck. Now we had time to think. There were four more deaths, two pilots and two policemen, to be added to the sickening toll of human suffering brought about in some way by an obscure theory of Arctic climatology. For most of that night, never dark enough to hide the wreckage of the helicopter, we scarcely bothered about our own situation : we thought only of the sudden ending to four good and useful lives, and of the suffering it must bring to four more human families. I felt a particularly savage responsibility. These men had died because of my thinking—suppose I was wrong? Suppose there was nothing to find in this Arctic wilderness—that Dr Braunschweig and his boat were on their way to the South Seas for some reason that none of us had guessed at. Suppose . . .

But this was morbid futility. Like soldiers these men had died carrying out their duty, and if my thinking was wrong it had been wrong in good faith. And I hadn't sent men to their deaths without going with them—it was blind chance, or some strange dispensation of Providence, that Keller, Ruth and I were not lying with them on the snow-covered hillside. If I went on giving way to self-pity it was more than likely that our joining the dead would merely be delayed. We had to have some plan of action, to save ourselves and, if possible, to carry on the fight.

Ruth and Keller slept or dozed through some of that awful night, which was why I was left to my own miserable thoughts. Around six in the morning I opened three more cans of our self-heating soup, the only means we had of getting a hot drink. It went down well, and I was thankful to have companions to talk to again.

"What do you think we ought to do now?" Ruth asked.

"It's hard, but I'm sure the right thing is to do nothing for a bit," I said. "Our best hope is that they'll send up the big plane to look for us. The helicopter is at least twelve hours overdue by now, and they'll realise that there must have been a disaster. I don't know how visible the wreckage is, but we can collect materials for a fire, and light it the moment we see or hear a plane. That had better be the next job. Do either of you want any more breakfast? There seems quite a good variety of biscuits and tinned meats, also some honey and jam."

Ruth said she didn't think she could eat anything but Keller and I decided that we should all eat to keep up our strength, and we persuaded Ruth to join us at least to the extent of consuming a biscuit spread with honey. After breakfast we got to work, collecting everything burnable from the wreck, and salvaging the broken bottom of a fuel tank which still had several gallons in it. We brought the fuel to our bonfire, but kept it in the broken tank until we were ready to light it.

The fog had gone with the night, and it was a clear morning. From our height on the peak that had wrecked the helicopter we could see over most of the landscape. There was another fairly high peak a mile or so to the west and there were distant mountains to the east and south, but northwards the land seemed to fall away in a ragged series of crevasses. "We're fairly well placed for being spotted," Keller said. "Our peak and the one near it must stand out for miles."

That was comforting, but no sight or sound of an aircraft came to justify our hopes. The hours dragged on, and at midday I thought we should do what we could to attract attention. "Let's take some of the stuff from our bonfire and make a smaller pile," I suggested. "The filling from some of the lifejackets should make a good smoke. A column of smoke will be visible to an aeroplane for much farther than we could see the speck of a plane in the sky."

We used about a quarter of our burnable material, poured a few pints of fuel on it, and set it alight with a match thoughtfully provided with our emergency rations, although both Keller and I carried matches of our own. The fire blazed up well, and there was a satisfactory pillar of black smoke from the lifejackets. We filled our empty soup tins with ice and snow, and put them by the edge of the blaze to melt. When we had a fair quantity of water I boiled some of it in a couple of tins to make coffee from a packet in our rations. It had a curious taste, but it was hot, and a change from soup.

We scanned the skies anxiously while our fire burned, but saw nothing. We were tempted to keep the fire going by putting on more of our precious burnable stuff, arguing that it would be silly to waste the fire if a few more minutes might lead to our being seen. Self-discipline prevailed, however, and we let the fire sink into ashes without attempting to prolong it. We were bitterly disappointed, and a lot more worried than we allowed ourselves to show.

Worry, and every other thought, were shattered by a sudden scream from Ruth. She had gone about fifty yards along a narrow side-gully running to the left of our snow hut for a piece of necessary privacy and we could not see her, but her scream told us where she was. It was not a shout of elation on seeing an aeroplane, it was a cry of panic. Keller and I rushed towards her, some instinct prompting me to grab one of the rifles we had collected from the wreck as I jumped up.

It was as well. As we rounded a slight bend in the gully we saw Ruth cowering against a snow-covered rock, with a huge polar bear standing over her, one of its great forepaws raised about to strike. Keller, who was brought up to use a pistol, fired from the hip. At almost the same moment I sent two rounds from the rifle into the beast's head. In our sickening anxiety all action seemed to be delayed, like a cinema film in slow motion. It looked as if nothing had happened. The bear still towered over Ruth, the huge menacing paw stayed suspended. But its force, thank God, had gone. The animal swayed a little, then slowly keeled over, falling not more than a foot or so to one side of where Ruth was huddled against the rock. It was a miracle that it did not fall on top of her—goodness knows how much it weighed.

Keller pumped a few more pistol shots into the huge body to make sure of things, while I put my arms round Ruth and helped her to her feet. She clung to me, breathing in short quick gasps, then straightened the hood of her anorak and said, "What a sight I must look! Oh, Peter, thank God you came—and thank you both for being so quick. It came absolutely from nowhere. I was just tidying myself up when I saw it standing over me. Oh, Peter, do you think there are any more of them?"

I know little of the habits of polar bears, but it seemed likely that where there was one there might be others. "I don't know, but we should be all right with the rifles handy," I said. "And we'll make one rule now—no one goes away from the camp, even for a few yards, without a rifle guard."

The adventure with the bear at least took our minds off our own plight, but anxieties soon came back. As the day dragged into evening we speculated endlessly on what might be happening.

"It seems extraordinary that they haven't sent the aeroplane to look for us," Keller said. "Of course, we don't know what conditions are like at Gould Bay—there may be dense fog, or heavy snow, or something else to make it impossible for the plane to take off."

"Yes, and they've no idea where to look for us. We must have been miles off course. Both the pilot and co-pilot put in a lot of time studying the map, and if they'd expected high ground we'd never have hit the mountain. Either the map is wrong, or we weren't anywhere near where we thought we were. Visibility was practically nil, and in this part of the world it's easy for compasses to go haywire."

There could be plenty of reasons for the failure to find us, though apart from giving us something to think about there wasn't really much point in speculating on them. We should have to decide for ourselves what we were going to do.

"I think we should stay here for one more night, and if nothing has happened by morning we should try to find our own way out," I said. "We're not badly equipped. We have good clothing, we have rations for some time, and we have weapons. We can take a few soup cans of fuel with us to have some means of doing a bit of cooking, though we must take care to keep a reserve for making a flare. If we can cook, we can get fresh meat from the bear—I believe Eskimos set great store by bear meat. The problem is to decide where we should try to make for."

"How far do you reckon we are from the base at Gould Bay?" Keller asked.

"Frankly, I haven't the least idea. We may be a hundred miles, or we may have flown round in circles in the fog and be within twenty or thirty. There are some navigation tables in the helicopter, but I've been able to find only one sextant, and that is smashed to bits."

"Probably there was only one. It would be carried mainly for emergencies since almost all navigation nowadays is by radio."

"And the radio is beyond repair. . . We must go back to first principles and see if we can get even the roughest estimate of where we are. At least the charts are more or less undamaged."

I fetched the charts from what was left of the pilots' cabin and we spread them out on a flat-topped rock. They were good for the coast, but rather non-committal inland. High ground was

138

shown, and some peak heights indicated, but it was impossible to relate heights shown on the map to the broken landscape round us. What was clear was that there should have been no peaks as high as that which had wrecked us within many miles of the route we were supposed to be flying from Gould Bay to the northern end of the Robeson Channel. We were so far north that it was difficult to work out bearings. Keller's prismatic compass and my little wrist compass agreed with each other, more or less, but how their readings related to true north it was impossible to guess. The sun, still visible, was the best help here. Lacking a sextant we could do no more than estimate an angle for the sun, but our watches were still going, and taking a mean of the three of them we made a guess at G.M.T. From the navigation tables Ruth calculated where the sun should be at our estimated time, and this gave us a reasonable guess at the cardinal points of the compass.

Having satisfied ourselves where to look east or west we went back to the chart. The Robeson Channel runs roughly from north-east to south-west and what we thought of as the northern end was more properly the north-eastern end. We assumed that we were north of the channel itself—flying blind in fog we might have crossed the strait and be somewhere in northern Greenland instead of on Ellesmere Island, but that would have taken us even farther astray than we thought probable. We had to make some assumptions and we assumed that we were still north of the Robeson Channel.

"Presumably we're somewhere north of Gould Bay, but whether to the east or west of it is anybody's guess," Keller said.

"Yes. And I think it would be madness to try to get back there—we've no idea how far it is, nor which way to walk." I was poring over the map. "Our best bet is to try to find the coast," I went on. "As long as we keep going south with a bit of east in it we're bound to reach the coast, and maybe we can identify something on the chart and work out where we are. The sea is a lot kindlier than this awful wilderness, and on the coast we can hope to find some driftwood to make a fire, for cooking, or signalling. We might get another bear, or we might manage to harpoon a fish—there's hope of life on the coast that there isn't here."

Keller and Ruth agreed. "If we can find out roughly where

we are, we've only got to follow the coast in one direction or another to get back to Gould Bay," Keller said.

"In theory, yes, but it's steep-to in many places, and more or less impossible to walk along for any distance," I said. "But even if it means climbing cliffs and making detours inland, we shall know what we're doing. Everything points to trying to find the coast.

"There's another thing. We came here on a mission to try to locate Dr Braunschweig and to prevent whatever devilment is afoot concerning him. We may be in poor shape for an expeditionary force, but we're alive, and I feel that we should do what we can. If our earlier reasoning was anywhere near right, we may not be very far from wherever he was going in *Apfel*. Time is running out for him even more than it is for us. Once on the coast we may get an idea of where to look. We owe it to our dead companions to do what we can."

When should we start? Almost every reasonable consideration suggested that it would be wiser to wait for rescuers than to march off into the wilderness on our own. But twenty-four hours had passed since the crash without any sign of an air search. It seemed unlikely that a skilled crew anxious to get a plane into the sky would have been held up for a night and a day. I write "a night" but it must be remembered that there was virtually no darkness. The helicopter had become overdue when there were still hours of light available for a search, and we had all expected that our position would have been located during the night.

Assume that for some reason the transport plane could not take off—the base party would have radioed for assistance, and air help could have come from Greenland, northern Canada or the United States. We were a long way from civilisation, but in terms of flying time we were not in any sense out of reach. Had the radio failed? For experienced operators with first-class equipment that seemed improbable, but it was possible in these extreme northern latitudes. If there had been a radio failure they would not have been worried by losing contact with the helicopter, but the helicopter would still have become physically overdue, and radio or no radio we should have expected an air search.

Prolonged silence would create anxiety for the whole of our expedition, but how long would it be before my people in London and Keller's in Germany became sufficiently anxious to send help? We had no firm dates, no precise objective; we were hunting for Dr Braunschweig and might go almost anywhere. Search parties certainly would be sent to look for us, but not, we felt, for several days.

After the best part of two hours of discussion Keller summed up, "I think we should stay where we are until noon tomorrow. If there is no sign of a plane by then we must assume that *something* has happened which means that it's no use going on waiting here. Let us make noon tomorrow zero hour. If we have to act then, I think Peter's suggestion of making for the coast is the best thing we can do."

"The main thing now is to try to get some sleep," I said. "We must have someone on watch—let us take three-hour shifts. And the watchkeeper must have a rifle and look out for polar bears as well as aeroplanes. We don't want one of those brutes investigating our hut."

It was getting on for seven o'clock. None of us wanted food, but food was important, so we had some more of the self-heating soup and a few of our iron-ration biscuits. We gave Ruth the first watch, which meant that she could turn in around eleven and sleep through until five. Keller took the second watch, from eleven to two, and I went on from two to five. It was almost light when I turned out, a slight dusk rapidly becoming day. I walked up and down for a bit to get some circulation going, and then took post on a rock a few yards from our ice-hut.

From the rock I had a view that covered almost the whole sky, and all approaches to the hut. We took the danger from polar bears seriously and I kept my rifle handy. Nothing moved. The sky was cloudless, and I could have seen the tiniest speck of an aircraft many miles away. I checked our bonfire—several soup tins of fuel were ready to light, and I had matches in my pocket. The fire remained unlighted. It was too cold to sit still, so I patrolled the hillside round our hut, my ears alert for sound, my eyes lifting every few seconds from ground to sky. I wished I knew more about polar bears. The one that had so nearly killed Ruth was in good condition, so there must have been food even in this inhospitable land. I reflected that probably he got most of his food from the sea, and this was a comforting thought, for it suggested that the coast could not be very far away. On the other hand if bears needed the coast for food we should have to be particularly on our guard if we reached the shoreline.

My watch ended at five, and Ruth took over. I turned in for a couple of hours and dozed a little, but I was too restless to sleep. So was Keller. He got up when I came back to the hut, saying that he had had quite a good night, and would keep Ruth company. Soon after seven he was back with breakfast—a mug of ration coffee, which he had made by lighting a small fire, and a slice of corned beef on ration biscuit. After breakfast we didn't set any more formal watches because we were all up, but we did maintain our polar bear guard by making sure that one of us always had a rifle.

We were giving the party at Gould Bay until noon, but that did not mean that we sat around doing nothing. Our survival might depend on taking the right things from the wreck : we had to carry everything we took, so we dared not take too much. The ice wilderness we had to cross was rough and broken, and to be overloaded was to invite disaster. A particular problem was that we had no rucksacks—we had not contemplated an expedition on foot. We had canvas shoulderbags, and there were some sacks in the wreckage of the helicopter, but we had no convenient means of carrying loaded sacks. We considered trying to make a sledge from the broken blades of the rotor, but decided against it. The ground was too rough for sledge-hauling. Our backs would have to do for everything.

We took iron rations for ten days, deciding that if necessary we could make them last a fortnight : if in a fortnight we had got nowhere, we should have to survive on what we could find, or—more probably—resign ourselves to death. We took four soup cans of fuel. If we came across any driftwood, a quarter of a can would be enough to start a fire, but if we could find nothing burnable the fuel would be so much deadweight, for we had no sort of cooking stove.

For clothes we had nothing but what we stood in, all Arctic kit of the highest quality, and as far as clothing went we could scarcely have been better equipped. Shelter was another matter—we had no tent, and nothing that could be used to make one. But we had contrived to build our snow-and-ice hut, and what we had done once could be done again. The problem here was what to use for digging—to carry shafts of broken metal from the wreck-

142

age would add to weight, and also be cumbersome. In the end we were lucky. Searching farther down the hillside we came across the remains of the helicopter's toolkit, including a short trenching spade, and a sturdy machete, carried for what reason I know not, but a godsend to us. Keller and I both had pocket knives, but the machete would be enormously valuable for roughly shaping blocks of ice for building, or for cutting up driftwood, if we found any.

We decided to take a lifejacket apiece. We could walk wearing them, if we fell through the ice somewhere they might save our lives, and if we didn't use them as lifejackets they could be opened out to form makeshift beds. We packed such charts as we had into our canvas bags.

We gave much thought to weapons. If we contrived to find *Apfel* we might expect a hostile reception from Dr Braunschweig's captors. We might be outnumbered and we should have to play that as it came, using our wits rather than weight of armament. Weight was the operative consideration. Pistols we should have to carry, but did we need rifles? On the whole we thought not, but there was the problem of possible encounters with polar bears—against a massive bear a rifle was a more reliable weapon than a pistol. In the end we decided to take one rifle and sixty rounds—sixty because it divided conveniently into carrying twenty rounds apiece.

We had a sad duty to perform as we made our preparations for departure. We had hoped that rescuers would be able to recover the bodies of our companions so that they could be taken home for burial, and while we still believed that a rescue party would ultimately come we could no longer be certain. We could not simply leave our companions as they lay, but it was hard to know what best to do about them. The frozen ground made it impossible to dig graves, and while we feared that bears might ravage the hillside once we had gone we could see no way of protecting the bodies. In the end we laid them side by side, said a brief prayer, and covered them with snow. At the head of the mound of snow we built a cairn of small rocks and stones, and in the cairn we placed a tin containing the names of the dead and a brief record of what had happened, written on pages from our notebooks. We left the record in English and German.

"Zero hour," Keller said.

X

Our March

We were thankful to be doing something. Our way, it was simply a line of sight across the broken wilderness, began by going downhill. Then we had to turn a shoulder and had a mile or so of more or less level ground ahead of us to the next ridge. As we rounded the shoulder the peak that had wrecked us went out of sight. Keller began humming *Lili Marlene*, and I put improvised words to it,

> "Best foot foremost,
> Marching to the Pole,
> Only got to get there,
> Then we'll be . . ."

"Tired," Ruth put in.

"Won't do. Doesn't rhyme," I said.

"We will be, though!"

"What do you mean by 'Best foot foremost'?" Keller asked.

"I don't know. It's English of a sort. It means something like, 'Go on doing your best'."

"Well, at least that's what we are doing."

We might be doing our best, but it wasn't easy. What looked from the slope of the shoulder like a flattish expanse of snow-covered ground became harder going with every yard. It was criss-crossed with small crevasses, and the snow was mostly powdery and soft. We sank up to our knees in the better places, and frequently up to our thighs. Once Ruth seemed to disappear altogether. I was terrified that she had fallen into a crevasse, but it was merely a deep bank of snow. Even so, she took some getting out. We took over four hours to cover what could not have been more than a couple of miles.

That brought us to the next ridge, and when we reached the

slope the going became rather better because the snow did not lie so thickly, and was merely ankle-deep over rock or scree. We topped the ridge in growing excitement, hoping to see the sea, but the prospect ahead was the same apparently everlasting wilderness, a long flat valley rising slowly to another ridge. We had been walking now for some six hours, and needed a rest. None of us felt like floundering on, and the ridge we occupied seemed as good a place as any for the night. We climbed down a little way to an outcrop of bare rock, and found a cluster of rocks that made a sort of roofless shelter. It did not seem worth trying to build a snow house for one night, so we made ourselves as comfortable as we could among the rocks. That was not very comfortable, but it was a change from walking, and the faithful lifejackets made good cushions, though they were woefully short as mattresses. We could not make a fire because there was nothing to burn but we divided two cans of the invaluable self-heating soup among the three of us. For the rest we had ration-biscuits and one thin slice of corned beef apiece.

We set watches as before, Ruth taking the first, Keller next, and then me. No one got much sleep because it was too cold. There was nothing, not even a bear, to hasten the slow passing of that miserable night. We thought back to our igloo by the wreckage of the helicopter as a palace of comfort, where we had not only shelter but a whole pile of lifejackets to snuggle into. At five a.m. we had had enough of the rocks, and after a breakfast that was precisely the same as our supper, set off on our march again.

Although we had been marching only for half a day we had established a routine that seemed to have gone on for ever. We walked in single file about five yards apart, with Ruth always in the middle and Keller and I taking it in turns to break trail. We each led for half an hour, and then changed over. The man at the back carried the rifle. We ought to have been roped in that rough and dangerous country, but although we'd searched the wreckage carefully we couldn't find any rope. We did come across a small reel of telephone wire, and we brought this with us, thinking that perhaps it might come in for fishing line.

It was Keller's turn to lead when we set off, and within ten minutes we met a crisis. Like Ruth the day before, Keller just disappeared, but this time it was not in deep snow but into a

145

crevasse. Ruth stopped at the edge and in a moment I was beside her. We peered down, but could see nothing, the black walls merging into total darkness a few feet down. I called, and to our infinite relief heard Keller answer, "Okay, I think. But I don't know how to get back."

"We can't see you," I said.

"I can see you against the light. I'm caught on a ledge, but there's no handhold."

"How far down are you?"

"I don't know. Not very far, I think."

The telephone wire was our salvation. I tied a stone to the free end and called down to Keller, "I'm sending down a length of wire with a stone on the end. Try to catch it, and then I'll pull it up. That will tell us roughly how far you've fallen, and we'll think of some way to get you up."

I paid out the wire slowly until there was a shout from Keller, "Got it!" To my relief I had not used very much line. While I held the wire Ruth pulled up the stone, and we estimated the length of line from the stone to the reel. It was about fifteen feet. "Not too bad," I said to Ruth. But how on earth were we to get him up without a rope? A gap of fifteen feet is not really very far, but it is infinity if you have nothing to bridge it. The thin telephone wire was useless. I thought suddenly of the lifejackets. These were made in the form of breast and back buoyancy bags, with straps over the shoulders and long tapes to go round the waist, and since it may be necessary to haul an inert body out of the water the tapes were designed to be strong enough to take the weight. We took off our lifejackets and I tied the tape of Ruth's to the tape of mine. Opened out, the combined length of the jackets and tapes was a bit longer than the telephone wire we had used, so that we could get our improvised line down to Keller.

"Help coming," I called to him. "We're sending down our lifejackets tied together. Get a grip where you can, and we'll haul you up."

I lowered the lifejackets, and the tapes linking them were long enough for Keller to grip the shoulder straps of Ruth's jacket. Then we met problems. Without tackle, the vertical lift of a man is a formidable job, and we had to be careful not to be pulled into the crevasse ourselves, and not to risk fraying the tape on the ice edge. Our emergency lifeline took Keller's weight all right

146

and we raised him a few inches, but it seemed impossible that we should be able to lift him through fifteen feet. He solved the problem himself. "You can't lift me," he called up, "but if you can hold me I can keep a grip with one hand and scramble up the rock, I think. Keep the line taut."

It was a severe climb. Ruth and I kept the contrivance taut by moving back from the crevasse as Keller inched himself up. I prayed that my knots would hold. The climb seemed to go on for ever, but gradually Ruth and I moved away from the crevasse, and suddenly there came a marvellous moment when Keller's head appeared. He got his arms over the edge and rested, panting. "All . . . right . . . now," he gasped. "Many . . . thanks."

"Hold the end of the lifejacket in case he slips," I said to Ruth. "I'll go and help him up." The worst was over, but even with my help it was a struggle to climb out of the crevasse. At last Keller was sitting safely on the ground. "Get him some hot soup," I called to Ruth.

Keller was bleeding from a long scrape on his forehead, but it was not a deep wound, and although bruised and badly shaken he seemed to have escaped major damage. His jacket was torn, which was serious because its insulating value would be reduced, but his haversack was intact and he did not think he had lost anything. The soup revived him, and when he had drunk a few mouthfuls he handed the can to me. "Fair shares," he said.

"We're not sharing this—it's all got to go inside you. We didn't share your ordeal in the crevasse."

"You got me out of it. The two of you saved my life."

"Time for soup," I said firmly, and made him drink the rest of the canful.

With snow and a handkerchief, Ruth did what she could to clean up Keller's grazes. I carried a small first-aid box in my personal kit, and this provided some antiseptic ointment. In that icy wilderness I doubted if there was much chance of infection, but the ointment at least smelt good, and applying it made us feel that we were trying to do something.

Keller's rescue had occupied two hours, and left us all exhausted. Keller gallantly made light of his injuries, but he was shaken, and in the cold his bruised joints were stiffening. He wasn't really fit to go on, but we couldn't stay where we were. We could try to go back to the wreckage, but the effort of struggling back the way we had come would get us nowhere. If we went on, not much more effort might get us to the coast. Ignorance made for optimism, and it always seems better to try to go on than to go back. So I took over the lead. According to our routine Keller should have carried the rifle, but I didn't want to add an ounce to the weight he had to carry so I asked Ruth if she could manage it. She agreed at once. "It's not so much the weight of the thing that bothers me, but that I don't think the rifle should be with the man in the lead. If Keller had been carrying it we'd have lost it in the crevasse, and Heaven knows we may need it." We disentangled the now rather battered lifejackets from the contraption we had made of them, put them on again, and started.

With Keller's fall vividly in my mind I walked slowly, testing every yard of doubtful surface. This was as much fatigue as caution, for none of us was in any state to go quickly. In fact, however, the going improved somewhat, the ground no longer heavily crevassed, and loose scree changing to a firmer surface. We also began to climb towards the next ridge, a slope more pronounced than in yesterday's valley. I did not take in much of our surroundings for I kept my eyes on the ground immediately in front of me, making sure that I trod on earth or rock and not on some treacherous film of snow masking the edge of a hole. Keller marched on doggedly but his bruises made it painful work and he had to concentrate on keeping going.

Thus we owed our discovery to Ruth, who had the wits to look about her. I was stopped by a shout, "Peter! Over there!"

She was pointing to something on our right, a hundred yards or so below our line of march. My instinct was to slip the safety catch of the rifle as I turned, expecting to see a bear. But there was nothing obviously threatening us; indeed, for a moment or two I could not make out what was exciting her. Then I saw it, too—a marked change in the landscape, with what looked like a band of dark earth instead of rock, for some reason more or less clear of snow, falling away at a right angle to our route. "I'm not sure," she said, "but I've seen an exposed opencast seam before, and I think that might be coal."

Carefully watching where we walked, we went over to have

a look. The geology of the place was weird, but the whole wilderness was so bleak and dreary that local differences did not stand out unless you looked closely. Here it seemed in some remote past half a hillside had fallen away, exposing a lower stratum of the local structure. To get to the black band we had to climb down a steep cliff, not noticeable from where we were because we were on top of it. The cliff seemed to have sheltered the area immediately below it from snow, and also from the prevailing wind, for at the foot of the cliff it seemed slightly warmer than on top, though probably there was not much in it, and what we were noticing was the absence of wind. But the change in microclimate made a profound difference and there were tufts of a heather-like little plant growing here and there, the first green we had seen since our wreck. The black stuff certainly looked coal-like. In places the surface was broken, and there were some loose lumps. They varied in texture from a sort of hard peat to something more like coal. "It's either coal or lignite," I said. "As far as we're concerned it doesn't matter which, for whatever it is it ought to burn. Let's see if we can light a fire."

While Ruth and I had been examining the black band Keller had been resting at the foot of the cliff. "There's a good place here," he called to us. "It looks like a cave."

It was. It was not a big cave, not much more than a dent in the cliff, but it was shelter, with sides and a roof, and there was room for the three of us inside. Ruth and I carried over several lumps of our coal, and piled them just outside the cave. Using the machete I broke some into small pieces for lighting, and poured a little of our precious fuel over them. Then I put a match to the fuel-soaked coal, and our spirits rose with the splendid tongue of flame the match produced. Ruth went back for more coal from the seam, while Keller and I carefully built up our fire. Soon we had a really brisk fire crackling away, lovely to look at, and giving out a generous warmth.

As soon as we had our fire going we began to think that the one thing we really wanted was a cup of coffee. You can't have everything—we had a fire, but there was no handy snow. "I'll go back up the cliff," I said. "It won't take long, and the snow there will make better water than the thin stuff round here." Feeling that the cave was home I took off my bulky lifejacket to be freer to climb, collected three empty soup cans, and set off.

The site of our residence, however, turned out even better than we could have hoped. I had barely started to climb when I saw an icicle, and below it was a small runnel of half-ice, half-water. Some drops of water were running down the icicle. It was a spring, and for short periods of the year it would probably be proper water. It was more ice than water now, but there was plenty of it, and it solved our water problem—it was like having piped water on the spot! I filled the cans with broken ice and went back to the fire. They boiled quickly, and the meltwater from the ice was a big improvement on melted snow, which, however clean it looks when you collect it, always seems to give a grudging, muddy fluid. It also gives very little—a full can of snow yields only an inch or two of water.

With really boiling water, and ice rather than snow as the source of it, our coffee seemed the best we'd ever tasted. I leant against the rock-wall of the cave, stretched my feet towards the fire, and invited discussion of what we should do next. "My own view," I said, "is that we should stay here until tomorrow morning. We all need rest, and we're not likely to find anywhere better than this. The coal is a godsend in itself, and it may also be a valuable leading mark. We know that in some places in the region there is coal near the coast, and we may be within a mile or two of the shore. I shouldn't be surprised if this valley runs down to it."

"It doesn't seem to run in the right direction, at least, not in the direction where we thought we'd reach the coast," Ruth said.

"It may be too local for that to matter. We can't see the end of the valley from here, and it certainly looks as if it curls round that shoulder about half a mile away, which would make it about right. But I'd like to leave exploring until tomorrow, and concentrate on rest."

Neither Ruth nor Keller needed much persuading. "It's just after midday, now," I went on, "and I think the next thing is some food. It's a pity we've got nothing to cook, but at any rate we can be warm while we eat. After lunch, I think Rolf should turn in. We'll set watches as usual, but we'll leave out Rolf for four watches. I'll take the first after lunch, then Ruth, then I'll come on again,. then another turn for Ruth. That will give twelve hours to see what rest can do for getting over that fall."

"I'm not going to let you take any extra watches—I'm quite fit to stand my watch," Keller said.

"I know you'd do it, but it's not necessary," I argued. "You're a third of our total strength and we need you fit—apart from any consideration for you, our own survival may depend on your fitness."

Keller still didn't like it. "What about the lady?" he asked. "She needs rest, too. Let me share the first watches with you so that she can have unbroken sleep."

"There is no lady here. I'm an Oxford professor," Ruth objected.

We laughed. "There's no arguing with that," I said.

He gave up. I was not wearing my lifejacket, so we added it to his and Ruth's to make slightly better cushions in the cave. He turned in against one wall, and his need of rest was apparent for in a couple of minutes he was asleep.

Ruth was nearly as tired, but before turning in for her three hours off watch she stood outside the cave with me for a little. "Do you think we shall get through, Peter?" she asked.

"God knows," I said. "What worries me most is the extraordinary lack of activity by the Gould Bay party. There are eight of them there, well equipped, with good communications. It seems unbelievable that they shouldn't have sent up the plane to look for us, and if they did send up the plane it seems unbelievable that we didn't see or hear it. Nothing I can think of makes sense. I mean, you can imagine things like total radio failure which *may* have happened, but it's unlikely that radio failure, with skilled operators, would persist for more than a few hours. And even if they lost contact with the helicopter by radio they must have been alarmed when we became physically overdue. I sometimes wonder if there may be a traitor in the party, deliberately out to lose us. But I can't consider that seriously. Like everything else it doesn't make sense."

"No," Ruth said. "The party are all Air Force or police, and I don't see how your traitor could have got into it. I agree it's puzzling that they don't seem to have looked for us, but I'm less worried about that than you are, perhaps because I think mathematically. If you have a problem in maths that you can't solve with any known data, you proceed to look for something you haven't noticed before. And if you can't, because you haven't

151

access to any more facts, you put it at the back of your mind until you can get at some more facts. We know that there *is* an explanation for whatever may have happened at Gould Bay, and it's no use being worried because we don't know it. I'm much more bothered about whether we ourselves can ever get anywhere. And I'm bothered all the time about you, Peter. You're nowhere near fit for this kind of thing."

"We weren't a bad partnership in getting Rolf out of his hole, and it was sharp-eyed of you to spot this seam of opencast coal. If we can reach the coast we can probably get somewhere in time. We must concentrate on the practical side of life. And the immediate practical need is for you to get some sleep. I'll keep the bears away, and look after the fire."

I thought that one of the best things I could do during my watch would be to collect a good pile of coal. It did not have to be carried far, about sixty to seventy yards, but getting it from the seam was hard work. Without a pick it would have been hard to break into, but natural weathering had to some extent done this for us. Here and there, towards the edges of the seam, the surface was cracked and pitted, and lumps of coal could be pulled away by hand. With the machete to assist I could even be selective about the size of lump I took. I kept the rifle slung during my mining and coal-carrying work. I didn't want to find myself with a bear between me and the rifle.

No bear appeared, and after about a dozen trips I had a fine dump of coal beside the fire—enough, I thought, to last the night. In our present luxury there was no reason why the watch-keeper should not have a mug of coffee, so when I'd dealt with the fire I fetched another can of ice from the spring and brewed up. Another blessing of the fire was that you didn't have to keep on the move the whole time. I sat on a rock in the pleasant lee of the fire and savoured my coffee.

Ruth's dismissal of what I called the Gould Bay Problem was all right as far as it went, and was certainly a practical approach—why waste mental effort on a problem that you *know* you cannot solve? But my mind is not so disciplined as hers, and I couldn't stop thinking round it. The only solution that made some sort of sense was my wild theory of a traitor in the party. This was the place for practising Ruth's dismissal principle—if I couldn't see *how* a traitor could have joined the party forget it, and just assume that he had. If so, I thought that one thing followed—we must be near the mark, and there might be a real chance of coming across *Apfel*. What the three of us could do then I didn't know—time to meet that problem if and when it arose.

With coal-work, coffee and reflection my watch passed quickly. I was reluctant to wake Ruth and felt ready to extend my own watch, but she has a mind equipped with clocks as well as computers and within five minutes of the time my watch was due to end she woke herself and came out. I made some coffee for her, handed over the rifle, and took my turn on the lifejackets. With a slight warmth from the fire coming into the cave and a flicker of flame to look at, I felt that I had never been more comfortable in my life. I must have been more tired than I realised, for in spite of having so much to think about I was asleep almost as soon as my head touched the lifejacket, and it seemed only a moment later that Ruth was kneeling beside me, shaking my shoulder gently. "It's horrid to wake you up, darling, and I hate doing it, but you've brought me up to obey orders," she said.

Ruth had made up the fire before calling me, and there wasn't much to do. I was refreshed by my sleep, and I wanted to explore what I called Coal Valley, but my job was to guard the cave and it wouldn't do to move away from it. The day had clouded over and we seemed to be in for another bout of mist : exposed in the wilderness it would have been miserable, but with the fire and our cave we were all right. At ground level visibility was still fair, and I was contemplating a trip to the spring for ice when I thought I saw something move on the far side of the coal seam. I felt automatically for the binoculars which would normally have been hanging round my neck—but they had not survived the crash. I edged round to the cave side of the fire, so that the fire was between me and whatever was in the valley. Yes, there was definitely something. . . . A moment later I made out a monster of a polar bear, coming towards us. I slipped the safety catch of the rifle, and waited.

The bear did not seem to be put off by the fire, but he

advanced cautiously. Probably he had never seen a fire before, and was curious about it. I wondered if he could scent us, and hoped that the rather acrid smoke from the fire might disguise whatever scent we gave.

Although frightening, he was a beautiful creature and I had no wish to kill him. I hoped he would go away. But he didn't. He seemed in no particular hurry, and paused to sniff at a tussock of the heather-like plant growing near the coal seam. It was more or less on the line from the seam to the cave that I'd followed on my coal-carrying job earlier, and I wondered if I'd left some scent on it. If I had he was encouraged rather than discouraged by it, raised his head in a determined fashion and came on.

I couldn't let him get to the cave. And I couldn't risk firing too soon for fear of wounding and not killing him, and having a maddened animal rushing at us and thrashing about. A big bear is well protected by his massive fur, and I didn't know which part of his huge body to aim for. I decided that I'd wait until he got within certain range and aim for his head. But I still hoped that he would go away.

It was no good. He came on steadily, apparently determined to investigate the fire and the cave. When he was about a dozen yards away I aimed between his eyes and fired. He reared up in a kind of shocked surprise, stood upright for a moment, and then fell over on his side, to lie still.

The sound of the shot roused Ruth and Keller, and they ran out of the cave—at least one advantage of our state was that we never had to lose time in getting dressed, for we had nothing but the clothes we wore, and apart from the lifejackets it was too cold to take off anything. They didn't see the bear at once. "What's happening?" Ruth asked.

I pointed to the bear. "I think it's dead, but we'd better wait a little to make sure," I said. I could have pumped some more rounds into the body as we had into the bear that had attacked Ruth, but I didn't want to. That earlier encounter was different. Then the bear was threatening Ruth, we were desperately afraid for her, and we fought in hot blood. Now I had killed because the bear could not be allowed to stay near the cave, and not knowing enough about polar bears I did not know how to drive him off. I had not wanted to kill him, I should have preferred

154

him to live and leave us alone. I had no sense of triumph in the killing. I just felt sad.

The beast was dead when Keller saw it and he reacted differently. "Fresh food!" he said. "I shall cook a splendid dinner for us all tonight."

"You're supposed to be resting," I said. "We could certainly do with some fresh food, but Ruth and I will look after it."

"No. I learned how to skin a bear on my Arctic course—it was not a polar bear, but I expect it's much the same. Thank goodness we have the big knife. I've had five hours sleep, and I feel fine. What a marvellous place this is, house, fire, food and water all provided."

There was no point in trying to make him go back to rest. He looked better, and it was probably good for him to have something practical to do. The shock of the past few days had been worse for him than for us. We had merely been in danger for ourselves, but Keller had lost fellow countrymen and loyal subordinates from his own force, for whom he felt responsible. He was a German policeman investigating a crime that seemed to have been committed in Germany, but it was part of a complex network of events, many of which had happened in England, and he had met disaster in the Arctic because of the theories of an English investigator whom he had tried to help. It would have been understandable if he had felt some bitterness, but if he did he did not show it. He was a fine man and a magnificent ally. He had a right to cook bear steaks if he wanted to.

They were certainly good eating, and I'm afraid we made rather gluttons of ourselves. Partly this was because although we had food and fire, the conditions were primitive. We had nothing to cook with, and the best we could do was to cook our steaks in the embers, turning them with the machete. Keller and I had pocket knives, but Ruth's personal cutlery consisted of a pair of scissors and a nail file. Our meat was liberally coated with ash and we had to eat with our fingers, but with ration-biscuits to accompany it we made a princely meal. Keller cut a couple of big joints from the bear, and we put these to roast slowly in hot ashes, planning to take them with us cold next day.

Well-fed and comfortable we sat round the fire. "I'm much encouraged by the coal seam," Keller said. "It's another piece of evidence that fits. When you hear of something thousands of miles away there's an extraordinary sense of achievement in actually finding it. I feel hopeful about tomorrow."

"I feel less and less inclined to leave here. We could do worse than become settlers in the Arctic."

"It might be all right for you," Ruth said, "but I feel more and more that I want a bath. I wonder if I shall ever see a bathroom again?"

"Be hopeful, like Rolf. Tell me, Ruth, what exactly does this coal seam indicate?"

"I keep explaining that I'm not a geographer. You can work it out as well as I can. From very elementary knowledge one can say it proves that the whole of this region of the Arctic once supported extensive vegetation."

"That would require a completely different climate," Keller said.

"Yes, but we know there have been huge climatic changes over geological time. There's no doubt about that."

"The problem is the extent to which some residue of a past warm climate may linger on the seabed, or in certain warm currents," I said. "Do you think there's anything in it, Ruth? We're coming nearer to your own field in trying to assess mathematical probability."

"I can't give you any assessment of probability without having more facts. What I can say is that a mathematician of the calibre of Adrian Stowe, who you think was murdered in Hamburg, wouldn't have done as much work on the problem as he did if he hadn't thought there was something in it."

"There's very little doubt that he was murdered," Keller said. "The case was not really investigated at the time, for much the same reasons that the death of Dr Jackson in Cambridge was at first not thoroughly investigated. As soon as we reopened the Stowe case it was obvious that it was by no means the straightforward suicide that it was meant to look like. Somebody was sufficiently impressed by his work on the theory to murder him for it."

Ruth was silent for some time. Then she said, "The trouble is that mathematical reality and practical reality are not always the same thing. I mean, Adrian Stowe may have satisfied himself that the Arctic Calorific Syndrome had a mathematical reality without necessarily showing that it was likely to be of any practical use. Whoever killed him presumably thought that he had discovered something, but it wouldn't necessarily have any *practical* value."

"Think back to what seems like another lifetime, Ruth. Do you remember telling me that it didn't much matter whether my theory was right or wrong as long as somebody else was prepared to act on believing it to be right?"

"I do, vaguely. And I think that is really the point here. An open-water North-West Passage may or may not exist—for myself I think that it probably doesn't—but if rival groups both seriously believe in it then it's going to influence their actions whether it actually exists or not."

"We're here because we think it possible that a yacht has been able to sail as far north as the Robeson Channel," Keller said. "If a yacht really can get here, it certainly looks as if there's something in the open-water theory."

"I don't think that quite follows," I said. "It has always been possible to navigate these waters in some states of the ice—given a good crew and patience it's astonishing where a sailing vessel can get. The real question is whether there are geophysical factors making for favourable ice conditions in certain areas of the Arctic for all or most of the time. We're assuming that some people think there are such factors, that they can be identified and located. But that's all we're assuming : we're not assuming that they're right."

"Well, maybe we shall find out one day, maybe not. For tonight we're going to be comfortable, anyway. I'm going to take the next watch. I'm perfectly fit for it—indeed, after that dinner I feel fit for anything."

The night passed uneventfully, and both Ruth and I were grateful for the extra sleep that Keller's insistence on standing a watch allowed us. We were up at five, and with little to pack we were ready to start as soon as we had breakfasted.

The best walking was on the coal seam, but it didn't last long. It was exposed for only about four hundred yards, after which it went underground again beneath a rubble of broken rock and scree. It was a tiny speck in relation to the thousands of square miles of wilderness and I marvelled at our luck in Ruth's sharp eyes.

When the seam became broken rock we left it for slightly better ground a little lower in the valley. There were still scraps of that small heathery plant growing here and there, and an occasional bush like some sort of juniper, with sparse green berries on it. I wondered if the short Arctic summer would give them time to ripen : on the whole I hoped that we should not be around to see.

The valley narrowed as we descended it, and turned in a sharp dog-leg to get round a wall of cliffs to the north, or more probably north-east, of where we were. The valley bottom was now a ravine, enfolding a rock-strewn riverbed. Here and there were frozen pools, but later in the summer there would probably be water. The spring by our cave must have drained into the river higher up. As we made our way down, the going became more and more difficult, with the sides of the ravine broken by deep miniature gorges, which doubtless channelled water from the high ground into the riverbed.

We were halted by coming to a sheer drop where the watercourse in the ravine plunged over a cliff-like shelf of rock festooned with icicles, a frozen waterfall. It wasn't really very high, perhaps about thirty feet, but without ropes there seemed no way down it. And I wondered if there was any point in following the ravine any longer. We hoped that it would lead to the sea, and it still seemed possible that it did—it may have been imagination, but I thought that there was a feel of the sea in the air, and from time to time I seemed to sniff salt water. But if we were making for the coast this ravine-like valley did not seem a good approach. We knew from the pilot book that the Ellesmere Island shore of the Robeson Channel is often sheer cliff, and that where there are beaches they are mostly rough and broken. The increasing size of the watercourse in our ravine was a hopeful sign—it looked like the bed of a river not far from the sea. It did not follow that it reached the sea in some nice gentle river-mouth—it might simply cascade over a cliff. And since the pattern of the land, the varying strata making up the wilderness, seemed to be repeated, it looked as if the waterfall we had now come to might recur on a larger scale on the coast.

"I don't think it's worth going on here," I said. "Anyway, we've got to make a detour of some sort. I'm quite hopeful of the cliffside to our left. It's not sheer, it looks climbable, and if

158

we can get up it and over the ridge we shall by-pass the end of the ravine. If we're really near the sea we shall be going something like parallel to the coast, and not out of our way."

"You're the navigator," Ruth said. "We certainly can't go down here."

"What do you think, Rolf?" I asked.

"Well, you've made far more study of the charts than I have. It seems to me a choice of climbing the ridge, or going back. I hate going back."

"That's settled, then. You're a better climber than I am, Rolf. Do you feel fit to lead?"

"Sure."

It was hard work, but relatively straightforward, and only once did we have any serious rock-climbing to do. Keller had done a good deal of climbing, and he had a sort of natural instinct for rock, with a fine eye for a route. Whenever it seemed that we had come to an impassable place there was always a little shelf or gully that enabled us to get round it. The worst bit was a huge slab of rock about twelve feet high that blocked everything. To the left was a more or less vertical wall, and to the right a sheer drop. There seemed no way round the barrier, and the maddening thing was that from the top of it the cliffside rose quite gently, and it looked good going.

Keller stopped to consider, his eyes "reading" the rock. The corner between the slab and the wall offered what looked like a secure hold, but it was about eight feet up. "If you could stand against the wall and I could climb on your shoulders, I could just about do it," he said.

One of the legacies of my wounds and operations is that I am not able to lift anything heavy. Ruth knew this and I could see her eyes cloud with worry, but I put my finger to my lips, and shook my head slightly. I didn't think that Ruth could bear Keller's weight, and there was nothing else for it but for me to have a go. I found as secure a stand as I could. "Okay," I said.

I could not have climbed on Keller, but with one hand on my shoulder and the other on the rock face he hauled himself up successfully. He could now reach the hold quite easily, and the rest—for him—was child's play. His weight sent a sharp pain down my side, but he was up, and for the moment that was all that mattered.

But how could Ruth and I follow? Keller was already considering this. "It's quite good above the hold. If we had a rope there'd be no problem," he said.

"Lifejackets," I suggested.

"Possibly, but we may not need them. If Ruth can get on your shoulders as I did, I can reach her."

Ruth didn't want to climb on me, but she is much lighter than Keller and I could lift her to where with a knee on the rough rock she could scramble on to my shoulders. Keller is immensely strong. He took Ruth's hands and seemed just to swing her up.

Then it was my turn. "I think we'll have to use the lifejackets now," Keller said. "I'll knot mine and Ruth's together, and send one end down to you. Use it as a hold, with your feet on the rock. It's quite rough, and you'll be able to manage."

His confidence was more than mine, and without him I certainly could not have done it. Ruth sat on the top of the slab holding on to the lifejacket tapes. Keller stayed where he was when he had pulled up Ruth, wedged somehow on the narrow ledge that had given him a hold for getting up. He didn't leave my weight to Ruth, but took the middle of our lifejacket line.

It took two or three goes before I could get started. At first it seemed impossible to co-ordinate a hold on the lifejacket tape with footwork on the rock, but by using my knees instead of my feet I succeeded in crawling upwards a few inches.

"Fine," Keller said. "Just keep going." He helped by hauling, and at last he was able to grip my hands. He held me for a moment's rest. Then an indication of the tension with which he braced himself came in his return to German. "*Jetzt*," he said. Next minute, and how he did it I don't know, he swung me up as he had swung Ruth. She gave me a hand over the edge of the slab, and I lay there, sobbing with exhaustion and relief.

Keller joined us and patted my back. "You did well," he said. I couldn't say anything, but I held out my hand and he took it.

There was still about half a mile to go to the ridge, but the slope seemed relatively gentle, and the ground mostly exposed slabs of rock, slippery with snow, but good to walk on if one took care. I felt done in, with a pain in my side, and eager as we all were to get to the top I suggested that it might be sensible to halt for lunch. I must have looked in need of a rest, for the others agreed at once, and would not let me do anything. Keller collected snow to serve for a drink, an unappetising mush served neat, but there was nothing to melt it with. We still had some soup, but wanted to keep that for emergencies. Unpalatable as it was, the snow at least served to keep up our fluid intake. We were better off for food. Using the machete as a carving knife Ruth cut me a chunk of cold bear meat which although distinctly tough had all the virtues of fresh food.

After lunch I went off a little way by myself, partly to answer a call of nature, partly because I wanted to have a look at my wound. When I got down to it through my layers of clothing it was as I feared; it had opened, and was bleeding. There was little I could do about it. In my haversack I had some lint and plaster, and I stuck a pad of lint over the wound, hoping to stop or at least to check the bleeding, to prevent it from getting all over my clothes. I said nothing about it for the moment, and as the others were ready we started at once on our final climb to the ridge.

Even in known countryside there is always a lift of the heart in coming to a view, and in our condition in unknown territory we were almost breathless with excitement as we covered the last few yards to the ridge. What we expected I don't really know. Our immediate goal was the sea, and we all hoped for something that would indicate the coast. What we did see was the remotely possible in theory suddenly become real. Below us, and about half a mile away, anchored off a stony beach in a little bay of open water, was a yacht.

XI

In the Robeson Channel

As when I had shot the bear I had no sense of triumph. With the bear I had aimed, pressed the trigger of a rifle, and the rest had happened with mechanical inevitability. Now, the intense thought that had gone into the case of the Baffin Map seemed equally to have led to an inevitable conclusion. But it was not concluded. I could not doubt that the yacht in the little bay was *Apfel*, but who was on board her we did not know. I might have been right in some things, but gravely wrong in others. Our present condition was certainly not what we had planned.

The others, who did not yet know of my damage, were more cheerful. Ruth put her arms round me and kissed me. "Well done, Peter," she said.

"One is brought up to believe in reason but this seems more like magic," Keller said. "Yet it has been done by reasoning—your reasoning, Herr Colonel. I congratulate you."

"Come off it, Rolf—English for save the compliments until they've been earned. And I could have done nothing without you and Ruth. The question is, what do we do next?"

"We're rather on the sky line. Do you suppose they can see us from the yacht?" Keller asked.

"If they were looking, perhaps. But who would they expect to come out of this wilderness? Still, you're right. We don't know what we're up against, and it's silly to take needless risks. Let's get down among those rocks and have a talk."

The side of the ridge we were on now was steeper than the one we had climbed. It was also more broken, and it looked as if it turned into cliffs between us and the beach. We took shelter in a pile of jagged rocks a few yards from where we were standing. We could look down on the yacht, but no one on the yacht could possibly see us. The instinct of hunters and hunted was strong in us, and we began by talking in whispers until I said, "This is ridiculous. She's at least half a mile away, and several hundred feet below us."

Keller laughed. This broke the sense of high drama, and we all felt better for it. "Back to assumptions," I said. "We can assume that the yacht is *Apfel*, and that Dr Braunschweig is on board. If our earlier assumptions are anywhere near right we must assume that he is a captive, or subject to some restraint. We must also assume that he has played his part in whatever he was forced or persuaded to come here to do, and that the deadline for his liquidation is getting near. Therefore we can't just go away and leave the yacht while we try to make our way along the coast to Gould Bay to get help."

There was a sign of movement on the yacht. A figure—we were too far away to make out whether it was a man or woman—came into the cockpit and went on deck. I longed for glasses, but we had none, and that was that.

"How many people do you reckon to be on board?" Keller asked.

"Hard to guess. Going back to our original theory, you remember that I doubted, and I think you agreed, whether the kidnapping was a forcible seizure of Dr Braunschweig. Such evidence as there was suggested that he had stopped his car for someone he knew, and that he had left the car voluntarily. He may have gone on board the yacht voluntarily—that would have made things easier for the kidnappers. Once on board they showed their hand, and forced him to stay on board, because they wanted him to take them to the Arctic in *Apfel*. She's made good time in getting here, so there must have been enough for an adequate crew—I'd say at least three plus Braunschweig himself. Of course there may be more, but I think they'd try to keep numbers down because they wouldn't want to put in anywhere for food. They could pick up water at some uninhabited fjord on the Greenland coast, but they would have had to make port somewhere for food."

Keller reflected on this. "Three presumably tough people, and we are three, so at least we're equal there," he said. "But we don't know whose side Braunschweig is on—he may be here for reasons of his own, and have left a false trail of kidnapping to disguise what he was really up to."

163

"It's possible, of course. But from what we know of him it seems unlikely. As far as we know he is genuinely devoted to his wife and children, and a clever man could have found some way of going off without exposing them to the agony of thinking he'd been kidnapped. If Braunschweig wants to be rescued he's an ally. And we have the advantage of surprise."

"How do we use it?"

"To get on board. They don't know that we're looking for Braunschweig, and if we turn up as shipwrecked mariners they can scarcely shoot us out of hand."

"I'm not so sure about that. If they're planning to kill Braunschweig they won't want any stray witnesses. And if we've been wrecked we've disappeared anyway, and they've nothing to worry about if they want to shoot us."

"That's a good point. But I don't think they'd shoot us at once—sheer curiosity about us would make them let us come on board. And once aboard we can see what the situation is. We've got pistols, and if necessary we can shoot first. They can't see the pistols under these anoraks. I suggest we transfer them from our belts to our pockets."

"I don't much like it. But I can't think of anything else."

"I don't like being shipwrecked," Ruth said. "It will strike them as wildly improbable. What on earth were we doing in a boat in this part of the world?"

"Sound reasoning—I was thinking too much of getting on board. It's always easier to tell the truth, so let's nearly tell the truth and be survivors from an air crash."

"There are several airlines flying polar routes, but I think we'd better not be a big passenger aircraft," Keller said. "We can assume they have got radio, and any passenger plane lost in this part of the world would be a big story on the radio news. We'd better be survivors from a small private plane."

"Difficult to explain what a small private plane was doing here."

"Advancing knowledge," Ruth said. "I'm a genuine professor, and it's my job to advance knowledge. We're part of the Oxford North Greenland Expedition and we were flying back to our base—you'll have to think up a good base for us, Peter—when we lost our way in fog and crashed. The pilot and navigator were killed, and we've made our way to the coast."

"When did this happen?"

"Yesterday, I think. We don't want questions about where we've been and how we got here."

"We're a bit old for undergraduates. You might pass, Ruth, but Rolf and I wouldn't."

"We don't have to be undergraduates. Somebody's got to look after the young. I'm a professor, Rolf is a fellow of Balliol—Modern Languages—and an experienced mountaineer. As for you, Peter, I think you'd better be a bursar—out for the ride."

"Am I permitted to be married to you?"

"I hadn't thought of that. Probably not. I don't think tough, exploring women professors are likely to cart husbands around. Sorry. But if we're going in for make-believe it might as well be believable."

"All right. Where's our base? Somewhere on Disco Island, but we can be rather vague about it. The plane was a six-seater executive job, borrowed from—who shall we borrow it from? Oh, yes, lent to the expedition by one of our sponsors. We needn't go into it, but if it seems necessary it can be Allied International Foods. They're always sponsoring expeditions, and we're testing out their new nutritious breakfast cereal—you know, 'Work all day on three tablespoons'."

Keller was impressed. "Good thing you two aren't planning a crime! The cover seems to me all right, and I like being an Oxford fellow. What do we do if they've got a radio and offer to send news of us to the outside world?"

"They won't," I said. "The first thing we'd do on staggering in from an air crash would be to ask if they've got a radio that can send news of us. I'm sure that they have got a transmitter, but I'm equally certain they'll say they haven't."

"What if they're not like that and want to help?"

"Let them. Our plane was Echo Mike Juliet 773. Our names don't matter—they're not likely to know them. Oh, I suppose I can't be Blair if I'm not married to Ruth—I'll be Peter Jones. I can still be a colonel, in fact I'd better be a colonel, because a bursar would be quite likely to be a colonel or an admiral or something. There'll be some excitement on Radio Canada North, or wherever they send a message, and then a lot of puzzlement. It doesn't matter. By the time anybody has been able to work

165

out that we're a hoax whatever is going to happen here will have happened."

Having sorted out who we were, the time had come for action. Making sure that our pistols were handy in our pockets we started on the next stage of our walk. It was steep, and with the pain in my side I found it heavier and heavier going. After about a quarter of a mile the slope became a cliff and we stopped at the edge. It wasn't particularly high, perhaps a hundred feet or so, and it wasn't sheer—to get down would be a scramble rather than a climb. But with my side throbbing with pain, and, as I could feel, bleeding, I felt that I couldn't do it. I sat down and told them about my wound. They were very worried. "I knew that we shouldn't have climbed on you," Ruth said. "Oh, Peter, how are we going to get you out of this?"

"Perhaps we can get help from the yacht," Keller suggested. "After all, we don't *know* that they're all instant murderers. It is quite reasonable that one of the survivors of our crash should be injured. I shall go and ask for assistance to bring you down."

"That's not a bad approach. But I don't like your going alone. I shall be all right here. Ruth must go with you."

"Rubbish," Ruth said. "I'm staying with you."

"Of course. We're not going to leave you by yourself. And it is logical that one of our party of survivors should stay with the injured man."

Every instinct prompted me against this. "It would be logical if we were what we're pretending to be," I said, "but we're not. We know a good deal about that yacht, and the people who may be on board her, and what we know I don't like. There's no telling what sort of reception you may get. If there are two of you, you'll have a chance of doing something where one might be helpless. You *must* be together."

We argued about this for several minutes, but I insisted, and finally they agreed. "But I don't know what I'm supposed to do if there's a fight," Ruth said crossly.

"Kick, my darling. . . Please don't be cross. There may not be a fight, but there are a thousand ways in which two can succeed where one would fail. Don't let's risk disaster now because of my old injury. There's another thing. You've got to get down this cliff, and when you get to the yacht you want to be free for

166

action. Leave the haversacks here. You'll be coming back, anyway, and you can do without the weight."

We were not a united party any longer, but they accepted what I said. "I hate leaving you," Ruth said. "God bless you. Oh, Peter. . . Peter. . ."

"Good luck," I said. Having started, neither looked back.

There seemed no particular reason for me to be out of sight but natural caution suggested that it might be wise not to give away my exact position on the clifftop, so I found a rock from behind which I could see everything below without being seen. Ruth and Keller were about halfway down.

For this coast *Apfel*'s little bay was almost comfortable. On our side the beach ended quickly in the cliff, but on the other side there was a good stretch of flat ground before the land rose again. I could see the yacht clearly, and I watched someone come out of the cockpit and go on deck. Keller called out, "Ahoy, there!" The first reaction was on the beach. Someone ashore, whom I'd not seen because he was masked by some rocks, came running to the rubber dinghy drawn up the beach. Another person on the yacht rushed up on deck. Ruth and Keller were just reaching the foot of the cliff.

Suddenly I heard the unmistakable sound of an aircraft and saw a plane that had just crossed the ridge coming in to land on the flat ground at the head of the bay. Ruth and Keller were on the beach with about fifty yards to go to the man standing by the dinghy. They waved at him and began running. He made no move. When they were about thirty yards from him he drew a pistol and fired two shots. Both flung themselves down, but I didn't think they were hit. It was time for some diversionary action. I had the rifle, the man by the dinghy was within easy range and I aimed for his legs.

In my army days I shot for the Regiment at Bisley, and I have always been good with a rifle. My shot went home, the man with the pistol screamed and fell down. He was wounded, not killed. I sent another round to hit the stones beside him. Dragging his left leg he began to crawl behind the dinghy.

Ruth and Keller were still on the ground. Keller began to get up to go towards the wounded man when the ground in front of him was spattered by more bullets. The plane had landed and

167

three men had jumped out. They were running towards the beach firing from automatic weapons. They were sub-machine guns and made a lot of noise, but were not very accurate at that range. Keller went to earth again, and gallantly rolled in front of Ruth. My rifle was a far better weapon than a sub-machine gun. I fired at the leading man from the plane and my second round got him. The other two panicked and turned to run back to the plane. I sent several rounds after them, and the bullets must have been uncomfortably close, for they gave up running to the plane and threw themselves down. I thought it would be a good thing if some fire came from another part of the cliff, moved about a dozen yards and loosed off. Thank God for the haversacks—they held the extra rounds for the rifle that Ruth and Keller had been carrying. For the moment I had ample ammunition.

I forgot about my wound. There were Ruth and Keller to protect, and whatever strange battle this was to be won. My blood was up, and I was determined to win it. This gave me a surge of strength.

But what to do? As long as I was on the clifftop my rifle could dominate events below, and our enemies on the beach could not know how many men with rifles were on the cliff. I changed position again and sent a couple more rounds in the general direction of the men lying on the ground. They made no attempt to get up. The men from the plane had jumped out so quickly that I thought the pilot must be still on board. He was, and he also had a rifle. He got out of the plane, took cover behind the undercarriage, and blazed away at the cliff. Since he could have no idea where I was it was a waste of ammunition.

I decided that my most useful job at the moment was a holding action to pin down the two men who had gone to ground. I could probably have killed them, but I didn't want to kill unless it seemed imperative, and I could keep them where they were by sending a round every couple of minutes within a foot or two of where they lay. Then things started to happen on the beach. Keller and Ruth wriggled forward slowly towards the dinghy, behind which crouched the wounded man. They knew that he had a pistol because he had fired on them and were taking no chance.

When Keller was five or six yards from the dinghy he

motioned to Ruth to stay down, got up and rushed the dinghy. The wounded man was in no condition to show fight. Keller took his pistol and for the moment left him where he was.

Apfel was moored about twenty-five yards offshore. I could see another dinghy on deck, lashed upside down just for'ard of the cockpit. There were still only two people on deck, and while I was engaging the men from the plane they began unlashing the dinghy. When Keller got to the beach they gave up this, and both fired at him with pistols. It was fairly wild shooting. Keller kept his nerve, retreated to a clump of rocks and installed himself in a position from which he could cover the dinghy on the beach, and any attempted landing from *Apfel*, without being in the least danger from the yacht.

Then Ruth took a hand. I'm not sure whether she had ever fired a pistol in her life but she decided to have a go. Still lying down, she opened fire on the yacht. She was at fairly long range for a pistol shot and whether her bullets went anywhere near the yacht I don't know, but they were a useful diversion. The two people on the deck stopped firing towards Keller and turned their attention to her. At that range I thought she was probably fairly safe, but nobody shoots at Ruth with impunity. Although at fairly long range they were within reach of my rifle, and I brought them a little nearer by working my way a bit down the cliff. Then I let them have it. My second round brought down one of them, my third the other. Satisfied that they were out of action for the moment I swung round and sent a few more bullets to discourage the men from the plane who were still lying on the ground.

So far as I knew our only opponent remaining effectively in action was the man with a rifle behind the plane. It was difficult to know what to do about him, and he could be as dangerous as I was, although from his wild shooting into the cliff I didn't think much of him as a rifleman. Keller, however, had been taking in the situation, too. He called to Ruth and she went over to join him by the dinghy. I couldn't hear what he was saying, but I could make out what he was doing, and I was thankful to see that he was taking no risks with Ruth. Clearly he was leaving her to keep an eye on the wounded man and guard the dinghy, but placing her behind the rocks where he was. There might be no more danger from the yacht, but there might be other people on board and it was wise to take precautions. Then Keller began walking towards the men on the ground.

I could guess what he was hoping to do, and I had a part to play. My job was to provide a kind of miniature artillery barrage for him, continuing to pin down the men as he made for them. I should have to be careful as he got near to them because I couldn't risk hitting him, but I thought I could manage by firing slightly to one side of him as he walked. I felt a curious link between us. We were totally out of communication, yet I felt I knew in advance just what he was planning, and he (as he told me later) felt almost that I was beside him.

The men still had their sub-machine guns, which would become more dangerous as Keller got closer to them. I saw one of them trying to adjust his gun and I sent a round within a couple of inches of his head. That kept him quiet. The next thing was that Keller was standing over them with his pistol, ordering them to give up their guns. There wasn't much that they could do. Keller could have shot either of them with his pistol before they could bring a gun into action, and if they tried to move they could expect what they now knew to be fairly deadly rifle-fire from the cliff. Of course they did not know how many men might be covering them from the cliff, and this was another thing that sapped their spirit.

I saw Keller take the guns and throw them away. Then I understood the next move of his campaign. He ordered the men to get up, put their hands above their heads and walk in front of him towards the plane. He kept close behind them, using them to shield him from any fire that could come from the man behind the undercarriage.

There was nothing more I could do from the cliff, and it was time to try to join the action below. My wound had stood up to things so far, and though I was now conscious again of its hurting I was determined to ignore it. From the dawn of time men have somehow found renewed strength in battle, and I felt now that while I might pay later nothing was going to stop me from doing what I wanted.

I remember nothing of my climb down the cliff—earlier, I had thought that it was beyond me, but now when I came to a difficult place I jumped. I knew that Keller would need me in the battle of the plane, and willpower kept me going. When I got to the beach I started to run.

The trickiest job for Keller would come when he got to the plane. As long as he kept away from the plane, and kept the men in front of him, he was safe enough from the pilot; but while the pilot was in action with his rifle none of us was safe. Keller was obviously determined to put him out of action, but at close quarters they would be three against one, and if they showed any guts in turning on him and risking his pistol he would be in peril. It was absolutely vital that in those critical last moments I should be there to help.

It was touch and go. As they got up to the near wheel of the undercarriage the pilot dashed round it, getting behind Keller's shield provided by his captives. If the pilot had been a better rifleman events would have gone differently. There was a split second when he could have shot Keller with no risk of hitting either of the other men, but he was running with the rifle, and though he fired once he was too excited to aim and the bullet went harmlessly overhead. Even so, the men in front saw their chance, and when Keller turned to face the pilot they turned and made for Keller. I was perhaps fifty yards away. The pilot swung his rifle like a club and in a moment it would have crashed viciously on Keller's head. It didn't, because I broke the pilot's arm with a bullet a fraction of a second before his blow fell. At the same instant Keller shot one of the other men in the shoulder. When the third man saw me he put his hands up.

We had won a battle, but our situation was far from triumphant. The man from the plane whom I'd shot from the cliff was dead, but we had three wounded prisoners on land, and perhaps two more on the yacht. One of the enemy, now standing with his hands up, was unhurt—what was to be done with him?

Keller and I had no time for mutual congratulations, nor did we feel like them. "The first thing is to do something about the wounded, then we must go on board the yacht," I said. "Do you think there'll be a first-aid kit on the plane?"

"Quite likely." Speaking in English he asked the unwounded man, but the fellow didn't seem to understand. He tried German, and he understood at once. "Are you German?" Keller asked.

The man nodded. Speaking in German he said he didn't know if the plane carried a first-aid kit, but he would ask the pilot. The wounded pilot said Yes, there was a box of bandages and other things, and he explained where it was kept. Keller told the unwounded man to go and get it.

The first-aid box was quite well-equipped, but there was not much we could do with it. The pilot had a broken arm and I fixed this as far as I could with bandages and a couple of splints from the box. His wound was not bleeding much, and he said he felt more comfortable. The man shot in the shoulder was more badly hurt. Keller and the unwounded prisoner carried him to the plane and laid him down on the floor of the fuselage between the two rows of seats. It was a fair-sized aircraft, capable of carrying thirty or forty passengers at least, and comfortably fitted out. With seat cushions and some blankets that we found on a rack we made the prisoner as comfortable as we could.

"We'll get Ruth up here to look after him as soon as we can," I said. "Now we must get to the yacht."

We dared not leave either the pilot or the other man with the prisoner. The pilot had a broken arm, but he might still be capable of flying the plane. And the plane had radio—the last thing we wanted was for messages to be sent that might bring reinforcements, or alert people we had no wish to be alerted. Even to leave a seriously wounded man in the plane seemed a risk, but we felt we had to take it—we could not leave him lying in the open, for he would lose heat rapidly and die. Inside at least he had shelter from the wind, and he was well wrapped in blankets. He was barely conscious, certainly incapable of piloting, and we did not think that he could get up to work the radio.

Making the pilot and the other man walk in front of us we went down to the beach. Ruth ran to meet us. "Nothing has happened here and I have been frantically worried about you," she said. "Are you all right?"

"More or less," I said. "We seem to have won, for the moment, anyway. Look, my darling, can you go to the plane? There's a badly wounded man on board, and he needs looking after."

Ruth was not happy.

"I'd much rather look after you," she said.

"I can keep going. There'll be some sort of galley on the plane, and there ought to be some water. See if you can find any—the man may need a drink."

"But he tried to kill you."

"Yes. That doesn't matter now. We've got to do what we can for him."

She shrugged her shoulders. "I suppose so, but I don't like it."

"None of us likes any of this, my darling. We've just got to go on."

Keller was getting ready to launch the dinghy. The man who'd been hit in the leg was on the ground beside it. He couldn't walk, but I didn't think that he was gravely hurt. We decided to leave him, the pilot and the unwounded man on the beach while we went on board the yacht. Keller spoke to them sternly in German. "You will stay here, and you will not move from this spot," he said. "You have seen what the Herr Colonel can do with a rifle—if any of you try to leave the beach he will shoot you from the yacht."

Just before Ruth went off to the plane I said to her, "With any luck we'll join you soon. Keep your pistol handy. If any of this lot tries to board the plane, shoot. None of them has a gun. Stand at the door, and shoot as soon as anyone gets to the boarding steps."

Keller rowed, and a couple of strokes of the oars got us to the yacht. There was nobody in the cockpit. I made fast the dinghy's painter and we climbed on board. She was a beautiful boat, with a rather deep cockpit. A central companion way led down to the saloon. The door was open. A woman's voice called through it in German, "If you move a step farther I shall shoot Dr Braunschweig."

That halted us. "What do you want us to do?" Keller asked.

"You have wounded, perhaps killed, my husband," said the voice. "You have slightly wounded me, but not much. I have a gun. I have also got Dr Braunschweig—he is tied to the saloon table, and he can do nothing. I could shoot you, but I am prepared to make a bargain. My husband needs medical help. The aeroplane has come. I see that you have hurt the pilot, Hans, but he could walk to the beach with you and he can still fly. You shall help me carry my husband to the plane, and Hans can fly us somewhere where there is a hospital—he will know. There is plenty of fuel."

I whispered to Keller, "Keep her talking."

"Why do you think we should help you?" he asked.

"Because you have no choice. My pistol is already pointing at Dr Braunschweig's head. If you wish him to live, you must do as I say."

"Tell her we must find out if the pilot thinks he is fit to fly," I said to Keller in English. She heard. "I understand English," she said. "That seems reasonable. But only one of you may go ashore."

"I'll go," I said.

I got back into the dinghy and made a noise of fitting the oars to the rowlocks. I let out the painter, but I didn't cast off. Very quietly I eased the dinghy along the gunwale until I was for'ard of the mast. I'd noticed a forehatch which no doubt led directly to the fo'c'sle and a sail locker, but which would almost certainly also provide a way into the saloon. I made fast the dinghy to a cleat near the bow and climbed back on board. The hatch lifted easily—every fitting was of the highest quality—and, as I'd thought, led to a well with a sail locker to starboard and a door, probably opening to the heads or lavatory, to port. Another door led aft—that would be to the sleeping accommodation, I thought. It was, with cabin doors on each side. It was lighted by a skylight. Aft again was a central door, in what was presumably a bulkhead. "That will be the saloon," I thought.

Gambling that the woman, whoever she was, would be looking towards the cockpit I opened the door, rushed at her, and grabbed her arm holding the pistol, wrenching it upwards. She fired, but by then the pistol was pointing to the deck over the saloon, and the bullet went into the deck. Before she could fire again I'd twisted her arm so that she had to drop the pistol. At the same moment Keller sprang into the saloon from the cockpit. I had the woman only by the arm. She clawed at my face with her other hand, her nails drawing blood. Then she bit my wrist. She had a dreadful supple strength, and I doubt if I could have held her long. Keller's weight and the enormous power in his arms soon settled things.

"Frau Baumgarten, I presume," I said.

While Keller dealt with the woman I cut free the man tied to the saloon table. He was stiff, but seemed otherwise unhurt. "I have no idea who you are," he said in English, "but I am profoundly grateful to you."

"We came here to look for you," I said, "but it's a long story. The immediate job is to look after our wounded prisoners."

"The man on the settee is severely hurt," Dr Braunschweig said.

Heinrich Baumgarten did not look alive, but although unconscious he was still breathing faintly. He had been hit in the chest. We could do nothing for him at the moment. "I wonder if we could trust that pilot to fly us to Gould Bay?" I asked Keller.

"I can pilot an aircraft," Dr Braunschweig said.

"That changes the situation. We must get ourselves and the wounded to Gould Bay as soon as possible. There is a doctor in our party there."

"I hope there still is. Oh, everything has gone wrong." Frau Baumgarten was sobbing quietly.

I shook her shoulder. "What do you mean?" I asked.

"Don't you know what happened? Our men surprised a German Air Force party there, and they are being held as hostages. I do not know whether any have been killed or hurt."

Suddenly events began to fall into shape. If the Gould Bay party had been taken hostage it would explain why there had been no search for us. But who were these people? Questioning could wait. Our flight to Gould Bay became more and more urgent. We were the surprisers now, and in Dr Braunschweig we had an addition to our strength.

"I do not know what may have occurred at Gould Bay, but to get your husband to the doctor there seems about his only hope," I said to the woman. "Flying time to Gould Bay cannot be great—to get anywhere in Greenland or Northern Canada where we could find medical help would take much too long. We must start at once. You can help Herr Keller to get your husband into the dinghy."

Whatever evil she might have done, she was clearly devoted to her husband. We had nothing to fear from her while she was trying to help him. I went on deck and brought the dinghy aft. Keller and Frau Baumgarten lifted Heinrich Baumgarten and carried him as gently as they could to the dinghy. "He will have to be carried to the plane—we shall need some sort of stretcher. Have you anything on board that can be used as a stretcher?" I asked Dr Braunschweig.

"I carry a folding canvas stretcher, all cruising yachts should carry one. It is in the fore-cabin. I'll go and get it," he said.

Access to the yacht was access to a world of valuable things. While Dr Braunschweig was getting the stretcher I had a quick look round the cockpit, and found a coil of good line. How often had we needed rope! Now we had plenty of it.

There was room for all of us with the injured man in the dinghy, and I asked Dr Braunschweig to come ashore. "There is one fit man on the beach, and although he is one of our enemies I don't see why he shouldn't help to carry Baumgarten to the plane. I should like you to go with him. You will find my wife Ruth on board, looking after another badly wounded man. Perhaps you could have a quick look round the plane to make sure that you can fly it, and see what sort of charts they have. We want to go to Gould Bay, which is on the western shore of Kane Basin, between Hayes Point and Cape Frazer. We could almost do without charts and get there by flying down the coast, but it would be comforting to have a chart. When you've checked on all this, perhaps you'd come back here."

He agreed, and took the oars of the dinghy. As we grounded on the beach Keller jumped out to hold the dinghy. "You, there, come and give a hand with a wounded man," he called to our unhurt prisoner.

With the stretcher, we soon had Baumgarten ashore, and Keller explained in German what was to be done with him. "This man must not be left on the plane," I said to Dr Braunschweig. "When you come back, he must come back with you. Have you a pistol?"

He shook his head. "Rolf," I called to Keller, "have you got that pistol you took from the man by the dinghy earlier on?"

"Yes," he said. "It's in my pocket."

"Can you give it to Dr Braunschweig? He is unarmed, and he may need it."

Keller handed over the pistol, and the stretcher party set off. As they got to the top of the beach and could see the plane a couple of hundred yards away Dr Braunschweig cried out, "That is one of our planes—it belongs to my company. It is one of a fleet we have in Alaska."

I wanted a quick conference with Keller. "It's an enormous help that Dr Braunschweig can fly an aeroplane. I haven't worked out how far it is to Gould Bay, but it can't be much more than two hundred miles or so, less than an hour's flying time. Did you take in what that woman was saying to me?"

"About the hijacking of our party? Yes."

"Well, I think it's our turn to do the hijacking. With Gustav Braunschweig there are three of us now, with Ruth four, though I don't want Ruth engaged in a shoot-out if we can help it. We shall achieve total surprise. They'll see the plane come back, and have no idea that it's got a different crew. Our Arctic clothes are much like theirs, and they won't see that we're not the people they're expecting. They must be holding our chaps in the big transport plane—probably they're living on board, for it's all the shelter they have. We can just go on board and open fire at once."

Keller nodded. "We must shoot to kill," he said. "Hijacking an Air Force plane is an act of war." As on other occasions when we were both deeply moved we acted rather formally and shook hands.

"We must take all the wounded, but we don't want our fit prisoner with us. I suggest we leave him here. He can live on board the yacht and he can scarcely get away. When we've settled things at Gould Bay we can send back to collect him."

Again Keller nodded. "There's one thing, though. The yacht has certainly got radio. We don't want him warning his friends before we get there."

"Lord, no. We'll put the radio out of action. Braunschweig will know all about the radio. He's coming back now."

I walked to meet him. "I can fly the plane without any difficulty —indeed, I think I've flown it before. As I told you, it belongs to my company," he said.

"What about charts?"

"There are plenty of charts, but I don't think I shall need them. I have all this coast in my head, and I can find Gould Bay without trouble. Would you like to tell me who you are?"

"My colleague is from the German Federal Police, and I am a sort of English policeman. It's a long story and I can't go into it now, but you can take it that we are on your side. It is important that you should be on ours, for we need your help."

I explained briefly what seemed to have happened at Gould Bay, how we had come to be where we were, and why we were such a tragically small party. "With determination I think we can rescue our people, but it will not be without risk," I said.

"You have risked your lives to save mine. I am at your disposal for whatever you think I can do."

"Thank you. We are going to leave the man who helped you to carry Baumgarten here—we don't want a fit man who can turn against us in our party. I'm afraid he'll have to shelter on your boat, but I don't see that he can do much harm. Do you carry radio?"

"Yes. We have very good radio."

"It must be put out of action. What is the simplest way to do it?"

"Remove the tuning crystals—it cannot be worked without them. And we can remove the aerial."

"We'll do both. I know nothing about the man, but it is possible he is an expert. If we succeed at Gould Bay we shall send back to arrest him. What about your boat? She is a beautiful boat."

"Yes. . . . But for you I should have sailed her to my death. She will be perfectly safe here. Some time, some time when all this is over, I shall come back and sail her home."

Dr Braunschweig and the prisoner had not brought back the stretcher, but we needed it again for the man wounded in the leg, who couldn't walk. Keller sent the prisoner back for the stretcher, and told him to run. While he was getting the stretcher Dr Braunschweig and I rowed out to *Apfel* and dealt with the radio. "Are there any weapons on board?" I asked.

"The Baumgartens had pistols—they are probably in the saloon. The other man who was hurt on shore also had a pistol, but that is the one I now have. I don't think there are any more. The Baumgartens occupied my cabin, to starboard. It might be well to search their things."

It was. We found two revolvers in a canvas holdall, and re-

178

moved them. Dr Braunschweig's uninvited guest would have neither radio nor gun.

We made him help to carry the lame man to the plane, and the rest of us then went on board. When we told him that he was staying he lost his nerve and screamed. "You are leaving me to die. How can anyone survive in this wilderness?"

"You have a comfortable yacht, with food on board, and a dinghy to take you out to her. Clear off! When it is convenient for us we shall send back to have you arrested."

We put all our wounded aft, the two seriously injured men lying on the floor, the others free to sit as they chose. Frau Baumgarten crouched on the floor beside her husband. Keller went forward with Dr Braunschweig. I stayed aft with Ruth, and to keep an eye on the prisoners.

Dr Braunschweig knew what he was doing. He started the engines, and let them run for a few minutes. When he was satisfied that they were running smoothly he turned and taxied into the wind. Then he revved up and we took off. Although it looked fairly flat the ground was unpleasantly bumpy, but Dr Braunschweig handled the plane well and we were airborne without incident.

In Dr Braunschweig we had not only a pilot but an expert navigator. He flew with complete confidence, and fifty minutes after taking off we began the descent to the gravel bank at the head of Gould Bay. To our relief the big transport plane was still there, but there was no other sign of life. This was not greatly worrying, for the plane provided living quarters, and there was nothing in that desolate landscape to attract anything outside.

We had made our plans, and we knew exactly what we were going to do. Dr Braunschweig was going to put down the plane near the big transport, and taxi to within about fifty yards of it. As soon as we were stopped we would open the door and put down the steps. Keller would go first, then me, then Gustav Braunschweig. We would not run, but walk normally. We should climb the boarding steps of the big transport, not bunching, but keeping close together, one step behind each other. We expected the entrance door to be shut to keep out the cold, but it was unlikely to be locked. Keller would open the door and we'd walk straight in, shooting to kill at anyone who was not of our party.

179

Braunschweig, who did not know our comrades, would not fire except to protect us. Ruth would stay on our plane, to guard the prisoners.

I have a sharply clear recollection of walking to the big transport, my heart pounding and my throat dry. The light seemed exceptionally clear. In the cold air I could see Keller's breath, and I thought it looked rather beautiful against the blue Arctic sky. Yet of what happened when we entered the big plane I remember little. Keller fired once and shouted to everybody to put their hands up. I did not have to fire at all. The commander of our party recognised Keller, and saw at once what was happening. There were two armed men guarding the eight members of our team. Keller's shot killed one. The other was so astonished that he did nothing, and in an instant the commander and an airman were on top of him. There was little fight in him and he surrendered almost at once. There were three other raiders on board, one making coffee in the galley, the other two asleep. The airmen of our force rounded them up quickly and with the line I'd brought from *Apfel* lashed their hands behind their backs.

Ruth had been miserable when we left, and she might have heard Keller's shot. As soon as I saw that we had won I went back to her.

XII

Diplomacy

THE GERMAN AIR FORCE doctor and nurse came with me when I went across to Ruth. He examined Heinrich Baumgarten first. "I can do nothing," he said. "I fear that he is dead." Hilde Baumgarten was huddled on the floor beside him. "I think he died a few minutes ago. At least we were together," she muttered. Skilfully folding some blankets the nurse made two of the aircraft seats into a bed and persuaded Frau Baumgarten to lie down. Taking a hypodermic syringe and a capsule from his bag the doctor prepared an injection and left the nurse to give it to her while he looked at the other wounded men.

The man shot in the shoulder by Keller was in a bad way. "I think he will live," the doctor said, "but I shall have to operate. I cannot do it here—he must be moved to the bigger aircraft." He asked the nurse to collect two men to carry him across. The pilot and the man I'd hit in the leg were in considerable pain, but neither was in any particular danger. The doctor dressed their wounds and gave them both injections.

Then it was my turn. The doctor did not much like the look of my old wound, but when the nurse had cleaned it up I thought it might be a lot worse. The doctor put in a couple of stitches where the wretched thing had opened up and gave me some pills which, he said, would help to prevent infection. I should have to go back to my own surgeon when I got home, but for the moment he thought that I would do. Ruth disapproved. She wanted to use the smaller plane to have me flown to hospital somewhere forthwith, but I said that it was out of the question. There was urgent work for Keller and me. I was sorry about Hilde Baumgarten's injection because there was so much that I wanted to ask her, but she was a woman and a patient as well as a prisoner, and I did not try to interfere with the doctor's treatment. In addition to the shock of her husband's death she had a flesh wound in her thigh, where my bullet had hit her. It was not a serious wound, but it was painful. I could not help admiring her for taking no notice of it in her concern for her husband. The doctor thought that she might be fit for questioning in the morning.

While the doctor and nurse tackled the emergency operation Keller and I had a conference with the Air Force commander. He was grieved to learn of the crash and loss of life in the helicopter party. He did not know that we had met disaster because he was hijacked before the helicopter became overdue. The hijacking was, as we had thought, carried out in total sudden surprise. He had only the doctor, nurse and a radio operator with him when the other plane appeared, because he had let the rest of the party go off to see if they could hunt a polar bear. There was nothing for them to do while waiting for us, and he did not want them to sit around playing cards. The arrival of the other aircraft was a welcome bit of excitement. The commander was walking across to offer the visitors a drink when armed men jumped down from the plane and seized him. After that he could do nothing. There were nine men in the party and they forced the doctor, nurse and radio operator into the navigator's compartment on the big aircraft, and locked them in. When the others came back from their hunt—they had seen no sign of a bear—they were seized and overpowered as they entered the plane. They were allowed no access to radio, and thus lost contact with the helicopter. The raiders knew nothing of the helicopter—had they known that it was at large they might have changed their own plans. When Keller and I turned up the commander thought that we must have come back in the helicopter.

The account of the hijacking was interesting, but it didn't answer any questions. Who *were* the armed men, prepared to seize a German Air Force plane, and to open fire on anybody who happened to be in what they seemed to regard as their private part of the Arctic?

"Did you get any idea of who this gang is, and what they are doing here?" I asked the commander.

"Not really. They were more concerned to question us."

"What did you tell them?"

"As little as we could. I said that we were on an Arctic exercise, primarily concerned with detailed air-navigation in the vicinity of the Pole."

"Did you identify the leader of the gang?"

"I think so—at least he was the man who did most of the questioning, and who seemed to give instructions to the others. He has not come back."

"Then either he is the man we left on the yacht, or the man who was shot when they opened fire on us on leaving their plane. I'm inclined to think he is probably the dead man. The man we left on the yacht seemed a rather spineless individual."

"I should recognise him if you recover the body. What are you going to do about the man on the yacht?"

"He will have to be collected and taken back to Germany."

"When do you think we ought to collect him?" Keller asked.

"I've been thinking about that. Timing is a critical problem. We ought to report our casualties as soon as possible, and I think we should try to recover the bodies for burial in Germany. That could be done on foot, but it would take days, and we haven't really got a strong enough party. It could be done much more easily with another helicopter. That means getting one brought out."

"There would be no difficulty about that," the commander said.

"I'm sure there wouldn't be. But the moment these deaths are reported there will be a tremendous news story, and we don't know yet who is behind it all. Do you think we could maintain silence for another twelve hours, until tomorrow morning? That would enable us to recover the man from the yacht, and give time for some hard questioning."

The commander didn't like it much—all his instincts were to report our situation forthwith. I didn't like it either; it was hard on the next of kin that they should remain ignorant of what had happened. But Keller supported me. Neither he nor I could give orders to the Service people, but the commander's own orders were to assist us and after some discussion he agreed to do as we asked. Then we had to decide who should collect the man from the yacht. I didn't want to go, and I didn't want Keller to go, for he was needed to question our German-speaking prisoners. In the end the commander decided to go himself, with three airmen. He could pilot the smaller plane, and we showed him on the chart precisely where the yacht was.

Ruth, Keller and I then got down to work with Dr Braunschweig. He still knew next to nothing about how we had come to look for him. He also wanted to send a radio message to tell his wife that he was safe. I hated the thoughts of his wife's continued agony but I had to steel myself and tell him he must wait.

I gave him a quick summary of events since Sir Anthony Brotherton had come to us with the first ransom note. "So," he said—he spoke excellent English, but this was the expressive German "Zo"—"I do not understand everything, but now I understand much more than I did. You know something of the Arctic climatic theory. I took it very seriously, and I wanted my company to investigate it in the utmost detail. Consider the advantages to the western world if it were no longer dependent on oil from the politically turbulent Middle East. There is plenty of Arctic oil—we have but touched the fringe of development there. The difficulty is in getting it out. There is a pipeline now from Alaska to the west coast of America, but such pipelines are hugely expensive, and there is always trouble with those who do not want the ecological balance of wild places to be upset. I am indeed sympathetic to them, but they are often ignorant and create alarms that are not justified. Big oil companies are, of course, much hated and distrusted—yet even those who hate us depend on what we do. We are not the soulless vandals we are made out to be. . . But no matter, there is no time for this. Imagine the value of a sea route for oil from the Arctic to Europe and the east coast of North America—quick, clean transport with no interference with anybody's land.

"To my astonishment Sir Anthony did not support me, and since he is by far the most powerful man on our board I could not hope to persuade a majority to go against him. Nor did I want to quarrel openly with him and others of my colleagues. So I determined to find out for myself whether a North-West Passage in the far north offers a feasible route. I had a most able mathematician on my staff in an Englishman called Adrian Stowe. He shared my enthusiasm, and gave invaluable help on the theoretical side. As his work progressed I became more and more convinced that a far northern passage does exist."

"It might exist mathematically and yet not be of any practical use," Ruth said.

"That is just what Adrian Stowe used to tell me. I am not a mathematician in your"—he gave a little bow to Ruth—"or Adrian Stowe's class, but I spent many years as a chemical engineer, and I am not wholly ignorant of maths. It was, indeed, because I understood the limitations of a theoretical approach that I was determined to investigate the passage physically. Fortunately I was equipped to do so. I am a navigator, I have had much to do with sea transport, and I had my own ocean-going yacht. Then Adrian Stowe died."

"He was almost certainly murdered," I said. "In England, two other experts in the Arctic climatic theory, who were his friends and colleagues in his work, have also been murdered. Did you suspect that Mr Stowe's death was not the suicide it was made out to be?"

Dr Braunschweig was silent for what seemed a long time. Then he said slowly, "I cannot say that I *suspected* . . . sometimes I *feared.* You must understand that all my life I have been immersed in my work, I have not thought of such things as the murder of a colleague. What has happened since makes me realise that I ought to have thought of such matters, but I did not."

He was shaken and distressed. I let him recover himself and asked, "What happened on the day you left Hamburg?"

"I was driving to my office when I saw Heinrich Baumgarten standing by the roadside. He recognised my car and waved at me to stop. I thought he was my friend, so I did stop. He said that his car had broken down some distance away and he had walked to the main road to try to get a lift. Could I drive him to his home? Of course I said yes. I ought to have realised that his story was improbable—a man in his position had only to telephone his office and a car would have been sent out to him at once. I thought of that later, not at the time."

He paused, and went on, "I suppose it took about twenty minutes to get to his house. He asked me in for a cup of coffee, but I wanted to get to work and declined. However, he pressed me, saying that Hilde would be most disappointed if I did not go in, that I need stay only a few minutes, and that he wanted particularly to show me a photograph of a boat he was thinking of buying. Stupidly I gave way.

"Hilde was very friendly, asked if my wife and I could have dinner with them one day in the following week, and made coffee for us. I remember nothing more until I woke after dark, lying fully dressed on a bed. I had a severe headache. I know now that the coffee was drugged, but at the time I thought I must have had a heart attack and that the Baumgartens were looking after me. A few minutes after I woke Heinrich came in, accompanied by another man. Both had pistols. Heinrich said he was sorry to upset me, but that he needed my help. He had, he said, to go to England secretly, and he wanted to go on my yacht. I asked why he needed a pistol, and why he could not simply have asked me to help him as a friend. He said I did not understand. I said I would have nothing to do with it, and wished to go home. He then said 'That is why we have pistols. I'm afraid you must do as I tell you.'

"I had little choice. Heinrich and the other man—he is called Arnold, but I do not know his other name, and he is the man who was wounded when he was ashore from *Apfel*—made me get into a car, and drove me to the waterfront. I thought of shouting for help, but it was late at night and there was nobody about. And the man Arnold kept his pistol pressed into my side. We got into a biggish dinghy, and Heinrich rowed. It was some distance from *Apfel*'s mooring and we must have been in the dinghy for nearly an hour. I wondered why we did not use an outboard, but realised that he did not want to make a noise. He brought us to *Apfel* and the three of us went on board. Hilde was in the saloon, still friendly, and gave me coffee and some food. I was hungry then, and glad to eat.

"After this Heinrich said that we must leave, and that we must go out under sail because he did not wish to attract attention with the engine. He told me that I must handle *Apfel* because I knew her. He and the other man helped to get up the sails, and now it was Hilde who kept close to me with a pistol.

"Perhaps I should have wrecked *Apfel*... Somehow I couldn't. I was still very much in a daze. We sailed out and when we were well away from the mooring the dinghy was cast off and left to drift. Heinrich said that we would set a course for Harwich in England, and that as we were now standing out to sea he could handle *Apfel* and I could go to bed. I was permitted to use my own cabin, but they locked me in.

"I suppose I was still affected by the drug, for, surprisingly I went to sleep, and slept until nearly six a.m. I looked out of my porthole, but could see no sign of land, nor anything to indicate where we were. I banged on my door, and soon afterwards Heinrich came. He was still polite. 'I'm afraid I misled you yesterday,' he said. 'We are not going to England.'

"I asked, 'Where are we going?'

"He told me that it depended on me, but that he hoped I would co-operate. I asked what the devil he meant, and he said he understood that I was planning a voyage to the Arctic. If I was prepared to navigate, he and Hilde and his friend would help me to get there.

"It was my own fault. I had liked Heinrich and Hilde, they had sailed with me for weekend cruises on *Apfel*, and while I think I was always discreet about my real purpose I made no particular secret about wanting to sail to Greenland. He told me that he and Hilde had been on board *Apfel* several times without my knowledge, and stored her for a long voyage. We need not put in anywhere save, perhaps, for water, and we could do that when we got to Greenland. All they wanted me to do was to navigate, though if I would help to work the ship we should all get on better.

"What could I do? I was totally in their power, and I *did* want to go to the Arctic. I thought that the best thing I could do was to play along with him, bide my time, and escape when I could."

"You would not have been allowed to escape," I said. "You would not have returned from the voyage. I'm inclined to think that we found you in the nick of time—that the aeroplane was to evacuate the Baumgartens and the other man and that you would have been shot out of hand. I think you had given them what they wanted, and that they had finished with you."

"You may be right. . . even if you are only partly right I am infinitely in your debt."

"That does not matter. Rolf Keller and I were simply doing our duty. What does matter is whether you have formed any idea of why they kidnapped you and made you take them to the Arctic."

"Heinrich was never explicit, but you cannot live with a man on a boat without getting some impression of his motives. Heinrich controlled—largely owned—a flourishing oil engineering business. Much of his work was in the Middle East, and in our conversations I gained the idea that he was also interested financially in oil production in the Middle East. From one or two things he said I think that he was a considerable shareholder in the Arabian Sands Oil Company, a smallish independent company that we took over. The majority of the shares were held by banks as nominees. I was against our making any further investment in the Middle East, but I was outvoted by my colleagues on the board. Finance is not my own field, and I did not know the details of the shareholdings we bought out in taking over Arabian Sands—maybe they were so well disguised that nobody outside the nominee banker actually knew. I suspect that Heinrich was deeply involved, but I don't know."

"You said that you thought the plane that brought the raiding party belonged to your company."

"I don't think it—I *know* it belongs to Unol. Shipping is my chief administrative job in the company, but all transport comes under me, and I was concerned in buying a fleet of those aircraft for service in Alaska and other areas where we need to transport personnel by air."

"Could it have been used as it was without the connivance of someone in the company—someone in a senior position?"

"You are implying what I do not want to think about."

"It has got to be thought about."

"I suppose the plane could have been stolen, but it would not be easy."

"Let us go one stage farther. Do you consider it probable that the murder of experts in the Arctic climatic theory and your kidnapping were organised by people in the company fearful of the effects in the Middle East if a new North-West Passage could be found?"

"Within the company, perhaps . . . within the oil industry, certainly. There is very much at stake."

"Have you any idea who the people in the plane are?"

"No."

Keller and I next turned our attention to the pilot of the invading aircraft and the other members of his party who were fit to be interviewed. We got nowhere, because all refused to say anything except to demand lawyers. "There's no point in wasting time on them," I said to Keller. "They'll have to be turned over to the Canadian police, and they can be searched and interrogated later. I think we ought to radio the Canadian authorities now. It would be simpler to keep everything in our own hands, but we can't. Various crimes have been committed on Canadian territory, and while the Baumgarten woman and the man who sailed with them from Hamburg can be extradited to face trial in Germany, the others will have to be dealt with by the Canadians. There'd be appalling diplomatic trouble if we just took the whole lot back to Hamburg."

Keller agreed and we called in our own radio operator. The Royal Canadian Mounted Police maintain a number of posts in the Arctic. The nearest seemed to be on Baffin Island, and we had a radio frequency for it, but the post was at least seven hundred miles away from us and we did not know what sort of transport they had available. Also the whole affair was so complicated that it seemed best to get in touch directly with Ottawa, and to leave it to the Canadian authorities to decide what to do. Sir Edmund Pusey's department at the Home Office has a liaison officer in the Canadian police, as it has with most of the world's major police authorities, and I'd taken the precaution of putting his name and his position at Canadian police headquarters in my diary.

So we duly called up Ottawa, established a good RT link, and were lucky enough to find that Commissioner Tom MacDonald was in his office. He was intelligent and understanding, and didn't waste time asking questions. I gave him a brief outline of what had happened and he said "Right, I'll come myself. How many prisoners do you have?"

I told him, and explained that some were injured and in need of medical attention. I also said that if he could provide a pilot we had a plane available which could take the prisoners, doctor and nurse, and a Canadian police guard. He thought that might be helpful, and told us to stand by.

Waiting on that desolate, snow-flecked gravel plain was nerve-racking, but we had no choice. The commander's return with the prisoner from *Apfel* broke the monotony, though this man, like the others, refused to say anything. Keller reported our dealings with the Canadian police to the commander. He was unhappy at the delay in starting back for Germany, but accepted its necessity. He was also relieved that we had at least done something to straighten out the complexities of waging what amounted to a private war on someone else's territory.

Ruth had been helping the German Air Force nurse to look after the wounded. Soon after the commander's return she came to tell me that Frau Baumgarten had woken up and was asking for me. "I wonder what she wants," I said.

"I don't know," Ruth replied, "but maybe it's because she is English. She is shattered by her husband's death and she probably wants to know what her own future is likely to be."

"I don't think I can be of much comfort there," I said grimly.

I was now certain of at least one thing in the maze of events, and I put it to Hilde Baumgarten as soon as I saw her. She looked pathetic lying on a cot under Air Force blankets, but I could not let sentiment get in the way of questioning her.

"Tell me why you helped in the murder of Dr Jackson," I said to her.

She did not attempt denial. She said wearily, "So you know about that. Who, exactly, are you?"

"I represent the British police. My colleague is a high-ranking German policeman. You were engaged in an international conspiracy, and it had to be met internationally."

"How much do you know?"

"I know that you were at a party attended by Dr Jackson on the night he died, and that you persuaded him to drink far more than was good for him. Later on that same night I think you went to his house, entered his bedroom through the french window, and helped him to take an overdose of pills. Oh, and you deposited an amber bead under the carpet near the door."

"You might have been there. . . .You know, I liked Charles Jackson—I was a student of his once. It was a long time ago. . . . Yet he had to be eliminated. . . ."

"Why?"

She did not answer for several minutes. Then, as if she were

190

talking to herself, she went on, "You never think of retribution, that it can happen to you. . . It seemed so safe. There was all the money in the world, and the League Against Political Injustice to make it safer. You won't have heard of LAPI, but you soon would have. Heinrich invented them to take care of the liquidation of Gustav Braunschweig. Now Heinrich is dead, and I don't know what will happen to LAPI. They would have been so useful. . . ." Her voice trailed off, and she went into a trance-like state. I had to shake her out of it, and said roughly, "You talk of murder and kidnapping as if they were a sort of private game. Do you realise how serious your own position is?"

"Oh yes, but I don't care now." She came back to consciousness, but seemed utterly detached from what she was saying. "Do you understand what Gustav and Jackson and everybody mixed up in their wild Arctic imaginings were trying to do? They wanted to kill Mid-East oil, they wanted to ruin everybody with interests in the Middle East. Naturally we couldn't let that happen. I don't know if their mad theories would have worked, but it was bad enough that they should start people thinking of the Arctic as a real alternative to the Middle East. If we could finish them, we should have power throughout the Middle East. If anyone was difficult, all we had to do was to hint that we had the secret of the North-West Passage. . . . And if you have power over the Middle East you have power over the whole world." Her voice trailed off again.

"You talk about 'we'. Who do you mean by 'we'?" I asked.

She did not answer but lay back with her eyes closed. I called the doctor. He felt her pulse, lightly lifted one eyelid. He looked concerned and puzzled. He put his stethoscope to her chest, listened for a moment, then shook his head. "I think she's dead," he said. "There was no reason for her to die."

"Can you die of sheer frustration—and, perhaps, a broken heart?" I asked.

"For all our knowledge, death, and life, remain mysterious. She had a severe shock, of course. But nothing else, her wound was trivial. And the sleep I gave her should have eased the shock. She is beyond help now."

"She is beyond a lot of other things. She was an evil woman, and death is merciful. At the least she would have faced many years in prison. She could have told us much more; now she has slipped away. Well, it can't be helped. And she did tell me something. What will you do about her death when the Canadian police arrive?"

"I can do nothing but report it. There ought to be an autopsy, but that is a matter for the Canadian authorities."

I went back to Keller. "Frau Baumgarten has cheated justice," I said. "She has just died, for no apparent reason."

Keller ran a hand through his hair. "That is awkward for us," he said in a worried way.

"She did tell me a little." I reported my conversation with her. "That seems to clear up the mechanics of Dr Jackson's death in Cambridge. We shall have to check what we can, of course, but it should be possible to confirm whether she was in Cambridge that night, and with luck there'll be some photographs of her at her home in Hamburg. Mrs Jackson may be able to say whether she looks like the woman she saw talking to her husband at the party. For myself I have no doubt about it—and she confessed readily enough when I put it to her.

"There's another useful bit of information—I think we'll find that the hijack party, who were employed to do away with Dr Braunschweig, belong to an organisation called LAPI—it stands for League Against Political Injustice. I don't know why they have an English name when they all seem to be German— perhaps, as we say, that's just put in to make it harder. It adds to confusion, anyway."

"I'm familiar with all our known terrorist groups, but I have never heard of LAPI," Keller said.

"You couldn't have heard of them. They appear to have been invented by Heinrich Baumgarten for the purpose—I don't think for a moment that they're a real terrorist group. They would have claimed responsibility for Braunschweig's 'execution'. And I daresay they would have been used again in various ways. We're dealing with some very nasty people."

Thirteen hours after our call to Ottawa the Canadians arrived. That was good going, for they had some three thousand miles to come, over some of the most inhospitable country in the world. We heard their aeroplane before we saw it, and were thankful to watch it come into view, grow bigger, and touch down safely. The German commander, Keller and I walked out to meet them.

I took to Commissioner Macdonald at once. "I've brought six men, the doctor and the nurse you asked for," he said. "It's only a ten-seater plane, and with the pilot we couldn't manage any more. I'm relying on your plane to take the wounded and the prisoners. One of my men is an experienced pilot. Who does the plane belong to?"

"It belongs to Universal Oil, and was stolen in Alaska by the people who brought it here," I told him. "But we have Dr Gustav Braunschweig, the deputy chairman of Unol with us, and in the circumstances he will gladly put the plane at your disposal."

"I've been in touch with your Sir Edmund Pusey in London," Macdonald went on. "He tells me that you are investigating crimes committed in England and in Germany, and, from what you tell me, on Canadian territory as well. If the plane was stolen in Alaska that brings in the Americans. What a muddle! Is there anything useful that we can do here?"

"Apart from collecting the wounded and the prisoners, I think nothing at all," I said. "Our German friends are most anxious to return to Germany, and the sooner the rest of the party can be taken to your headquarters, the better. If you approve, my wife and I will go with you, while my colleague Rolf Keller goes back to Germany."

"I'll be thankful to have you. I don't begin to understand what's been going on, and I'll certainly need you. Did you say your wife was with you?"

"Yes. She's an Oxford professor, by the way. At the moment she's helping to nurse the wounded in the big aircraft. Why she's here is a long story, which I'll tell you later."

The Canadian doctor and the nurse, with the guards for the prisoners, went off in the Unol plane. Macdonald had arranged for them to refuel at a depot of the Hudson's Bay Company en route for Ottawa. Ruth and I were to travel in the smaller plane with him.

As soon as the Unol plane was away the German party left. Keller would be back at the centre of things before I could be, and we arranged that as soon as he had reported to his Government, and Dr Braunschweig had had a chance to see his wife, he and Braunschweig would go to London to meet Pusey. I did not know how long I might be kept in Canada, but I could, of course, be in touch with Pusey from Ottawa. When the time came for Ruth and me to say good-bye to Keller our parting was brief and rather formal. We had no words and didn't need them.

The big German transport roared into the sky, circled, dipped its wings in salute, and soon became a speck on the flight that would take it home across the wastes of Greenland. I held Ruth's hand, drained of all feeling except of love and pride in her. Sadness for the toll of death would come later, and anger at the human ambition, greed and selfishness that caused it. Would justice be done? *Could* justice be done?

I was roused from gloomy reverie by Macdonald. "I've called up my people and arranged for a party to find the wreck of the helicopter and recover the bodies," he said. "There'll have to be a Canadian inquiry, but it was a military plane and the inquiry can be discreet. There will be no difficulty about repatriating the bodies to Germany for burial. We shall have to recover the body from your battle by the yacht, but again I think there will be no difficulty. Now that's fixed up, Colonel, is there anything to keep us in this forsaken place?" There wasn't, and a few minutes later we were airborne too.

Macdonald was a kindly host, and he fed us Canadian whisky, cold ham and bread that had been fresh that morning, until he was satisfied that we were in no immediate danger of death from hunger or thirst. Not until then did he begin asking questions. "How come we weren't called in before you went to Ellesmere Island?" he said politely. This was an awkward one, but we'd taken some precautions.

"It's not as bad as it looks," I explained. "Until we found the yacht at the end of the Robeson Channel we weren't at all sure that we were looking for our gang in even the right continent, and we didn't want to waste your time. There was evidence of a sort pointing to the Arctic, but our interpretation of it was all supposition. If we were right, we had to act quickly, because Dr Braunschweig's life was in danger from his kidnappers. But there was nothing we could ask you to do, because we had no idea of what was likely to happen. We weren't all that guilty of diplomatic bad manners. Our authorities, and the German Government, agreed on an exploratory expedition, and we decided that it could be regarded as an Arctic training exercise for a special detachment of the German Air Force. The German military people duly cleared the exercise with the Canadian Ministry of Defence. For all we knew it might be a matter only of flying out to Gould Bay, landing on the gravel plain, and conducting a few helicopter sorties without finding anything.

"We were caught up by events. Unknown to us, the kidnap gang was in process of taking off the people who'd sailed with Dr Braunschweig from Hamburg. Before leaving they'd have liquidated him, and doubtless sunk the yacht. When they saw the German plane at Gould Bay they seem to have panicked. Had they left it alone, they could have carried out all their plans without our being any the wiser. An announcement would have been made that Dr Braunschweig had been executed by a group called LAPI—that stands for League Against Political Injustice, and seems to have been a put-up terrorist group invented for the purpose. They wouldn't have said where the execution had been carried out, and nobody would have known anything of the goings-on in the Canadian Arctic.

"This is still conjecture, but I think it's safe to assume that the appearance of the German plane upset them so much that they decided it would have to be put out of action while they dealt with Dr Braunschweig and the yacht. From their point of view there was far too much at stake, nothing less than total domination of the whole Middle East oil industry."

"What do you think they would have done with the German air crew?" Macdonald asked.

"I don't suppose we shall ever know. The man who appears to have been their leader was killed. When the rest of them are questioned they'll say that they intended no harm to the crew, but I don't believe it. Hijacking a German Air Force plane is a grave matter. All the resources of the German Government and of the NATO alliance would have gone into the hunt for them, and they wouldn't have wanted men left alive who could recognise them if any of them were caught. They showed no hesitation in opening fire on us the moment they saw us near the yacht. I think they'd have taken the airmen one by one out of the plane, shot them, and hidden the bodies. They'd have left the empty plane where it was. It would have been found, of course, but they could hope that nobody would ever discover what had happened to the crew—it would have been yet another of the unsolved mysteries of the Arctic."

"If your helicopter hadn't crashed, you'd have gone back and been captured, too."

"Possibly. But I think we'd have found the yacht first—in flying time we weren't far from it when we crashed. There'd have been no one there but Dr Braunschweig and his kidnappers, and we had ample strength for dealing with them. We'd have reported by radio, and what they'd have done then, goodness knows. If they'd tried to bluff us over the radio, we might have smelt a rat. Or they might have come in force to attack us, in which case anything might have happened. We won as we did because we had every advantage of surprise, and used it. They knew nothing about the helicopter, remember, and they didn't know who we were, nor how many of us there were."

Macdonald considered this, "Surprise or not, the three of you didn't do badly," he said.

"The more important thing is what we're going to do next," I said.

We came down at a police post to refuel—the bigger Unol plane had to go via the Hudson's Bay station, because it could not have landed on the police airstrip. We were offered beds for a proper rest, but attractive as the offer was we declined it, and only stayed for a cup of coffee while the plane was fuelled. Both Macdonald and I were anxious to press on to Ottawa. When we were on our way again Ruth, who was utterly exhausted, curled up on a seat and managed a little restless sleep. I shut my eyes, but it was no good—my mind went over and over what had happened, trying to extract some meaning from it. Whom had Hilde Baumgarten meant by "We"? She and her husband were obviously leading figures in the conspiracy, but they must have had powerful support. I considered what we knew about Dr Jackson's murder. Maybe we could never prove it, but there seemed little doubt that the Baumgarten woman had acted as she had admitted. But something was wrong. I'd mentioned the amber bead to her, and she hadn't denied it. But how on earth could she have got hold of one of Ingrid Mitchell's amber beads?

I went back to what Dr Mitchell had told me. I had the

sharpest memory of her on that last day of her life, all defences down, and a growing understanding that if she had trusted the police much suffering might have been prevented. She wore the beads frequently, partly, perhaps, because of their association with Dr Jackson, but probably more because the rich glow of the amber suited her clear, dark skin. One day at the museum the string of the necklace had broken, and the beads scattered on the floor. All but one had been picked up—the remaining one was never found.

I tried to visualise the incident. What, exactly, had Ingrid Mitchell said? She had been surprised at my knowing—more accurately, guessing—about it, and then said something like, "Yes, it did break, one day when I was visiting Charles at the museum. As he'd given it to me he was a bit upset, and helped me pick up the beads." That would have been in Dr Jackson's office, later her own office. I had a clear recollection of it, a pleasant, light room, with a big desk, a fitted carpet, I thought three chairs, though there may have been four, and not much other furniture. The carpet was a paleish fawn; the dark amber beads would have shown up well on it, and with friction from the pile of the carpet could not have rolled far. Dr Jackson had helped her to pick up the beads—with two people looking there seemed even less chance of one's being missed. Could Dr Jackson himself have kept one for sentimental reasons? Possible, but it seemed hardly likely. Could there have been anybody else in the room? Ingrid Mitchell hadn't said anything about anyone else, but suppose Dr Jackson's secretary, afterwards her own secretary, had been there she might easily not have mentioned her.

The more I thought about it the more likely it seemed that some third person *must* have been in the room, to pick up, and keep, one of the beads. The secretary might have come in while they were hunting for them, or she might have been with Dr Jackson when Ingrid Mitchell called. She was so familiar a figure in the setting of the office that Dr Mitchell might just not have remembered her. What did we know about the secretary?

Next to nothing. I had met her every time I'd been to the museum but had no distinct impression of her, other than of a fair-haired, rather attractive young woman in her late twenties or early thirties. I had a vague recollection of hearing Dr Mitchell call her Joan.

Then I thought of something else—a remark that Sir Anthony Brotherton had made on the morning he'd come to see us about the second ransom note, when we'd told him of Dr Mitchell's death. He had not heard the seven o'clock radio news, and he was visibly shocked. In telling him about it I'd said that the Keeper of the Department at the museum responsible for the Baffin Map had been found murdered at her home. I had not then told him that Ingrid Mitchell had been shot, and he had asked, "Can you be sure she was murdered?" It was a remark that anybody might have made and I'd thought nothing of it at the time, but now that it came back to me after thinking of the chain of circumstance relating to the amber bead it seemed suddenly a distinctly curious thing for him to ask. We had not told him any details regarding the deaths of Dr Jackson and of Adrian Stowe—both had been murders disguised, for a time successfully, to look like suicide or accident. There had been a similar attempt, though a much clumsier one, to make Ingrid Mitchell's death look like suicide. Why had Sir Anthony thought there could be any doubt when I'd told him that Dr Mitchell had been found murdered?

All at once I knew what we'd got to do.

XIII

Two Telephone Calls

I'M WRITING THIS in the sadly familiar room in an Oxford hospital where they put me when I have to undergo more surgery. There was a gap of several months between the events narrated in the last chapter and what I am writing now. During these months the rest of a miserable story was cleared up, with little help from me, because after I'd put through a call from Ottawa to Sir Edmund Pusey I collapsed in Commissioner Macdonald's office and was rushed off to a Canadian hospital, where I was kept for a week until I was patched up sufficiently to return to England to begin another round of hospitals and doctors. So all the work was done by other people, but at least I managed to talk to Sir Edmund on the telephone before I packed up.

It was the early hours of the morning in Canada, but with the difference in the clock it was breakfast time in England. I felt things swimming round me and knew that I had to be brief. "There's no time to explain, but there are two things you must do immediately," I said. "You must find some way of detaining Sir Anthony Brotherton, and you must get Inspector Richards in Cambridge to detain a woman called Joan Benson, who was secretary to Ingrid Mitchell at the museum. I'm afraid I'm going to pass out for a bit, but Rolf Keller will be back in Hamburg about now and he can explain what's happened here."

When Sir Edmund tried to talk to me I couldn't answer.

As a boss Sir Edmund Pusey has some maddening characteristics, but he makes up for all of them by absolute loyalty to his staff. To ask a high Home Office official to detain the chairman of one of the most important oil companies in the world without being able to give any reasons was asking a lot, but Sir Edmund acted at once. He told me later that he was not at all sure what he was going to do, but he is not an ex-diplomat for nothing, and he decided to go himself to Sir Anthony's house in the hope of catching him at breakfast. "A man is often a bit off guard at breakfast time, and I think I hoped that I might make a glimmer of sense out of your extraordinary request by talking to him then," he told me afterwards.

He was too late. He got to the house to learn that Sir Anthony had been found dead in his bed that morning. Being Sir Edmund he was at once immensely helpful to the distressed household, but natural kindliness did not suppress his intense curiosity, and he soon began to learn things that shook even his long experience of human corruption. After helping the board of Unol to compose a guarded statement about the sudden death of their chairman he had two telephone calls in quick succession. One was from Inspector Richards to say that he was coming from Cambridge and needed to see Sir Edmund urgently; the other was from Keller in Hamburg with the news that he and Gustav Braunschweig were on their way to London.

I had rushed off to Hamburg and the Arctic leaving Inspector Richards with the murder of Ingrid Mitchell on his hands. Most criminal cases are solved by routine detective work, sometimes with the help of a bit of luck—but the luck doesn't come without the patient routine. Richards knew all that I could tell him of my visit to Ingrid Mitchell on the morning of her death, and acting from first principles he set out to establish the pattern of events concerning her before my visit. That took him to the museum and a long interview with Miss Benson who, apart from me, was the last person known to have seen Dr Mitchell alive. Richards had no reason to suspect Miss Benson, but as a matter of routine he asked about her own movements on the day of Dr Mitchell's death. She told him that a Mr Blair (I had abandoned army rank in my dealings with the museum) had called to see Dr Mitchell, and that Dr Mitchell had gone out with him, saying that she would not be back that day.

"Was it usual for Dr Mitchell to go off like that?" Richards asked.

"Well, it wasn't unusual. I mean, she didn't often leave the office for a whole day, but visiting scholars would come from time to time, and sometimes she'd go out with them, maybe for lunch."

"Who is Mr Blair?"

"I don't know, exactly. He'd been here before. I think he belongs to some institution in London, but I don't know about that."

"Did Dr Mitchell seem disturbed?"

"Not particularly. She wouldn't have any reason to be, as far as I know."

Knowing what had brought me to see Dr Mitchell, Richards was a little puzzled by that last remark, because Ingrid Mitchell had been very much disturbed by my visit, and an apparently intelligent secretary who knew her well might have been expected to notice it. Her lack of observation, however, or reluctance to speculate might mean nothing, though they alerted a small detective nerve. He continued his polite questioning.

"What did you do after Dr Mitchell left?"

"Got on with my work. There's always a lot of typing. She left several letters, and we're re-cataloguing the department, so there's a load of work to do. Oh, and I made a couple of phone calls."

"Do you remember who you telephoned?"

"Yes. I rang the printers asking them to hurry up with proofs of a paper on aerial surveying that Dr Mitchell is giving—was giving, I should say—to the Institute of Geographical Research, and I tried to ring a Mr Jeffery at Clare College about a list of maps he wanted, but he wasn't in."

"Where did you go for lunch?"

"Nowhere. I hardly ever go out to lunch. I have a glass of milk and an apple here."

"So you were in your office all the time until the police sergeant came with the news of Dr Mitchell's death—that would have been about four o'clock?"

"Yes."

He did not know it at once, but that was the Inspector's piece of luck, though he could not have benefited from it without more routine. Having left Miss Benson he decided in his careful way that he ought to try to confirm her telephone calls, and went to the museum's switchboard operator. She was an efficient middle-aged woman, working in a tiny telephone room that would have been condemned if the museum had been a factory. "Do all outside calls go through you?" he asked.

"Yes. It's a tiresome system, but there's no direct dialling from any of the departments and I have to get the numbers they want. This switchboard's hopelessly out of date and I'm always asking them to do something about it, but the Curator's an old man and he doesn't like telephones. He's due to retire soon, and I hope to goodness we'll get a new outfit when he goes."

"Do you keep a record of the calls you make?"

"I'm supposed to, as a check against people using the museum phone for personal calls, but there's only me, and a part-time girl who takes over when I'm off, and we can't do it. I've told the Curator several times, but he says it doesn't matter."

"So you wouldn't know of any calls that came from Dr Mitchell's office on the day she died?"

"Well, I might. It's not a proper record, but you see this pad? When I'm asked for a number I jot it down so that I know what to dial. I tear off the used pages every day, and put them in this old box file, where they stay until the box gets full. Nobody seems to want them, so then I just throw them away. But you're asking about yesterday, and the pages are still there. Let me have a look."

From the box she took the top dozen pages, covered with scribbled telephone numbers. "I tear off the pages in a batch, so the top ones are the beginning of each day," she said. "You're asking about the morning, so they should be on the first couple of sheets. Yes, here we are—119, that's the extension for Dr Mitchell's office, or rather, it's for the phone in her secretary's room, her own extension is 120. I have to put the extension so I know who I'm dialling for. There seems to be only one call during the morning, a London number—01 836 8365."

"You wouldn't know who it was?"

"No. I just get the number. But there was an incoming call. I remember now, because I couldn't put it through. I rang Miss Benson's extension, but I didn't get any reply. I tried Dr Mitchell's extension as well, but she didn't reply either, so they both must have been out. When I said there was no reply a man's voice asked me to get Miss Benson to ring 01 836 8365 as soon as she could. See, I've got the number written here, with my note, Miss Benson to ring."

"It's the same number that she herself rang earlier," Richards said.

"So it is. I have such millions of numbers that they don't mean a thing—that's why I have to write them down."

"You haven't got a time for the call."

"No, I don't bother with times. But it must have been before lunch because it's my writing. I go to lunch at one-thirty, when the part-time girl takes over for an hour."

"Did you get the message to Miss Benson?"

"Yes, but not until the afternoon—I'd say about three-thirty. I remember ringing her extension several times up to just before half-past one, when I went off, but she didn't answer. I tried again as soon as I got back, but she still didn't answer—I remember thinking that she must have gone out for a long lunch. It was at least half-past three before I got her."

"Did you get the London number for her then?"

"No. She said thank you, but she knew what it was about, and it could wait until tomorrow—that's today, I suppose."

"Has she rung the number today?"

The operator looked at her current pad. "No, she doesn't seem to have rung anyone today," she said.

The Inspector had had a heavy day, driving to Cambridge from London after leaving me in the early morning, calling on Mrs Jackson, as I'd asked him to inquire again about Dr Jackson's papers, and then putting in several hours at the museum. Mrs Jackson could tell him nothing—she could only repeat that as far as she knew her late husband's papers were at the museum. By the time he had finished talking to the switchboard operator it was late in the afternoon. He tried to get hold of me, but I was already in Hamburg, and he decided to concentrate on the inconsistencies in Miss Benson's story to him. Inconsistencies was a polite way of putting it; by next morning he was as sure as he ever had been sure of anything that they were lies. But why? The two invented local telephone calls seemed pointless, unless she did not know the ins and outs of the switchboard operator's methods and wanted to disguise the fact that she'd made a call to London—the operator might have remembered that she'd telephoned somebody, but not the number. Clearly she had not lunched on a glass of milk and an apple in her room—unless for some reason the switchboard operator was lying. Was there any way of checking? It was maddening that the switchboard lady was so vague about times, but really he had been lucky to have got so much out of her. He could go again to Miss Benson and challenge her statements, but there were several arguments against this. First, unless he could prove that she was lying she had only to stick to what she'd said, and he'd be no for'arder. More important, if he showed that he was suspicious of her she could alert other people, and he knew enough about the case to realise that there might be many others involved. He discussed things with his Superintendent, and they decided that they must try to find some independent evidence of Miss Benson's movements on the day of Dr Mitchell's death before doing anything else.

She lived in a flat in Cambridge, and normally drove to work in a blue Mini which she owned. The museum had a car park for staff and visitors, with one end marked off by white lines for the staff. There was no attendant, and no check on the coming and going of cars, so the only hope was to try to find out if anyone had noticed Miss Benson's Mini leaving or returning to the car park during working hours on the day in question. Hers was the only blue Mini among staff cars, so it was reasonably noticeable. Richards felt free to make exhaustive inquiries about cars because they could be related to Dr Mitchell—he himself knew that she had driven to her house with me, but the museum people could assume that the police were trying to work out her movements on the last morning of her life.

He got nowhere. Miss Benson had had her Mini for two years, and it was so familiar in the staff part of the car park that other users simply thought it had been there at the normal times. No one seemed to have been looking out of a window to see either Dr Mitchell or Miss Benson drive away. Inquiries round Dr Mitchell's home were equally fruitless.

What of the London telephone number? It was traced through the Post Office and turned out to be a call box. Since Miss Benson had apparently rung it and been asked to call back this was puzzling, and the Inspector was even more puzzled when he learned that it had been out of action for several days because of vandalism—the box was on a housing estate notorious for its social problems, and it seemed that it was out of action almost more often than it was usable. Had the switchboard lady written down the number wrongly? That seemed unlikely, because Miss

Benson was apparently put through without trouble when she made her call, and the same number had been written a second time when the operator had been unable to get a reply from Miss Benson's extension. The caller then had asked for a message to ring the number to be given her—that seemed ridiculous if the number was a call box, even one in working order. It was reasonable to ask someone to ring a call box at a given time when you can make a point of being there, but to ask for a call at a call box without any pre-arranged time makes no sense. Could it have been a code, and not a telephone number at all? That was possible, but if so how had the number apparently worked when Miss Benson asked for it in the first instance? Richards could make neither head nor tail of it, but the mystery increased his suspicion that Miss Benson knew something of Dr Mitchell's murder, even if she herself had not been directly involved. He reported all this to Seddon at the Yard, and concentrated on trying to find someone who might have seen the blue Mini.

There things rested while Keller, Ruth and I had our adventures in the Arctic. On the day that we were flying to Ottawa there were two dramatic developments. First, Richards had a second stroke of luck. A taxi-driver who had been on holiday came home to learn that the police were inquiring about a blue Mini which might have been in the vicinity of Dr Mitchell's cottage on the day of her death. He had had a fare which took him past her house, and he remembered nearly running into a blue Mini which in his view had been parked dangerously under a hedge where there was no footpath, round a bend in the road about a hundred yards from Dr Mitchell's drive. He was a good witness; moreover, he knew his fare, who was a man he took home quite often. This man confirmed the near-accident with the blue Mini. He and the taxi-driver were taken to the museum car park to look at Miss Benson's Mini, and while neither could swear that it was the car they had seen, both thought that it was like it. Richards and his Superintendent decided that thin though this evidence was it justified bringing Miss Benson to the police station for questioning. They also got a warrant to search her flat, and in a drawer of her dressing-table found a bundle of papers which looked like notes on the Arctic Calorific Syndrome. That was enough to detain her.

An even more dramatic development came on the morning

that Sir Anthony Brotherton was found dead. Seddon had been puzzling away at the mystery of the call-box telephone, and with the help of skilled Post Office engineers he suddenly solved it. There was nothing in the box itself to indicate anything but frequent vandalism, but examination of an underground cable some distance from the box showed that the line serving its number had been diverted. As long as the box was in use the diversion would not work, but the box could be put out of action by a simple switch and the line then served a telephone that was traced to Sir Anthony Brotherton's house. All that had to be done to make use of this means of secret communication was to put the box out of order.

When Miss Benson was told of Sir Anthony Brotherton's death she broke down under questioning, and the whole—or as much as she knew about the whole—of an extraordinary story came out. In a way it had started in Cambridge years before when she and Hilde Baumgarten, then Hilda Stevenson (she Germanised the spelling of her name to Hilde after her marriage) were both undergraduate students of Dr Jackson. Both got good upper seconds in geography, and got jobs in the Unol office in London, Joan Benson as a secretary, and Hilda Stevenson in the cartographic department dealing with surveys of oilfields. Hilda met Heinrich Baumgarten when he was on a visit to London to discuss a contract for pipeline engineering for a field in the Middle East, married him and went off to live in Germany. Joan was rapidly promoted, and became personal secretary to Sir Anthony Brotherton. She also became his mistress.

Whether the first alarm about the potential disaster to Middle East oil that a practicable North-West Passage might bring came from Baumgarten or Brotherton was never clear, but both soon became much involved in thwarting any ideas that Dr Braunschweig might have about developing new Arctic shipping routes. Both knew about Charles Jackson's importance in adding to knowledge of the Arctic Calorific Syndrome, and Brotherton's first idea was that he should be controlled by blackmail. An opportunity came when his secretary retired, and Joan Benson, a former student of his and now with magnificent references from Unol, applied for the job. She got it, and her combination of a good degree in geography with first-class secretarial experience made her very good at it. She soon became more or less indispensable to Charles Jackson, and she was able to keep Sir Anthony Brotherton informed of all his correspondence on the Arctic, and the general progress of his work. The main danger to the Middle East consortium seemed to come from the mathematical research by Adrian Stowe in Hamburg, and it was decided to eliminate him. The Benson woman said she didn't know much about this because it had all happened in Hamburg, but she made one damning admission—she had typed the name Adrian Stowe and prescribing instructions for taking one tablet on a chemist's label sent to her by Brotherton. Hamburg police still had the bottle with the label on it, and when it was shown to her she said it was the one she typed. Chemists' labels on medicines always have a reference number from which the original doctor's prescription can be identified. This label duly had a number, but on inquiry at the chemist's shop it turned out to have no relationship with any series of references in the dispenser's own files, and was obviously bogus. Joan Benson had sent the typed label to Brotherton, and knew no more about it. Presumably he had sent it to Baumgarten, but whether the barbiturate tablets that killed Stowe were obtained in London or Hamburg was never discovered. Baumgarten, his wife and Brotherton were all dead, so in a sense it did not matter, but Joan Benson's statement sufficiently established that Stowe's death was murder.

After Stowe's death events moved back to Cambridge. Miss Benson knew that Dr Jackson had been in constant touch with Stowe and had copies of his notes, and Brotherton decided that Jackson would have to be controlled or silenced. The plan adopted was to play on his known sympathies and human decency. Miss Benson came to the office one day looking haggard and distressed, and when Jackson asked what was the matter she confessed a pitiful story to him. Her mother, aged eighty, was in an expensive nursing home. Originally she had enough income from investments to pay the fees, but her investments had been badly managed, the income had all but disappeared, and now there wasn't enough money to meet the fees. Miss Benson had helped from her salary, but she couldn't go on. While she was at Unol she had forged shipping documents diverting a large consignment of oil to a friend, who had sold it on the so-called free oil market, making over £200,000. Half of the proceeds had come to her, and she was using the money to maintain her mother in the home. That was the real reason why she had wanted to leave Unol and come to Cambridge. Now there was a chance that the fraud would come to light, and the friend who had suggested it to her was asking for money to keep people quiet. She had paid him everything she had, but he kept demanding more and she didn't know what to do. As far as she herself was concerned she didn't particularly mind being sent to prison, but she was worried about her mother. It would be an appalling shock to her to have to leave the private home where she had been well looked after for years. She felt that her mother would die soon in any case, and if only she could keep things quiet for a bit longer at least her beloved mother could die in dignity and peace.

This story—wholly fictitious—was cleverly calculated to impress Charles Jackson who, with his wife, was making considerable sacrifices to keep his own mother in a private home. He asked Miss Benson how much she needed, and at first her requests were quite modest. It was a struggle, but he found the money for her. Then the demands were increased, culminating in the suggestion that he should steal the Baffin Map from the museum. By this time Jackson was himself ill and desperate, but he couldn't contemplate stealing the map and, as we had learned from Ingrid Mitchell, he had given it to her to keep safe. When Miss Benson discovered that the map was missing and that Dr Jackson had not taken it she, Brotherton and Baumgarten became greatly worried. They decided that Dr Jackson was probably about to go to the police, and that he would have to follow Adrian Stowe into oblivion. They also wanted to get the copies of Stowe's notes from him. Miss Benson knew all about his treatment for depression, and she knew the name of the drug that his doctor had given him. Brotherton or the Baumgartens—again we could never know which—obviously had access to pharmaceutical information, for they learned of its fatal combination with alcohol. Miss Benson knew of the forthcoming Cambridge party from Dr Jackson's diary, and the conspirators worked out a quick plan for getting rid of him. Hilde Baumgarten came over from Germany, gatecrashed the party with no trouble—there were people coming and going all the time—and Dr Jackson was delighted to meet one of his old students. She kept his glass liberally supplied with gin, and when his wife and Ingrid Mitchell took him home she must have followed them in a car she had hired for the occasion. She had more or less admitted to me that my reconstruction of events in Dr Jackson's bedroom was right and although we could get no farther because of her own death, the Cambridge police found a car-hire firm which had hired a car to a lady on the day of the party, and on being shown a photograph of Hilde Baumgarten thought that it was like what they remembered of their customer. There was damning incidental evidence in the amber bead, which Miss Benson *had* picked up when Ingrid Mitchell's necklace broke, and had kept in case it might come in useful. She admitted that she had given it to Hilde Baumgarten.

Here oil politics became rather mixed with personal emotion. Miss Benson lived in hopes that Brotherton would divorce his wife and marry her, but she knew well enough that Sir Anthony had an eye for attractive women—and that plenty of women had found him attractive. She was jealous of any other women who might come into his life, and when she told Brotherton that Ingrid Mitchell had been appointed to succeed Dr Jackson at the museum he remarked that he had met her when she was doing a thesis on Alaska, and had thought her a most interesting girl. There is no evidence that Ingrid Mitchell ever met him again, but the remark was enough to make Miss Benson dislike and distrust her, and if she could have been involved as a suspect in any way, Joan Benson would have been delighted.

As things turned out, no one was suspected of Dr Jackson's murder, but Hilde Baumgarten had been disappointed on going through his desk. She had the twenty-five minutes that Mrs Jackson was away driving Ingrid Mitchell back to Cambridge, and she was a cool, efficient woman. There was plenty of time to get the pills into the half-drunk Jackson, and then to tackle his desk. There were some notes, but nothing like as many as she expected, and she knew enough about the Arctic theory to realise that Adrian Stowe's papers were not among them. She took what she could find and—fortunately for us—had time to stage the setting for Dr Jackson's accident a little too perfectly by wiping his glass and imprinting only his own fingerprints on it. But this wasn't noticed at the time, there was the amber bead to lay a false trail if necessary, and from the conspirators' point of view everything worked splendidly.

But they still didn't have the copies of Stowe's notes that they felt sure must exist. There seemed two possibilities, first that Dr Braunschweig had them, secondly that they might be in the possession of Ingrid Mitchell, who was known by Joan Benson to have been working with Dr Jackson on the Arctic theory; indeed, it seemed quite likely that both might have copies of the all-important Stowe papers.

The Benson woman kept a close eye on all Dr Mitchell's movements, reporting everything to Brotherton via the secret telephone line. He knew at once of my original visit to the museum—indeed, when he brought us the first of the Baffin Map demands I had told him that I intended to go to Cambridge. My second visit seemed more sinister, and when Dr Mitchell hurriedly went off with me it appeared more dangerous still. Miss Benson denied that she had overheard any of my conversation with Dr Mitchell about the map, and there was no listening device linking her office with the secretary's room that we ever found, though there would have been plenty of time for Joan Benson to have removed one. I didn't believe her denial—without a listening device she could easily have overheard us by opening the door to her room slightly, and listening behind it. It did not matter. What did was that as soon as Dr Mitchell had gone off with me she rang Brotherton, and he told her that she must follow us to Ingrid Mitchell's home, get in as soon as I had left and search the place for the Stowe papers, dealing with Ingrid as might seem necessary.

Miss Benson appeared completely frank about her part in the murder, but neither Inspector Richards nor I wholly believed her. Her story was that Brotherton had given her a pistol for contingencies when she first went to the museum, and that she had shot Ingrid Mitchell because it seemed the only way to search the house. I think her motives were more complex. She hated Ingrid Mitchell, partly because she was afraid of her in relation to Anthony Brotherton if they ever met, which was always a real possibility in her mind, partly because she was jealous of her position in Cambridge. She herself was a geographer, and at the back of her contorted mind I think there may have been an idea that she might succeed to the post of Keeper of the Arctic Maps. The amber bead seemed significant here. It was Joan Benson who gave it to Hilde Baumgarten, in the hope that Dr Mitchell might somehow be implicated in Charles Jackson's death.

Why was Brotherton so upset when he heard of my second visit to Ingrid Mitchell? Here we were still left only with conjecture. Joan Benson was an important cog in the anti-North-West Passage intrigue, but she was no more than a cog. She could explain the use of the Baffin Map in an attempt to get an unbreakable hold on Charles Jackson, but its later use as a ransom demand for Dr Braunschweig remained puzzling. Did Brotherton and Baumgarten really want the map in order to destroy any possible hint of the existence of a North-West Passage farther north than anyone else had apparently ever looked? Dr Mitchell said that the map had really very little bearing on the Arctic calorific theory, except in indicating navigable water for William Baffin three centuries ago. But then she was an expert, understood the immense range of seasonal variation in the ice, and knew infinitely more about modern theories of warm currents than did Brotherton or Baumgarten. I think they *did* regard the map as important, and for mixed reasons. They did not want any reminder of Baffin's last voyages, and they did not know what had happened to the map when its disappearance was finally reported to the Cambridge police by the museum. They judged Charles Jackson by their own standards, and when he refused to have anything to do with purloining the map they assumed that he must be mixed up with Dr Braunschweig in some way. But Jackson was a pure scholar, knew nothing more than he may have learned incidentally from Adrian Stowe of Dr Braunschweig's commercial interest in the Arctic theory, and after Stowe's death rather distrusted Braunschweig. The map was of a piece with all the other planning that went into the affair—it was over-subtle. A plain demand for money on Dr Braunschweig's kidnapping would have explained his intended murder well enough, and would not have taken us at once to the Cambridge Museum. Of course, the Brotherton-Baumgarten partnership would have had to put up with ignorance of the whereabouts of the map, but no one investigating an apparently political killing of Dr Braunschweig as an industrialist would have had any reason to go looking for him in the Arctic.

Only exceptionally clever plotters would have thought of involving the map. Brotherton and the Baumgartens *were* exceptionally clever. Were they *too* clever? And why was this dreadful puzzle contrived at all?

XIV

Out of the ruins of Troy . . .

THE ONLY PERSON left alive with first-hand knowledge of the conspiracy was Joan Benson, and although she had played a major part in events at Cambridge her knowledge of the inner politics of Universal Oil and the oil industry was a little out of date. Dr Braunschweig knew much more about recent events, and detailed financial investigations by Keller in Hamburg and George Seddon in London suggested that the original impetus to stop the development of a North-West Passage for the transport of oil at any price came from Heinrich Baumgarten. He had a profitable engineering business founded by his father, but he was ambitious for power in the oil industry itself, and invested heavily in the Arabian Sands company. When that company ran into difficulties he saw his only hope of avoiding personal ruin in a takeover by a larger group, and as things turned out the only group with whom he had a practical chance of doing business was Unol. Any hint of geographical discovery which might damage the value of shareholdings in the Middle East, even temporarily, would, as he saw it, have devalued his investment in Arabian Sands to a point which would have meant bankruptcy for him personally. But how did he get Sir Anthony Brotherton on his side?

On the face of it, Sir Anthony had almost everything that a man can hope to obtain from life—money, position, power. A search of his house brought to light a vile collection of obscene books and films, and further police inquiries showed that he was deeply involved in pornographic sex. But he was shielded by an apparently normal marriage, and in a position to pay for discretion. How much Lady Brotherton really knew of her husband's secret performances never became clear—she seemed to have been content to lead her own life, enjoying her position in the world, and not asking questions. There were no children, and she may have been genuinely ignorant of her husband's affairs, though how far her professed ignorance really extended we could never determine. There was nothing to indicate that she had played any part in the conspiracy, there was no charge that could be brought against her, and she remained an enigmatic personality, important to her husband socially, but quite possibly unimportant in any other way. There was some evidence that Hilde Baumgarten had indulged Sir Anthony's tastes from time to time, and Seddon unearthed an undocumented possibility that Sir Anthony had diverted Unol money to support shares in Arabian Sands before the merger. Financial dealings here, however, were of such intricacy, involving nominees from Hong Kong to the Channel Islands, that proof of this could never be obtained. If Sir Anthony had been committed in such a way then he, too, might have faced ruin if the Arabian Sands deal had been upset.

Good work by the Metropolitan Police in London, and by the German force in Hamburg, cleared up the incidental mysteries. The German police reckoned that they rounded up all of those involved in Baumgarten's League Against Political Injustice who remained alive. The leader, and the one really important man in the outfit apart from Baumgarten himself, had been killed in the shooting round the yacht. He was a promising young engineer working for Unol in Alaska, and had ideological convictions on the need for terrorism to combat big business. It was he who had obtained the Unol plane. The others in the plane were professional crooks, recruited for money. The German authorities obtained their extradition for the attack on a German Air Force plane, and they got stiff prison sentences. None of them seemed implicated in the real conspiracy, or even to know much about it, so it did not come up at the trial.

The only one of the major conspirators left to face trial was Joan Benson. Her case bristled with complexities, for Sir Anthony Brotherton was dead, and although his part in the murders was clear to us, he could not be charged and cross-examined. I was patched up sufficiently to share in the questioning of Miss Benson, and although she was undoubtedly a murderess, I felt a good deal of pity for her—it seemed damnably unfair that she alone should be left to be charged with murder. And her case was different from the rest—her ambitions were in her emotional attachment to Sir Anthony. She had been genuinely in love with him, and believed that one day he would marry her. It was necessary to question her about his sexual practices, but she flatly refused to believe in them. Having admitted her part in the murder of Ingrid Mitchell, her remaining object in life seemed to be to protect Sir Anthony's memory, and to keep his name out of things. With a plea of guilty there was no need for anything much to come out at her trial. Inevitably she was sentenced to life imprisonment, the judge adding a humane rider that the prison authorities would observe her mental state and see that she got any treatment she might need. Pusey, Inspector Richards and I were all convinced that she had been at least partly out of her mind for some time, and that she was more than likely to end up hopelessly insane. I think I almost hoped so.

Partly fortuitously, partly by the greatest care in handling the prosecutions in both German and English courts, publicity about the North-West Passage was avoided at all the various trials, but it was hard to decide what to do about Sir Anthony Brotherton. An inquest had to be held, and it would have upset Foreign Offices and Departments of Trade throughout the world if it came out that the chairman of one of the greatest of international oil companies had been murdering people, and attempting to murder his own deputy chairman, to prevent research into a possible North-West Passage route for the transport of oil. And the effect on oil markets would be incalculable. With Dr Braunschweig in the chair, the board of Unol was at one with the British and German Governments in wanting nothing to emerge about the North-West Passage theory. But how was Sir Anthony's suicide to be explained? Legally, no explanation was required—a coroner could return a verdict of suicide without speculating on any reason for it. But the suicide of the chairman of Unol was a news story of vast proportions, and every newspaper and news agency in the world could be expected to assign teams of reporters to cover it.

If you want to keep the press away from one story, give them another one. The library of obscene books and films discovered in Sir Anthony's house, and the lurid aspects of his secret life were enough to give the press a field day, and a prominent man's fear of being found out was enough to offer a convincing reason for suicide. This was what happened. Tampering with the call box to provide a secret telephone number was a fact, and a man had been duly convicted for it. Police evidence of investigation of the call box, all of which was true, if not quite the whole truth, indicated that Sir Anthony might have good reason to fear that his activities would come to light. Press and television enterprise after the inquest got hold of various girls whose sensational accounts of orgies brought fat cheques for themselves and acres of material for the papers and "investigative" television programmes. In the mass of sensational disclosures the oil industry itself was ignored.

Behind the scenes, the Unol board did what it could to help those who had suffered from its chairman's crimes. The dependents of the German airmen and policemen who had lost their lives in the Arctic could be helped by substantial grants in addition to their Service pensions. I was back in hospital when Ruth brought Mrs Jackson to see me, and I was allowed to tell her of what was being done for her.

"I promised to visit you again when I knew more of the story of your husband," I said. "I can't keep that promise literally because you have had to come to see me, but I can reinforce what I told you in Cambridge—that you and your daughter can be very proud of your husband. He was an honourable man, killed in doing what he saw as his duty. His illness, which led to so much suffering for you, was the direct result of his own generous behaviour in trying to help a woman who deserved no help—but he could not know that."

"There is a lot that I don't understand," she said, "but I do realise that Charles genuinely believed the story of that dreadful woman who murdered Ingrid Mitchell. It would have been better if he had told me about it—but then he wouldn't have been Charles. He thought it was her secret, and he could not talk about it, even to me."

I kept to the end the thing I most wanted to tell her. "There's something more," I said. "In recognition of your husband's work the Universal Oil Company has arranged to endow a Jackson Chair of Polar Geography in the University of Cambridge. That will give him the kind of memorial that perhaps he would most have liked to have."

At this point she broke down and cried. Ruth put her arms round her. "Try to think of the Jackson Professorship," she said gently. "If your daughter follows her father, as you think she may, perhaps one day she will be the Jackson Professor at Cambridge. That would be something to look forward to."

"If I can keep her at school . . . I'm sorry, I shouldn't be talking of this now, but Charles spent most of our money on that woman's blackmail."

"It is I who have to say sorry . . . I was so excited about the professorship that I clean forgot to tell you something else," I said. "In more personal recognition of your husband's work the board of Unol has decided to make you a grant which will mean at least that you never have to worry about money again."

Money could do nothing for the parents of Adrian Stowe and Ingrid Mitchell, but there was one injustice that could to some extent be righted. Adrian Stowe's death was formally recorded as suicide, and was felt by his mother and father as a slur on his memory. Hamburg police traced some of the other guests at the Baumgarten dinner party on the night he died, and although it was a longish time ago they established with reasonable certainty that Hilde Baumgarten had been absent for about half an hour during the evening. That would have given her time to drive to Stowe's flat and put the deadly bottle of false saccharine tablets by his bed. His death was clearly murder, but neither of the Baumgartens was alive to be questioned or charged. In the end the police made a statement saying that further evidence that had come to light made it certain that Stowe could not have taken his own life, but that since important witnesses had since themselves died the matter could not be carried farther. The records of the British Embassy were changed to death by misadventure. This was not very satisfactory, but it comforted his parents a little. The memories of Adrian Stowe and Ingrid Mitchell were perpetuated by Unol with the endowment of a Stowe Readership in the Mathematics of Climatology at Oxford, and of a Mitchell Lectureship in Arctic Studies at Cambridge. "I suppose it is not exactly profiting from murder, but the universities haven't done badly out of all this wretchedness," Ruth observed.

"*Nunc seges est ubi Troia fuit*," I said, delighted to air my little Latin to a Professor of Mathematics who had none. "It is better to get a crop of some sort from the ruins of Troy than

217

nothing. And if you go into the history of the peaceful colleges of Oxford and Cambridge you will come across a fair bit of violence in the lives of some of those who endowed them. They did very well by Henry VIII, for instance. There aren't many princely patrons around nowadays. Thank God that big business can sometimes be generous as well as grasping."

I was sick of the sight of the contraption by my bed that held a plastic bottle to drip something or other into my right arm. My left arm was sick of holding Boswell's Johnson and, if I tell the truth, I was getting rather bored by Dr Johnson. Ruth couldn't come until the evening and it was barely the middle of the afternoon. I put down the book and was staring miserably at the ceiling when a nurse came in to say I had a visitor, and did I feel well enough to see him?

"I shall be thankful to see anyone," I said. "You have neglected me for hours."

"I haven't. And anyway, you are supposed to be asleep."

"Well, I'm not. Bring him in."

It was Dr Braunschweig. "I was horrified to hear that you were back in hospital," he said. "I should have come two or three weeks ago, but you will understand that I have been frantically busy. I hope you got my letters."

"I did, and thank you very much for them."

"I have to thank you for saving my life."

"Bosh. You have to thank Rolf Keller, several brave German airmen and policemen, and a host of people whose names you will never know. We all owe our lives to other people, all the time. Tell me of the interesting things that have been happening —I'm horribly out of touch in this place. I know, of course, of your generous gifts to Cambridge and Oxford, and they have warmed my heart. But I don't know what is happening in your company. Have you taken over as chairman?"

"I have been acting as chairman—that was unavoidable. But I'm not sure that I want to go on indefinitely. My colleagues would probably elect me, but it would mean moving to London, and abandoning work in my own field. There are other good candidates, and in all the circumstances I'm inclined to think that—how shall I put it—a chairman less personally involved in these unhappy events would be better for the company. But that can be determined later—for the moment, I am carrying on."

"As far as we have been able to make out the inspiration for the whole dreadful business came from Baumgarten. But I'm not at all clear why."

"You know as much as we shall ever know. Heinrich was a strange man, and I think that Hilde was an even more powerful personality. They were extraordinarily thorough. They both actually travelled to Brazil before coming back to kidnap me, and Heinrich arranged for various letters he had written to be posted in Brazil to his firm in Germany, safely covering the time that he was with me on *Apfel*. He made a mistake in putting my car in his own garage—but it was quite a clever mistake, and he thought that he would be back before the car could be found."

"He reckoned without the Hamburg police."

"And without you . . . But we are not to talk of that."

"But why do it at all? He was a rich, successful man."

"He stood to lose a lot of money over Arabian Sands. And he wanted power. So did Hilde."

"And Sir Anthony?"

"He wanted power, too. And as we know now, he was vulnerable in various ways. I think Hilde had some hold on him, but that may not have been very important. He wanted supreme power in the Middle East, and he was afraid of me, though I didn't realise that at the time."

"And now? Will the North-West Passage work?"

Dr Braunschweig was silent for some time. Then he said, "In the way that Sir Anthony and Heinrich feared, as a surface route to Europe and the eastern seaboard of America, I think not. Or not yet. Perhaps it needs only a small change in local climate—possibly there was such an interlude in William Baffin's day. But as things are, I see no immediate possibility of a North-West Passage as a practicable route for surface tankers. I emphasise the word 'surface'. I am convinced that there is much reality in the Arctic calorific theory, and the remarkable voyage of the US submarine *Nautilus* has already proved that there is a practicable route for underwater transport. Given the need, we could develop submarine tankers that would ferry oil from the Arctic by a north-west route without great difficulty. It would require huge investment, and I think they would need to be nuclear-powered—and the world is not ready for nuclear-powered oil-tankers. There are no shore bases for them—and think of the outcry at bringing nuclear-powered submarines to existing oil terminals. My own view is that they would be as safe as any other form of shipping, but that is not yet the world's view. We shall maintain a small design staff to work on the problems—it is our job to think not years, but decades ahead. And the mere possibility of an under-water route for oil from the Arctic may yet have political advantages. But I think not yet—there is too much invested else-where. And yet, who knows? We cannot know the future, but we must be prepared for it."

"So all this dreadful toll of life was not wholly waste?"

"I cannot define 'waste'. It was part of what may come to be seen as a historical process. It was futile, and unnecessary, but Charles Jackson, Adrian Stowe, Ingrid Mitchell, even you and I, may have helped to shape the future."

My next visitor was Sir Edmund Pusey. He greeted me cheer-fully. "I have some news for you," he said. "I am delighted to tell you that the Prime Minister has decided to recommend Her Majesty to confer a knighthood on you."

"Good Lord! I'd far rather you got me out of this place."

"You must just be patient. I have had a word with your surgeon, and he is impressed by your constitution. He assures me that you are progressing as well as can be expected."

"As well as *he* expects, perhaps."

"He has a world reputation, Peter. And now he has an even more distinguished patient."

"Don't think I'm ungrateful. But what on earth am I to say to Ruth about becoming Lady Blair? She dislikes being Mrs Blair, she much prefers to be a Professor."

"Leave Ruth to me, Peter. I have not served time in the Foreign Office for nothing. I shall break the news to her in the most delicate and diplomatic way. And she will be proud of you—you'll see."

"That's all very well. But how is this thing to be gazetted? No one knows anything about our job."

"Your knighthood is to be in the Military Division—no one ever asks questions about that. And if anybody does raise the matter, 'for public services' covers a multitude of sins."

"I suppose I should say thank you."

"It would be gracious. By the way, there is one other thing. When you are feeling fitter, there's a rather tricky little matter on which I should be glad of your advice . . ."

AUTHOR'S NOTE

My Arctic climatic theory and William Baffin's map are imaginary, but the wonderful sub-polar voyage of the USS *Nautilus* in 1958 is real, and so are the finding of a seam of coal by the Nares Expedition in 1876 and the report by the Oxford University Ellesmere Island Expedition in 1935 of flat ground suitable for landing aircraft near Gould Bay. All the human characters in my story are imaginary.